Praise for *Geographies of the Heart*

"Years of secrets, resentments, and words left unspoken force a family to examine the fragile complexities of the heart. A tender yet powerful journey, where bitterness gives way to the determination it takes to stitch lives back together."
—Beth Hoffman, *New York Times* bestselling author of *Saving CeeCee Honeycutt*

"Caitlin Hamilton Summie writes like waves cross large oceans. Words, sentences, chapters and stories build with a complexity of wind, current, and underground tectonic force until they crash toward their resolution onshore. Her debut novel, *Geographies of the Heart*, is a new force of nature that readers of Summie's work will love. Intense, searching, intimate in the moment and sweeping in its range, this novel is an oceans-wide meditation on the inseparability of family, and the redemption of loss."
—Andrew Krivak, author of *The Bear*

"*Geographies of the Heart* is both riveting and moving, its characters rendered with painstaking and loving attention. I got to know them very well, and the author made me care about them. Caitlin Hamilton Summie is not afraid to go deep, to explore the fears and emotions most of us spend so much time trying to conceal. I loved this novel. I only wish there were more like it."
—Steve Yarbrough, author of *The Unmade World*

"An accomplished, confident debut, with complex characters you'll be rooting for."
—J. Ryan Stradal, bestselling author of *Kitchens of the Great Midwest* and *The Lager Queen of Minnesota*

Praise for *To Lay to Rest Our Ghosts*

Winner, Phillip H. McMath Post-Publication Book Award

Silver Winner, Foreword INDIES Book of the Year Awards for Short Stories

A Pulpwood Queen Book Club Bonus Book for June 2018

"What is remembered; what is missed; what will never be again…all these are addressed with the tenderness of a wise observer whose heart is large enough, kind enough, to embrace them all without judgment…intense and finely crafted…her stories reach into the hidden places of the heart and break them open to healing light, offering a touch of grace and hope of reconciliation."
—*Foreword Reviews, starred review*

"Her compelling writing reminds us of the power of a well-delivered narrative…Summie's stories emphasize [our] shared humanity, and there is something accessible, recognizable and timely for everyone."
—*The Vail Daily*

"This debut collection works together to form a Cubist portrait of grief…Summie's ghosts linger."
—*The Minneapolis Star Tribune*

"…Summie is our modern Chekhov."
—*Savvy Verse & Wit*

"The stories center on the complexity of family relationships with such empathy and humanity that novelist Steve Yarbrough called the book "nothing short of magnificent."…Summie grounds readers in reality just as they become lost in her beautiful prose…*To Lay to Rest Our Ghosts* does not shy from life's hardest moments, but its sorrow is not gratuitous. Summie is a writer who approaches life as a whole,

both good and bad, rooted in history and place, and her elegant prose shines in this collection."
—*Chapter16.org (also appeared in The Knoxville News-Sentinel)*

"The universal issues and dilemmas at the heart of Summie's stories and her focus on families give *To Lay to Rest Our Ghosts* wide appeal. You'll want to talk about these characters as if you knew them, and you'll want to revisit these stories more than once."
—*BethFish Reads*

"...a collection of eloquent, grace-filled stories that offers readers a mirror into their own souls. If you enjoy the spare, affecting writing of Kent Haruf, read this. Buy two copies, one for yourself and one to give someone you love."
—*Hungry for Good Books*

"...Summie writes elegantly...Like a landscape painter, she creates memorable images: a wheelchair-bound man stuck in a muddy rut, a young mother pulling a line of children through a whiteout."

—*Kirkus Reviews*

Geographies of the Heart

A Novel

Caitlin Hamilton Summie

Fomite
Burlington, VT

ISBN-13: 978-1-953236-39-5
Library of Congress Control Number: 2021941461
Fomite
58 Peru Street
Burlington, VT 05401

01-04-2022

CREDITS

Chapter 2 first appeared in slightly different form as *Cleaning House* in *South 85 Journal*

Chapter 3 first appeared in slightly different form as *Whole New Worlds* in *JMWW*

Chapter 5 first appeared as *Patchwork* in *To Lay to Rest Our Ghosts* by Caitlin Hamilton Summie, published by Fomite Press

Chapter 6 first appeared in slightly different form as *Beginnings* in *JMWW*

Chapter 11 first appeared in slightly different form as *Geographies of the Heart*, in *Long Story, Short* and then in *To Lay to Rest Our Ghosts* by Caitlin Hamilton Summie, published by Fomite Press

Chapter 12 appeared in slightly different form as *Taking Root* in *Belmont Story Review* and in *To Lay to Rest Our Ghosts* by Caitlin Hamilton Summie, published by Fomite Press

For my family

Disconnected
Sarah
Fall 1994

ON THEIR FIRST DATE, Sarah wore jeans and a red sweater, to catch the auburn color in her hair. No make-up. She usually wore some, but not then. She didn't want to. She just wanted to be herself.

She'd met Al in the library early in the week, in an unusually long line for reference help. After chatting about the wait and the weather, and just before she stepped up for her turn, he'd invited her out for a coffee at the Campus Cup.

The Campus Cup was just shy of being a dump, but students and faculty alike loved it, the lumpy chairs and scratched tables and maroon curtains, pulled back now to let in the last of the late afternoon light. The Cup served coffee or tea in mismatched saucers and cups, and there was no background music, just the hum of conversation. Sarah loved the Cup, and she often squirreled up there with books and tea at her favorite table in the corner by the front window, if she could get it. On rare occasions, she'd bump into her younger sister, Glennie, but Glennie most often studied in the library and only popped in to fuel up. She never lingered, so Sarah thought of The Campus Cup as her place. For Al to suggest it gave her confidence in him, even if it was a logical choice.

She saw Al now, half-standing up from his chair, waving, blushing. He was as she remembered, with his Scandinavian white-blond hair, the blue eyes, those dimples. He was tallish and on the heavy side, not that she was petite, and she was grateful they'd be sitting down. It would be easier to look him in the eye.

When she reached his table, Al held out her chair. Who did that besides her Grandpa? The gesture charmed her, and Sarah smiled her thanks. They smoothly navigated the awkward subject of who was paying. Sarah imagined that any offer to treat would be waved away and asked for a coffee but declined his offer of a cookie. Lately she had been eating too many of those, as the stress of her final semester took its toll, but the stress was less from schoolwork than her job search, which hadn't yet yielded any results.

Settled later, after making a careful landing with their blue cups and red saucers, Al looked at her brightly, quickly glanced away, then looked back. And just as quickly, a scruffy, gaunt young man appeared, pausing to readjust his heavy backpack as he passed their table. At least that's what Sarah thought until he lifted his hand in a half-hearted wave.

"Hi, John," Al said. "John, this is Sarah."

She held out her hand, and John stared at it, then shook it more forcefully than necessary, as if to make up for his not having understood what to do with it in the first place.

"I just wanted to let you know that I read the book you suggested. I didn't, uh, I didn't agree. With some things," John said. His voice was soft, and he seemed nervous, taking his time getting his words out and fiddling with his backpack strap, but Al never interrupted or tried to fill in his words for him.

When it was clear that John was done speaking, Al said, "I'd love to know what you thought of it. Do you want to come to my office hours tomorrow?"

John nodded. "Okay. I'll come by. Not this week. Maybe next week."

"Looking forward to it."

John nodded again and hoisted his backpack higher on his shoulder. "Okay," he said, and with a glance back at Sarah, "Bye." But he didn't leave.

"I'm glad you stopped," Al said, smiling.

And then, still nodding, John left, bumping people with his backpack as he passed, apologizing his way out the door.

The exchange was painful to watch, and Sarah admired Al's patience. Or maybe, she thought, it was actually kindness.

"Are you a professor?"

"Almost. I'm a Ph.D. student in the Religion Department. How about you?"

"I'm a marketing major. I graduate this December, so I'm in the middle of a job search."

She took a sip of her coffee. "Why religion?"

"I've always been interested in it. I was like John. I read a lot when I was young. It's hard for me to explain, but I'm interested in its role in people's lives. Maybe in redemption, or the hope of it."

"Redemption? All I want to do is sell Cheerios or something," Sarah chuckled.

"I get this question a lot, but I don't really have a great answer. I think I'm still figuring it out myself. It's why the B.A. became an M.A. and is now a Ph.D."

Something about his truth nagged her, perhaps because she was ready to move on in her own life. She wanted to be solid, set, ready, employed. "I thought when we graduated, we were automatically adults." Her tone was light, but his reply, when it came, was pensive.

"Adulthood is hard."

"Well, spare me some pain. What's hardest?"

"Making friends," Al said, blushing again. "It's hard to make friends without classes and dorms and parties. Where do you meet people, you know? And I'm not even talking about dates. I mean friends. How often can you go hang out with people in the department? Even if your old friends are still your friends, you want to meet new people, too."

And that's when something recalibrated for Sarah, made her tilt her head and begin to listen with the same care Al had listened to John.

They settled in then, over cooling cups of coffee and no cookies, moving to a larger table as the crowd thinned so they could put their feet up on the extra chairs. She bought the second round, as she called it, and Al laughed. They talked about her job prospects, his thesis chapter from hell, how her sister, Glennie, was a grind and did nothing but study, how he was an only child. They talked about how much they loved dogs, but neither had one, and how great it would be if the

Campus Cup had a resident hound. They talked until Al peeked at his watch and said that sadly, he had a lecture to finish.

"What class?"

"It's the survey class, Religions of the World."

"Do you like teaching?" she asked, having noted a stutter when he'd talked earlier about his students. Except for the rare exception like John, he'd said, they lacked intellectual curiosity.

"Sometimes," Al said. "But I love it on days when you see a student catch on and light up. I love that light."

"The light makes it worth it?"

"Yes, absolutely. Doesn't connecting with someone in a real way always make it worth it?" He held her gaze then, and she didn't look away.

At the end of their date, after a sweet hug goodbye and his promise to call, Sarah stood for a long time on the sidewalk. It was dusk, and there was a slight chill in the air that was nighttime coming, and a feeling inside her that she didn't know. She watched Al walk down the street. He lumbered really, then disappeared into the crowd, and she took a deep breath. She wished she had some place to go and so she ate at the Village Wok, then cruised down the sidewalk hoping to bump into a friend and get swept up in a plan or even a direction. In the end, she walked home and called Glennie.

"Hey, it's me. The date went well."

"That's great. What's he like? Will you go out with him again?"

It took Sarah a minute, then she said, "He's shy, but he knows who he is. He's mature. And yes."

AL REFUSED TO STAY OVER at her place. Ever. So she stayed at his place. He had a wide double bed and shelves made out of plywood and cinder blocks. Most of the books were religious in orientation. One book, with a red binding, almost sent her home her first night. The white block letters on the spine spelled out Men, God and Faith. She thought he might be an Evangelical. Not Al. The only thing he was evangelical about, he said, was football. Gophers and Vikings. And high school hockey.

Al lived with his friend, Todd, who did not approve of Sarah's frequent visits.

"You're just lucky she's not in your class," Todd said once, in front of Sarah. He spoke as if she wasn't there, looking over her head to Al, who stood beside her in the kitchen, plate in hand, waiting for her to dish out baked chicken and potatoes.

Sarah had eyed Todd. He was a stocky farm boy from the south of the state, a friend Al had made in undergrad, with whom he stayed in close touch, with whom he had shared many a drunk, many a fear.

"I'm almost graduated," she said.

Silence descended. That's how she described it later in a phone message to Glennie. Silence rolled in like fog, but Sarah didn't leave.

"She's not in my class, she's a marketing major, and she graduates in December. We're talking two months," Al said over dinner.

Todd didn't answer. He shook his head. "It doesn't matter. It's the ethics of the thing."

That did it. The word ethics. Al didn't want to be unethical. He didn't want to raise questions about his judgment. Al began to meet her at less popular coffee shops, canceled late night plans, until she finally cornered him in the religion department office.

He was wearing corduroys with a thick grain, soft brown leather shoes, and a white shirt. He looked like an undergrad, with his easy smile, his deferential stance, the bent knee, his hands in his pockets as he waited his turn to ask the department secretary a question.

When he looked up and saw her, Al blushed. He walked with her down the hall into his office, which he shared with another Ph.D. candidate. The redness seemed to drain out of his face. Then, in a voice too quiet for her comfort, he asked, "What are you doing coming here?"

She remembered this moment all her life, the first time they argued, the first time she wanted to jut her chin out, the first time she was scared of losing him, and so scared at being scared that for a moment she didn't answer but looked around his office, which she'd never seen before, at the pictures of Jesus clustered above a desk.

"Are these yours?" she'd asked.

Al glanced at the posters. "Yes," he said, "because I study Christianity." He looked back at her. "That was flippant. Sorry. But look, I can't have you coming here like this."

"I didn't realize," she said, "that my student status bothered you this much, that coming to visit would do this."

Al stared at the floor.

"Aren't you a believer, too?" she asked, glancing at the Jesus posters.

"I would never want to jeopardize your future," she added.

Still, no answer, not even a sound, and so she left, shutting the door gently behind her.

She waited, hoping for him to call. Her mother called instead, wishing her good luck on finals. Glennie called to say hello, to hear what was up with this new man, and where was Sarah anyway? Sarah was on the couch, ignoring their phone messages, flipping through magazines. She was scribbling notes in her last classes, distracted by the buzzing lights, by the boy in front of her who smacked his gum, by thoughts of Al, teaching in another building, for students just like her.

AL WAS A LISTENER. He'd curl around her and stroke her hair when she was angry, let her speak the anger away. He'd offer advice only if she asked, or only, as he said, if she promised to listen to it.

"Don't get mad," he'd say.

"I won't."

"You have to promise, because last time you did get upset."

Sarah learned the technique from him, she thought later, the long listening, and the respectful quiet, and then, slowly, her response. And she remembered this most, in the long afternoons when he didn't call, that she would have most liked him now, for his advice on how to deal with his silence. She curled up on her bed, pulled the covers around her, and hoped.

They had only dated two months. She'd dated her high school boyfriend for over a year and hadn't felt half as sad when they split up to attend separate universities. She thought about calling Al, but she stayed curled up on her bed, thinking about Halloween, when they had first made love, and Al had gently pushed her down on the bed and kissed, first, the side of her neck. She curled up into a tight ball, wanting him.

"You have to get out of bed," her housemate Ann said. "This isn't healthy."

And it wasn't. It was self-indulgent, but she felt like being self-indulgent, and so she stayed. Even when she got up for finals, or even, once, for a Christmas party, she had no stamina and ended up back in bed, in a ball.

On Thursday nights, they used to cook dinner together. The same dinner, their favorite. Baked chicken with paprika on top, green beans with plenty of butter, and mashed potatoes with gravy. Afterward, they made strong coffee, to study together, but often, side by side on the bed, they pushed the books away and made long, slow love.

Every memory made her hungry or horny or sad or all three.

Ann, finished with finals early because she was a dance major, refused to let Sarah feel any sorrier for herself than she already felt. Ann had the body of a whippet—taut, lean—and she spoke the way she looked, without excess.

"Your butt will sag by thirty. Get up and exercise."

"There are other fish in the sea. In fact, at his size, you should qualify for two good boyfriends next."

What Ann didn't realize, none of the girls, really, was that part of what Sarah loved about Al was his bulk. The girls noticed his blue eyes, his dimples, the white-blond hair they said reminded them of summer and the beach and bonfires. But they spoke carefully, avoided mention of his size until the break-up. For Sarah, his roundness was its own attraction. She loved the way she could bury her face in the soft warmth of his arm, the way, pressed together, they felt solid, impenetrable, strong.

Ann, persistent, dropped in every day, sometimes twice.

"Today you will eat."

9

"Today you will stay out of bed for four hours in a row."

"Call Pillsbury. They liked your resume, and you need a job. Besides, you might score free baked goods."

They started calling Al Doughboy, Ann and the other girls in the house. They stopped when Sarah told them, for the first time, that she liked his size. Then Ann asked, for the first time, what Sarah needed to do to shake the blues.

"I want to get out of here," she said, "and go someplace new."

Ann, of course, had an idea for that, and they spent the weekend in a rundown Radisson in Minneapolis. They crammed five girls into a single and held a slumber party. Sarah didn't invite Glennie. Glennie had never even met Al, the way the semester had gone, though Sarah had a tickle of guilt about that, something her dad had said on the phone recently, about Glennie not doing well.

"This," Ann said, as she passed the joint, "is the way slumber parties should be."

"I should tell him I'm sorry," Sarah said, picking up the phone, but Ann grabbed the receiver and set it back down.

"Call when you're sober," she said.

"I can't."

"Then just let it go."

IN HER CAP AND GOWN, Sarah thought she looked much older than she felt. And when she marched into graduation with the other hundreds of graduates and stared at the teeming crowd, which moved like an amoeba, she was less than jovial, but she drank from the bottle of champagne that circled the rows.

Sarah knew she wouldn't call Al, and so later she packed her bags, took down her photos, her bulletin board, her poster of France. Put her life back into boxes, and finally, when there was nothing else left in the room, not even the boxes themselves, disconnected the phone.

"Hoping for a call?" her dad asked, stroking his beard, which she noted had more gray in it lately.

Sarah nodded.

He patted her back.

He'd taken off from work to help Sarah pack the last of her things, easy enough for him to do as an administrator at the U. Her rental was nearby, and it wouldn't take long. Maybe his lunch hour. Glennie had arrived too late to help. Her father had hurried across campus though he was far from trim, and he'd arrived before Glennie, who was only one block down, but this is the way it had been lately. A block had become a sea and then a sea, an ocean. Sarah and Glennie had hardly seen each other all semester, and Sarah thought Glennie looked tense and thinner. Glennie had always been tiny, delicate, like a willow branch, all legs, long golden hair, and blue eyes. Beautiful, intense, a reed of a girl who had no interest in her own looks and often seemed perplexed that others did. But she looked rail thin now. Had Glennie's sophomore year started that badly? Could it be the cut of her clothes? But maybe it was just Sarah's perspective. *She* was thinner and tense. She hadn't been eating much.

"You okay?" Sarah asked.

"I'm fine."

"You just look really thin."

"Everyone's asking. I'm fine."

The lost weight made Glennie's eyes look bigger, and she had the hint of a ghost about her. Was she down one size? Two? On Glennie's frame, that would be a noticeable loss. Yet she hadn't shared a single confidence or worry in how long? Sarah couldn't remember. But Sarah hadn't made time to check on Glennie either. She'd been so consumed with Al.

"Do you want to talk? Go get a coffee later?" she asked.

Glennie didn't reply.

"Glennie?"

"No. I'm fine, like I said. Nothing to discuss." Glennie sounded like she was about to slap someone, her reply coming out fast; her words, clipped.

I don't even know you right now, Sarah thought, and the thought shocked her. Somehow, she had let a door close between them, and she was determined, absolutely determined, to get it back open. If things were done with Al, that was one thing. A deeply sad and devastating thing, but she would heal. Eventually. But things couldn't be broken with her sister, even if her sister was broken.

It hurt a little to see Glennie. She had that enviable golden hair and stunning blue eyes.

"Al has similar coloring," Sarah said. "Like you're both direct descendants of Vikings."

Glennie tucked her hair back. "Let him go, Sarah," she said softly.

Of course Glennie would suggest moving on, not that there seemed like any option. Glennie was like a firefly with romance. She burned out fast. No man had held her attention, not even other Pre-Meds. It mystified Sarah, but what Glennie loved was medicine. There were no phases in Glennie's life, no other interests. Like a competitive ice skater aiming for the Olympics, she had one passion, one goal. Sarah thought it probably had to do with their grandparents. They'd grown up with all three generations living in one house, and doctor appointments, prescriptions, and health scares were woven into the fabric of their childhoods. At age six, Glennie apparently had asked for a stethoscope of her own. She was still waiting for one. But now she planned to earn it.

Dad appeared at the door, winded, cheeks red from the cold. "I've got it all loaded in your car. Gotta get back soon. Is that everything?" When Sarah nodded, he handed over the keys, then said over his shoulder, "I'll be in the car. You can drop me back at the office."

"Thanks, Dad."

Sarah scanned her room one last time. Bare now, tape stuck to the walls, black scratch marks the landlord would paint over for the next occupant. Silent. She grabbed the phone. Glennie threw an arm around her as they left, whispering, "Al wasn't worth it anyway."

Sarah nodded. She didn't feel like arguing, but she also didn't agree. She believed he was.

Glennie had a paper to finish, for which she had received an extension of a few days, but she stayed long enough on the sidewalk to wave as Sarah pulled the car out. Sarah didn't dare wave back. She'd probably wreck. She'd always needed two hands on the wheel.

Her dad was quiet during the drive, looking out the window at the new snow, falling lazily.

"She's too thin," he finally said.

"I know, but she won't talk about it."

"I thought she'd talk to you, even if she won't talk to anyone else."

"Can you call someone?" Sarah asked.

Her dad shook his head no. "I did, but they said she's over 18. I can't make her go see anyone."

"Do you think she's too thin, like dangerously thin?"

"I don't know."

Glennie was on her own because that seemed to be what she wanted, out in uncharted territory, with an enemy only she could see. But Glennie would handle this. She wouldn't let anything deflect her from her dream of becoming a doctor. Sarah might not have known her sister was struggling, but *she* knew it.

Carefully, Sarah pulled alongside the curb outside her dad's building. For a moment, they sat in silence. Adulthood sucked, she thought. So much for the freedom to chart your own course. Her sister might already be going off the rails. Sarah had no job. And when had her dad not known something?

"Thanks for your help," she said when he opened the car door. "I'll see you tonight."

"Glad you're coming home."

Sarah smiled but wished she'd had a choice. Ann had accepted a job as a receptionist at an accounting firm in St. Paul and was moving into an old house with three friends. They'd all wanted Sarah to join them, but Pillsbury, Sarah's last hope for work, had never replied, and so she pointed the car toward the highway and the ranch style house where she grew up. Toward the red maples and the wide lawn and the Christmas lights blinking hello through what was, suddenly, a thicker, heavier snow. Where her mother was probably looking out the front door because of the weather, hoping Sarah had taken the back roads, and her grandparents were likely waiting at the kitchen table, which had a view of the driveway. Sarah would go home, and she would start her job search over. She'd try not to miss Al, and she'd spend time with Glennie. They would bake cookies, if Glennie felt comfortable with the idea, and maybe take a sleigh ride with the Johnsons. If Glennie wanted to have a snowball fight, they would have a snowball fight. If Glennie wanted to watch movies, they would watch movies. Sarah would travel whatever distance it took to reach her, wherever Glennie was, however alien a place, however vast. Sarah would reach her in the end, though. She would help her. Sarah felt sure of that. Because the Macmillans endured. They believed in the power of family bonds. If they had nothing else, they always had each other. And Sarah would always honor that legacy.

Cleaning House
Sarah
October 1995

IN THEIR DUSK-LIT NURSING HOME ROOM, my grandparents seem at peace with the half-darkness, in that space between what they know and what they don't. It's as if the shadows suit them, soften the edges. Promise a gentle passing.

But none of that is true.

As their day nurse, Kirsten, said on the phone yesterday, "You did something. I don't know what. But this situation has been going on for days now, and you need to get over here and fix it."

I know Kirsten well enough now to have heard the laughter in her voice, but there was a sharpness in it, too, that sent a wash of fatigue over me and stalled me for an entire day. I'm the default caregiver, still being unemployed. I can't seem to market myself so maybe this field isn't for me, but at least temping has allowed me to care for my grandparents in moments like these. Dad gets two personal days. Glennie is even more unreliable now that she wants to take the MCAT early, next semester, the wrong time to push herself if you ask me, but she doesn't ask, just pops in sometimes to prove she's okay. And Mom has to ask for time off weeks in advance at the garden center because she's the manager. It doesn't matter to the owners that these are her parents, and I know she loves her job. Still, I'm not sure how to handle everything, I want to say, standing here in the nursing home hallway. No one has time to listen, though, not really, not when there are health crises almost every day in the nursing home and deadlines and rigid, rule-following bosses. I could imagine what Kirsten would say anyway, and I could even imagine her saying it.

"You're as good as your mother with them." Her dyed blond hair in a tight ponytail, showing hints of dark brown at the scalp. The deep wrinkles in her forehead. Baggy eyes. Baggy scrubs, solid purple or ones with flowers. Eyebrows raised as if to warn me. Kirsten could be thirty or fifty, but I bet she is closer to thirty. She has her hands full every day, and her sympathy for me is limited, and I understand. Who needs angry eighty- and ninety-year-olds?

My grandparents have been arguing, and the argument has escalated into barks with my name in them. Sarah!

Then suddenly this morning, silence. They will not talk to each other. In fact, they will talk with no one.

Except, apparently, me.

Kirsten phoned to update me after their breakfast, and I said I'd be by before they ate dinner. And now here I am, on this crisp October evening, gathering courage before crossing the threshold, wondering what I've inadvertently done that has made my grandparents, married for a remarkable 61 years, stop speaking to one another and the staff.

The door to my grandparent's room is pushed back against the wall, and three black numbers form a diagonal down the white paint: 129. Someone has taped construction paper leaves to the door announcing their 61st. Congratulations, Catherine & Ed!

Grandpa lays quietly in his bed, hands in constant spasm, his middle grotesquely enlarged. Grandma, in a chair by the foot of his bed, stares fixedly out into the hallway, her same determined glare suddenly fiercer. She's wearing a navy sweat suit, which bags around her legs. Her hair lies flat on one side, then swoops up on the other. Her scalp shows through in spots. She slumps, but she stays where she is, right by Grandpa. She waits. She can't see me, but she will try. For as long as it takes.

She's the only brave one in the whole damn family.

MY GRANDMOTHER WANTED me to have the china, which had gone to the oldest grandchild for five generations. She told me over the phone early last May, slipping the news into a discussion about how to clean my moldy shower curtain. She referred to it as my shower curtain because she refused when discussing anything remotely intimate to acknowledge that Al might use the item, too. Thrilled as she was that we were back together, she wasn't thrilled about the living arrangements.

We talked on a warm day, a bee buzzing kind of day, when Al and I had looked around the house and each chosen a chore. Al decided to clean out the fridge, which for him meant eating all the leftovers. That accomplished, he'd disappeared into the back yard. I'd peeked out the kitchen window at him, momentarily forgetting Grandma. When I looked back at my notes about how to clean the shower curtain, I'd scribbled add china.

"Back up, Grandma," I'd said.

"Back up to what?" she'd asked, sounding tired.

"To the china part."

"Oh," she'd said. "Well."

I'd fiddled with my pen like it was a baton.

"I've mentioned this on and off for years, Sarah. I'm leaving my china to you," she'd said.

"Why?"

"Because I'm leaving the silver to Glennie."

"No, I mean why are we talking about this?"

"Because I'm cleaning house, too,"

I didn't want the china. I don't really want anything, except what I already have, a pale orange sweater she knitted for me my freshman year of college and the few photos she parceled out last Christmas. But what I want isn't the point, though I have trouble remembering that. The point is that she wanted to give me something, me and Al, and she wanted to give it then, before she got to the now, in which on bad nights I pop in for a visit and find her sitting in the nursing home hallway strapped into her wheelchair, picking at the scab on her head.

"Be gracious," she'd said finally as our conversation wound down.

"About a moldy shower curtain?"

She didn't think I was funny. She said, "You're being flip. How's Al?"

I peeked out the window again and saw Al bent over our vegetable patch. He seemed to be examining the garden. He seemed to be debating.

"He's trying to weed."

"Trying? Is he actually doing anything?"

Grandma loves most everything about Al, except what she interprets as a certain lack of decisiveness. It's hard not to love Al, with his big dimples and white-blond hair, as if it has been bleached. But her love came around slowly, after she recovered from our decision to live together.

"Is he going to ask you to marry him or not?"

Grandma had sounded perturbed, and I remember thinking, It's my life. I couldn't be pressured into doing what I wasn't ready to do. She blamed Al for my reservations. She expected me, after all, to believe in marriage, as if her success ensured mine.

I stared out the window at Al, who had begun to vigorously pull up my basil. I didn't stop him.

"Grandma," I'd said, "I'm not in the mood to talk about weddings or death."

"You never are," she said. Her voice shook. "Did it ever occur to you that I might need to?"

I was trying to think of how to tell Grandma I was sorry, but the apology got lost in my rising anger, tempered slightly by the fatigue of being at odds with her, and then she said, abruptly, "Oh, never mind. Why do you want to clean your shower curtain?"

"I want to get the mold off."

"Pitch it," Grandma said, and then she hung up.

That was on May 2nd, just before her 88th birthday, the celebration of which was postponed by a late-night phone call, by a sudden family conference in the emergency room of Abbott Northwestern Hospital. By the sudden move here.

IT'S TIME, I THINK NOW. Overdue. Time for me to accept the china. Time for me to grow up.

Time for me to go into the room.

"Grandma," I say, stepping through the door.

She doesn't respond.

"Grandma." I raise my voice and find that place between volume and clarity that she can hear.

Her smile is wide. She brings both hands together, as if she's going to clap, once, but then her hands part, and she puts one arm out, and I hold onto her more than she holds onto me. With her free hand, she slaps at Grandpa's feet, and he jerks, scowls at her, and then sees me. He laughs and holds out his hands.

Grandpa looks like someone inflated him. Seeing him rounded in the middle and with arms and legs thin as sticks, I fight back tears. He's ballooned in the middle from age and constipation, and probably from arguing with Grandma. Arguing with her is enough to constipate us all. I know from experience.

I bend and give him a kiss. He's unshaven, and his cheeks are hollowed. He smells. I don't know what he smells of, urine maybe, maybe old age, but the smell is sour. If he knew, he would die of embarrassment.

"Who is it?" he asks.

"Sarah," I yell. "Are you kissing every girl who comes along?"

He laughs and nods long after my joke, and I know he hasn't heard. I hold his hands firmly in mine.

"How are you?" I ask.

He laughs and nods again. He pats my hand. "I'm going to sleep," he says and turns away.

I look at Grandma.

"He does that," she says. She shakes her head. She holds a hand out to me, and I take it, stretching myself out between the two.

The last light is fading and the sky takes on a dark blue hue. I let go of their hands and turn on the lamp on Grandma's nightstand. Her pajamas, rose-patterned flannel, drape off the bed onto the floor, along with a white crocheted blanket. Not warm enough. She needs heavier blankets, year-round. I pick up her pajamas, fold the blanket over the metal bars alongside the bed. They're the kinds of beds advertised on TV for people with bad backs. They adjust. That's what the whole place is about: adjustment.

Grandma is preoccupied. She presses her fingers against her mouth and taps lightly, repeatedly. With her other hand, she absentmindedly digs at the scab on her head. To stop her, I touch her shoulder, and she snaps to attention.

"I wanted to talk to you." She pats my hand with each word, and her pats are soft, her skin is soft.

I pull my chair closer. "Kirsten said you'd been nagging her to call me."

"I don't nag. I politely insist. There's a difference."

I don't argue.

"We need to clear some things up," she says.

"We're clear."

Grandma sits up a bit in her chair, leans forward. Her frown is deep, and there's a flash in her eyes, a spark that I'm glad to see, sort of.

"We're not clear," she says. "We are not clear yet." She spits out the last word. She will always have the last word.

We are all small women, my grandmother, my mother and me. Only Glennie is tall, and with her thick golden hair, she's a siren. She hasn't realized what we know, that men are waiting for her to notice them. I am short. I am plainer. I have an honest face, my mother says, clear blue eyes, a strong jaw, hair an auburn color that makes her think of late September and falling leaves. My mother is poetic. My sister is graceful. I look at my grandmother. We have the same determined jaw, she and I. We have the same eyes. We are the strong ones.

"What's not clear between us?" I ask.

"The china." Grandma waves her hand in the air. She picks at her scab again, and I take her hand in mine.

"Thank you," she says softly.

TIME CHANGES THINGS SLOWLY at first, like the seasons. The leaves turn yellow, the color deepens, and then suddenly some are red, and fall arrives, as if overnight. I've decided that's how age works. First, there is a gray hair, a wrinkle, a dull ache in one's joints, but the changes are small and easy to accommodate. When Grandpa couldn't see to drive and Dad told him to stay off the road, he and I waved good-bye to his Chevy Impala as they wheeled it away to the junk yard. Then I helped to drive him places, to the hardware store; the Donut Shop, where the old Navy men meet to tell tales; to the basketball games, where he swore loudly every time the high school team lost, which happened more often than not. Looking back, I can see the slow sequence of changes, but it's a jarring and sudden awakening when Grandma cannot climb the stairs, when suddenly, her body no longer works right, and I'm wiping her feces off a wall.

Last May, I met my family at Emergency. They'd rushed Grandma there, uncertain what had happened, uncertain anymore what qualified as a crisis.

Dad was watching for me, looking across the lobby to the entrance, but he missed me entirely. He was wearing jeans and an old wool sweater and a pair of ratty old loafers. He had his hands thrust into his jeans pockets, a look in his eyes that was inscrutable, and his chin thrust out, all gray beard and defiance.

Mom stood outside a set of swinging double doors, peeking down the hall each time they swung open. Grandpa was rifling through the magazines on a nearby table, then he straightened the pile, and then he stood, hands behind his back, and watched the doors as well. I reached them just as they each moved closer, just as a doctor came through and turned to them.

"She exploded," Mom told the doctor, her mouth a thin line, her face newly haggard and pale.

"She's losing control, Mrs. Macmillan," the doctor replied. He was an emergency room doctor, a stand-in for Doctor Kline.

"She tried to get to the toilet," Mom said, and then, "We can't keep up." Her voice sounded firm, as if she was trying to convince herself.

The doctor nodded. What could he say? There was nothing to say. There was no way, after a certain point, to keep up.

We walked Grandpa down to see Grandma. She was sleeping, eyes shut tightly, face pale. Grandpa's hands shook, but he reached out, stroked her forehead, brushed the hair out of her eyes, and finally sat holding her hand, occasionally adjusting her blanket, occasionally drifting off himself. Mom took root on the other side of the bed, keeping an eye on them both.

Later, Dad and I talked to Dr. Kline, who said Grandma should probably not go home. Sometimes, Dr. Kline said, life straightens out the wrinkles on its own. He knew a nursing home that had a room. He was on the board. I remember thinking that he sounded like a travel agent talking about a hotel, something small and clean and temporary, and then I realized that was exactly what he was talking about.

A nurse walked Grandpa back out to the lobby and guided him to a chair. Dad bent down, hands on his knees, and talked into Grandpa's best ear. He told him what Dr. Kline had said. Grandpa nodded. His voice was steady when he said, "Wherever she goes, I go."

Grandpa and Grandma moved to the nursing home a week later. In the meantime, we shuttled Grandpa back and forth to see Grandma in the hospital. The garden center relented and let Mom take time off to care for them. We filled in the nursing home application. Question fifteen. Please list a funeral home.

That night in the emergency room, we were clear eyed, unblinking, calm. Yes, we understood. Yes, we knew this was for the best. I called Glennie. She was at the library, according to her roommate, and I knew this was probably true although it was nearly three a.m. She fell asleep there often, curled up in the chairs down by the humming pop machines, locked in for the night. But that night I wished Glennie had a boyfriend or a hobby, that she had a life beyond organic chemistry and DNA, a life beyond her future dreams of medical school. I wished she was with us.

Later, as light came back into the sky, Dad and I returned home and wiped down the bathroom wall. We threw away the towels hanging on the rack. We closed the door.

"YOU NEED TO LEARN TO ACCEPT A FEW THINGS," Grandma says to me now. "I need to accept some things, too. One of them is that I'm here. You need to accept that we are going to die."

She catches me unprepared. "I know that," I say, and my voice sounds light, surprised.

"No, you don't."

"Grandma, I understand."

Grandma shakes her head. She slumps back into her chair. "If you knew that, you'd listen."

I'm afraid to reply, so I sit and wait for her to speak. Grandpa's hands still spasm, and I stare at them, wanting them to stop, afraid that they will. Grandma seems to know where my gaze falls.

"You do what he does," Grandma says. "You turn off when you don't want to talk. You turn away."

Grandma lifts herself out of her chair part way, pauses, then sits back down. I try to help, but she's too heavy. I press the call button.

She swats Grandpa's feet. "Wake him up."

I hesitate.

"Wake him up." She raises her voice, and I lean over and tap Grandpa awake, tap until his eyes open slowly, and he looks at me.

"Tell him I'm giving you the gift now. Tell him not to turn off."

"What gift?"

"The gift we're giving you. Don't argue."

She presses a buzzer near her chair. Soon Kirsten knocks on the door, then comes inside. Without a word, she lifts Grandma from the chair and sets her walker in front of her. Grandma leans heavily on it. After Kirsten leaves, Grandma walks slowly over to her dresser drawer and pulls out a box.

Grandpa shakes his head. "I told her you wouldn't want this," he says. "I don't want her to do it."

Grandma grips the box in her hand, turns, and I'm shocked that she lets me guide her.

I think about ritual, about the passing on of china, of linen, of antique furniture. To me, family history is made up of stories more than material goods, and the thought of wanting something, of saying, yes, I'd like the china, seems crude. I want the stories. I want connections, and the rituals that forged them, like Grandpa and Grandma's October favorite anniversary meal (beef stew and biscuits), Dad playing Santa each Christmas, my annual snow fight with Glennie. I want only to remember. I can't believe that one day she'll be gone; that Grandpa will be gone; that I'll turn from the stove on Thanksgiving, turn from stirring the gravy, and not see them waiting at the table to taste; that I'll walk down the aisle, one day, far away, and they will not be sitting in the front pews; that their stories are ones soon I will tell, and never as well.

"Here," Grandma says, having returned to her seat and taken a breath. She thrusts the box at me, and when I hesitate to take it, she nudges my hand with it. "This is for you."

I take the box. It's made of a rough, hard material, and the white has yellowed.

"I'm not giving you the china."

I stare at her.

"I'm giving it to Glennie. She likes it. She might use it. You won't."

I smile, but I don't feel much like laughing. Grandma smiles at me, too, and her smile is a steady one, determined. "I'm also giving you my tea towels," she said. "You make more messes."

I laugh, and the laugh is like a bubble, and it lets the tears loose.

"Just keep one or two nice," Grandma says. "Keep the ones with my good embroidery for nice."

Grandpa clasps his hands together as if he's praying, and his hands still shake. Grandma waits for me to open my box. Inside, on a piece of soft, old white rag, is her wedding band. It's dark in spots and needs a good rubbing clean, but it is there, with sixty-one years of marriage wound around it, slightly tarnished, but still holding firm.

I can't touch it. I just stare at it. I raise the box in the air, hoping Grandpa will see the motion, and he does. His eyes follow my hands. He takes a deep breath.

"That," Grandma says, sounding triumphant, "you will use."

I give Grandma a kiss, then Grandpa. He holds my hand and whispers in dulcet tones, "I didn't want her to do this yet. I wanted her to have it all her life."

I say thank you, but my voice cracks, and I'm not sure he hears.

"Whenever you're ready, you use that," Grandma says. "He's mad, but I want you to have it now, when we're able to give it. He'll talk to me soon. He'll talk to me."

I leave the ring in the box and slide the cover back down. I sit with them silently for a long time in the room that is not their home, in the place that is temporary and cold, and watch as the last light slips in a breath from the sky and the deep darkness seeps in, as winter takes over. Grandma eases herself back into her chair, and Grandpa, wide awake in the growing darkness, trembles. I tremble, too. Only Grandma is calm. Only Grandma is at peace. Only she is ready.

Whole New Worlds
Sarah
December 1995

My grandfather saw the beginning of the Bolshevik Revolution. He stared from the deck of the U.S.S. Greenlet toward the thin strip of land that was the shore, and he thinks he saw puffs of smoke, the distant beginnings of a new war as the other died. His ship was outside Vladivostok. He was 15, and now, at 92, he isn't sure he remembers what happened in Vladivostok correctly. His memory slips. He calls me by my mother's name. He lies in his bed in the nursing home, voice thin as paper, and whispers pieces of stories. I try to catch them. I catch what I can. I create our history out of the pieces, pick them up, fit them together. Puffs of smoke.

I'm sitting in the gray half-light of early morning, alone. Just like Grandpa, I can't think clearly. He's looking back; me, forward. Try not to look at the borders, at the possibilities, I tell myself. They are boundaries into whole new worlds.

Grandpa lied about his age to get into WWI, running down to enlist with his buddy Jimmy Kantor before either of their mothers could stop them. Later, he insisted the Navy find him a place in WWII, even though he was considered too old. In my own life, I have never known such courage, and rarely such clarity.

The kitchen is cold, and I'm wearing my favorite wool sweater and a long flannel nightgown, the same outfit I wore yesterday, and the day before. I couldn't sleep, and I slid out from underneath the heavy weight of Al's arm and came downstairs. I stole his fuzzy bear paw slippers to wear, and each step I made on the hardwood floors sounded like I was being hushed, from restlessness to calm. Upstairs, Al snores softly. He's sound asleep, head under his pillow, arm thrown over mine.

"I can't believe you two planned a vacation in Iowa," Mom had said.

I called her last week to let her know we'd be out of town, to ask her to feed the cat. Alber hates to be alone. If somebody doesn't come over and lavish him with praise on a regular basis, he'll take revenge on the plants.

"We're staying in an old farmhouse," I said.

"Where else would you be staying?" Mom paused. "Whose idea was this?"

"Al's." I felt the conversation degenerating. "Mom," I said. "We just want to get away for a while."

"Oh, trust me, you will."

We rented the house for the days before New Year's, hoping to escape into a quiet and calm that the previous months had not allowed. I had a feeling then, in the way planning the trip made Al more buoyant, in the way he crossed days off on his calendar, that for him the vacation meant more than escaping a trying three or four months. Last week, when I wasn't looking, the box with my grandmother's wedding ring disappeared from the top of my dresser, and now, almost through our vacation, packing to leave, I wait for him to give it back to me.

The Realtor reminded us the amenities were few, just before we signed the rental contract for one of the few properties that fit his budget.

"No coffee pot," she said, raising a penciled brown eyebrow, gauging our response. Her name was Mrs. Swenson, and she had an office right down the road from Al's office at the university. Mrs. Swenson wore a bright red jacket and gold earrings. She smoked thin cigarettes.

"No coffee pot?" she said, and her voice rose at the end.

We stared at her blankly.

"No washer and dryer." Again, the eyebrow went up, and again, we were silent. "No shower," Mrs. Swenson continued, "only a bathtub."

Al leaned forward. He smiled. He said, "Does it have toilet?"

The eyebrow stayed up. "Yes," she said.

"Inside?"

"Yes."

"Then we're dandy."

I had watched Al sign the contract, his hand gliding over the page. It seemed so easy, being definite.

This morning, when I put a kettle on, blue flame hissed and sprang from the burner, and there was something beautiful about it in the darkness. Outside, for miles, the view is of snow and trees. There are no lights lining any highway, no garbage truck that thunders past, flashing yellow lights across the ceiling, nobody telling me that what my ads really need are borders to give them a little pep. Out here, lost in the long land that is farmland, I sit at a kitchen table of solid maple, and drink tea that is hot and strong. Later, I'll drive down a dirt road, bump along until I reach pavement, and then glide past field after field, just for the fun of it, just to feel open space, wide open space, like I haven't felt for a long time.

"Will you feed Alber?" I finally asked my mother when we spoke on the phone last week. Lately, we've communicated by telephone, sending ourselves from one side of Minneapolis to the other, over the snowy roads we refuse to traverse, over the long gray landscape of winter.

"I'll even take him for walks," she had said.

I doubted Alber could make it more than two yards, but I didn't say so. Alber could use exercise, like Al. They're a pair. They stretch out on the couch together and watch college football on fall Saturdays. On occasion, I've even seen Al slip Alber a victory potato chip when the Gophers scored.

"What's happening?" Mom asked. "You're planning to quit your job, now you're enamored of Iowa."

I knew she was joking, but underneath the joke, she didn't understand. For months now, Al has been like a signal man on a Navy ship who waves flags at boats on the horizon. The signals are sometimes subtle, sometimes not and then must be decoded, but the message is clear. Where will we spend the holidays next year? How do I feel about the ring my grandmother gave me, her ring, the ring she has slipped off her finger already, for me, now? That's what he asked me when I brought it home and showed it to him in October, placed on a white cloth in a small white box. He asked, "Is that the one you want?"

I think, being honest with myself, which sometimes is hard for me to do, that Al was willing to wait for me until he started hanging out with my Grandpa. Al's signaling started with Grandpa, who has decided I need to hurry up so he can be here to see it all. Al's signals are like the smoke in Vladivostok that warned Grandpa at age fifteen that something was beginning, something big.

LAST SEMESTER, Al taught in the mornings. He rode the bus to campus to lecture in Religion 125, Religions of the World. In the afternoons, he stopped by the nursing home. He climbed off the bus early to do so, switched lines, and walked the last block. He had no living grandparents.

The first time he visited, he brought flowers for Grandma. Grandpa made him leave the room, and when Grandpa yelled for Al to come back in, Al pretended not to notice the whoopee cushion. He took his seat, in the chair between both beds, and sat down hard. Grandpa roared. He laughed so hard, he cried; and even Grandma, who bit her lip, who said that cushion was the worst toy in the world, even she began to giggle. Al's visits became a regular activity, a daily ritual, and Grandpa kept his checkerboard open to their last game. Their game was always open; they never finished. Al played every afternoon, because it was the one thing Grandpa could do. Grandpa could grab his elbow to move his arm, pick up the pieces, and slide them slowly across to a space. There were times when he couldn't see black and red, so Al told him the color.

"Red," he'd yell. "Black."

But he never moved Grandpa's pieces for him, and he never played to lose.

I caught them recently, huddled together, whispering after their game. I'd dropped by on my own, and there was Al, sitting on the foot of Grandpa's bed, telling him a dirty joke. It's a favorite memory already, Al leaning over, speaking directly into Grandpa's good ear, if he has one anymore, and Grandpa, hand on Al's shoulder, holding himself still and listening. I smile remembering how Grandpa tilted his head back, laughing long and hard.

GRANDPA WAS THE FIRST to realize that Al was the one. Grandpa knew before I knew. I don't know how. Usually, Grandpa isn't observant, but Glennie, insists that when it comes to us, Grandpa is a hawk. He zeroes in, she says, he watches.

Al and I met at the library during my senior year of college. That year I invited Al to Thanksgiving, even though we'd only been dating a few weeks. His parents lived in Chicago, and he couldn't afford a ticket home. He was part-way through his Ph.D., too, and he had a thesis chapter to write.

On Thanksgiving Day, given the miserable performance of his football teams, Grandpa ensconced himself at the kitchen table, in the way of the busy dinner preparations, and drank his second scotch of the morning. I walked into the kitchen, and there he was, surrounded by china plates, dipping his hand freely into the salad for croutons. I walked randomly throughout the house, waiting for Al to arrive.

Grandpa and Dad had a saying, an excuse, for drinking scotch. They pretended they'd seen a snake downstairs, then come up waving their hands in front of their faces, fanning themselves, and collapse into chairs. They said the only cure for seeing a snake was a glass of Glenlivet.

When the doorbell rang, I tried to beat Grandpa to it. Who knew what Grandpa might say if he answered the door?

Grandpa got there first.

"What do you want?" he asked, opening the door, glass in hand.

"Hello, sir. I'm Sarah's boyfriend, Al, and I'm here for dinner."

The cold air streamed in through the door, and I stuck my head out around Grandpa and smiled at Al. Al wore a white shirt and a beige sweater and a pair of pressed pants. He carried a bouquet of flowers and a bottle of red wine.

"Grandpa," I had said, hoping to prompt him to let Al inside, "This is Al. I told you about Al, remember?"

Grandpa sniffed. He said, "Al, I saw something frightening this morning. I saw a snake."

I wilted a little.

Al paused. He said, "Sir, if you have seen a snake, then you deserve that drink."

Grandpa stepped aside, and with a flourish of his hand, asked Al if he had seen any snakes. Al shook his head. No, he said, he had not seen a snake, but he could have sworn he'd seen a bear in the middle of 35W on the drive to our house. He got a double.

I worried how my parents might feel, climbing up from downstairs with Grandma to say their first hellos. I worried about what they would think of Al. My grandmother reached the landing first, then my mother, and they didn't seem to notice the drink, or to think twice if they had. Maybe the bouquet distracted them. Dad reached the landing and made his way to me.

"What's his name again?" Dad asked.

"Al," I whispered in his ear, and over Dad went, hand extended, saying "Al, Al, Al," repeating the name to cement it in his memory. "Welcome. My, there are a lot of snakes out today."

"There are even bears," Al said.

It was like water, his arrival, a smooth transition. Add a boulder to the stream and the stream works around it. No upsets, no tension, just the rearrangement that comes with multiplying. Al said later that he'd needed that scotch. He'd been nervous as hell, having all my family standing around him at the kitchen table, asking question after question, under fire.

Grandpa had winked at me later, as Mom fluttered around Al, thanked him for the flowers, as Grandma reached for his hand to tell him a story. He had winked at me and laughed to himself, and I realized that he'd planted that drink in Al's hands, that it had been his gift, his mercy.

Before Christmas, Grandpa called me. He never called because he had trouble hearing over the phone, but one day, he picked up the receiver and probably turned up the hearing dial by using his magnifying glass.

"Sarah?" he said.

For a minute, I think we were both stunned, him at having successfully completed the call, me at hearing his voice.

"I want you to take me to the mall," he said.

Grandpa hated the mall.

"Sure," I said. "When?"

"Today. Could we go today? I want to get Al a Christmas gift."

"You do?" I felt pleased, really, like somebody in my family ought to get Al a present. He, after all, had presents for them, albeit small ones. He'd bought Grandpa a new whoopee cushion.

"What are you getting him? "I asked.

"Slippers," Grandpa said.

I picked Grandpa up that afternoon. He wanted to be dropped off, so I spent the free hour looking around the shops myself, and we met later. He said nothing, and I never thought to ask. Slippers were slippers.

Later, Grandpa called again.

"Time to deliver it," he said.

"Deliver what?"

"The gift."

THE gift. I didn't notice the wording then, slow to realize how special Al was to Grandpa.

Then Al and I broke up, making the gift exchange bittersweet.

Then we got back together.

Now here we are, a year later.

The light is in the sky now, spreading, like a stain. Upstairs, Al sleeps on. Finals are over. Before we left, he graded a hundred essays about Buddhism. He now hates Buddhism. More than that, though, he hates what freshmen have to say about it.

"Buddhism is an act of faith. So is love," he quoted from a student paper. He was sitting at the kitchen table the night before we left, final papers spread out in neat piles in front of him. "Oh God."

The small happinesses, the small things. These are what keep me going. Al at the kitchen table, red pen out, correcting comma splices and failed logic. Al singing in the shower. Me half-asleep, snow coming down outside now, and that's all, that's my world.

Whole new worlds, I think, staring out at the snow. Lines shift. Lines change. Boundaries are redrawn. Whole new worlds, created out of bits of the past, from what is passed forward, accepted again, taken and renewed. This, too, is an act of faith, the going forward, the continuing on.

To family, my grandfather had thundered, raising his glass, years ago. We are a dynasty in our own right, with our feet planted in the soil of a new country, the generations traced back to Vimmerby, to Glasgow, to Sarahstina, for whom I was named. I was named for a woman who fled her homeland, created a new life, recreated herself. I have never asked why she fled, why Grandma uses that word in particular, as if she had a fear too big to stay in the country, a fear only distance could swallow whole.

"What are you afraid of?" I speak out loud, my voice low, breaking the stillness in the kitchen. I imagine Al marching downstairs with Grandma's white ring box, maybe tucking the ring in the pocket of his robe. I don't know what I will say. Can I say, may I have twenty-four hours?

"What is so frightening about the possibility of marriage?"

I have no answers for myself. I have no answers at all.

IMMEDIATELY AFTER WE'D RENTED THE HOUSE, I dropped by the nursing home to tell Grandma and Grandpa we'd planned a vacation. The deposit receipt seemed to burn a promise through my purse.

As I walked through the double doors into the main reception area, I saw Grandma seated in a fold out chair in the front row of the current events lecture. The current events lecture took place every night before the first dinner shift, and the regulars wheeled themselves down in time to get the best seats, the seats right next to the speaker.

Grandma was a streak of teal blue sweat suit, a white head craned toward the podium, as I passed by. She didn't lift her head. She didn't move her body. She listened. The speaker, a young woman, a volunteer, read the headlines slowly and loudly, "Today in Angola." I knew my grandmother well enough to know that in her mind, she traced the name back. Angola, before it was Angola, was what? A hand shot up in the air as I rounded the corner, and a strong voice asked the volunteer to repeat. "Today in An-go-la."

I heard Grandpa muttering as I walked into their room. He lay in bed with a stuffed cat on his chest. He was talking to the cat, little words, small words that I couldn't understand. His feet and hands shook as usual, but not his voice. I wished I could bring Alber over. Alber would stretch across his chest and not wriggle away. He'd love the attention. He'd never want to leave.

I bent over and gave Grandpa a kiss, and he laughed. He wore his favorite baseball hat, a gift from Mom. The hat said he was the world's best dad.

"I'm going on vacation," I said, and he nodded. He said nothing, asked me nothing. He hadn't heard. I pulled up a chair, took his hand in mine and talked on, knowing he wouldn't hear, but thinking he might catch bits, like Grandma, a word, something to keep his mind busy.

I told him about the farmhouse, how an old farming family built it back in the early days of the century, how the hard wood floors sagged in spots, apparently, and the curtains on the kitchen windows were crocheted in a fading white and pale pink. I told him what Mrs. Swenson told me.

"Where's Al?" Grandpa asked, interrupting me, hands shaking, feet in spasms, as though he was itching to move.

"Working," I yelled.

Grandpa nodded. "Are you going to marry him?"

The question hung in the air between us. I felt a creeping fear rise in me. What word had he heard? Al's name. Maybe house. Maybe nothing. Maybe he simply had our potential marriage on his mind.

Grandpa said. "You oughta' marry him." He looked at me, raised his hand. "You have the ring."

"I don't want to get married," I said. I meant to add to the word "yet" but the word never made it out of my mouth.

Grandpa hadn't heard. Deafness can be selective. He hears what he wants to hear.

I changed the subject, a good strategy, I thought. "I quit my job, Grandpa. I'm going to get a better job. I know I wanted to be at Pillsbury, but my boss is terrible. Forgets deadlines. Loses drafts. Blames me. I'm going to start looking again."

He nodded, picked up his cat, stroked the fake fur. "It's good to have a job," he said. "Everybody should work. My first job was at a grocery," he said. "I delivered groceries. No, not the first time. I worked inside first."

"What did you do after groceries?" I asked.

"The war." He patted my hand, held his cat tightly. He muttered the story of Vladivostok, again, a favorite. "I was afraid. The smoke, I didn't know what it was. I thought we were going to have to fight. I was on watch, and I called to a friend, and he watched with me. We watched that smoke, it was smoke, I think, and we never went in. We were ready to go, even though we didn't know what we'd face."

I fitted the blanket around him as he spoke, like he used to do for me. He seemed to be telling his cat, not me, reciting. His words trailed off, puffs of smoke themselves, final outbursts splitting into silence. I had closed his blinds, returned my chair to its proper place, when I turned and saw him watching me, following my movements.

"Don't make a mistake here, Sarah," he said.

His words trailed after me, a hoarse whisper as I breezed out the door. I turned. He'd turned, too, to watch me leave. To him, I was a gray shadow, indistinct, shapeless, a trick of light.

AL POUNDS QUICKLY down the staircase. He pulls his slippers off my feet.

"Traitor," he says, grinning.

Then he retreats.

Al comes downstairs, for good, when the full light has reached the sky. He has nothing in his hands, no fist curling around a hidden treasure. Out in the glare of sun and snow, nothing moves. Nothing I can see anyway. I make him a cup of tea.

"What have you been doing?"

"Thinking."

He shuffles across the hard wood floor in his slippers, and the slippers remind me again of Grandpa, and I look out the window at the line of trees, the only distinct shape in view. Al sips his tea.

"Everything okay?"

I nod.

We're quiet. The kitchen fills with something I don't understand. I think of Vladivostok. I think of being 15 and scared shitless and looking out at the smoke, not knowing then exactly what it was.

"Al," I say suddenly, and Al comes to me.

Loss. I am afraid of loss.

Al rubs my arm and asks nothing. He is simply there.

AL AND I BUILD A SNOWMAN in the yellow light of morning. We build him outside the kitchen window, and the air, like ice, burns our faces, makes us hurry. We roll the snow, push it down the only decline in land we've seen for miles. We roll his middle, and we roll his head, and we stand back. I give him my scarf.

"What's wrong?" Al looks for a twig with which to make arms.

"What do you mean?" I stay right where I am, feet planted firmly in the snow.

"I mean, what's eating you?"

I think, be honest with him. Be honest with yourself. I say, "I'm afraid. I'm afraid of losing people."

There is no wind here, nothing to stir the snow, or my words. Nothing that will take my words and send them away. What I say carries, is clear, stays with us.

"I'm afraid of being left."

Al kicks the snow with his boots, and snow flies up, falls. He puts his hands on his hips and leans back. He stares at the sky. "If you don't trust me, we have nothing."

I can't say that I trust him. To say so would be a lie, and so we stand there, him staring at the sky, me at him. It's cold, suddenly, and I close my eyes and let the cold flow into me, think of freezing, right here, right where I am. I don't want to be without him.

"If I tell you that I can't predict my future, but I always see you in it, will you marry me?" he asks, still staring at the sky.

"Yes," I say the word carefully. I enunciate, and for a long time neither one of us moves, we stare at the snowman. I accept, and the world moves on. We let the word sink into the quiet.

AL IS EATING SUGAR CEREAL, as my mother would call it, the kind of cereal kids love but shouldn't eat. He loves mornings, and sugar cereal, and his bear paw slippers from my Grandpa. He loves me. He's wearing his flannel pajamas and plaid robe, both of which he has had since college, both of which are full of holes. "You're quiet," he says.

He's right. I haven't said much this weekend, except "I do."

We leave tomorrow. We'll drive at night, letting the truckers guide us home. We won't see a city for an hour, and then one will reach out to us, slowly at first, the McDonald's by the county line, the increased traffic of semis, the convenience stores and gas stations, multiplying, fanning out, as we drive in. Classes start again soon, and Al has to teach another section of Religion 125. The class starts at eight am.

"That in itself is ungodly," Al said, just before we left for Iowa, staring at the schedule he'd received.

I'd laughed, and he had, too. We had a vacation planned then, a place to go and get away, and it didn't matter how bad our jokes were, or his teaching schedules, or that I had, that very day, resigned my position at Pillsbury.

"What will you do now?" Mom had asked, when I'd called about her feeding Alber while we were gone.

"I will start by breathing slowly in and out," I said.

I accepted Grandma's ring but didn't put it on. I accepted the possibility of marriage only because she insisted, insisted that I recognize cycles, her death, my beginning, and I refused to wed the two. Now we are going home engaged. I can imagine what my grandfather will say. He will make a joke at first. He will say, "Engaged in what?"

But he'll laugh, and my grandmother will nod, and in the midst, as I turn from face to face, ring on my finger, telling them the story over and over until they hear, faces blurring, I'll move easily, having faith in the turn.

Whatever It Takes

Al

2000, recalling late 1994 and early 1995

SARAH'S GRANDPA, ED, NEEDED TO STOP DRIVING. His sight was worse than his hearing and with that combination, we all knew we had a time bomb on our hands. Despite being the in-law, I got the job of telling an ninety-some-odd-year-old man to hand over his keys.

"You're kidding me," I said, when Sarah told me. The memory remains vivid: I had a beer in one hand, a bowl of potato chips in the other, and a Gopher game on in the living room. I was in my pajamas and had almost made it to my favorite chair, the only one with a footrest.

"Nope."

"It didn't work last time, when your Dad made him get rid of the Impala. He just went out and got that Volvo." I chuckled.

"But this time he really has to stop, Al. You know that as well as I do. This isn't funny."

"Why not have your mom tell him? Or you?" I was still holding my beer and chips, and I used them to gesture. Carefully.

Sarah, my beautiful auburn-haired Sarah with that squareish chin and the strength of Rome, sagged a little. Her voice sounded small when she said, "We think he likes you best."

I lowered my head, pinched my lips together. It's kind of heartbreaking to hear that you're the favorite when you aren't even blood.

But I did the deed. One morning at Larch's Donut Shop, the place Ed loved to go to visit with other veterans like himself and swap tall tales, I joined in for a round of crullers. I had to buy the round, of course, but at least they let me sit with them. They were proprietary about their table, all those crusty WWII vets who gathered every Thursday, when there was a doughnut morning happy hour.

The group was mostly Navy, though over time some Army crashed, which caused the occasional good-natured fight, especially during football season. Of course, for the Army/Navy game, they placed bets. Real ones. Real big ones.

While Ed was free with most of his memories, Larch wasn't, not if you hadn't served. He never shared any details of his service with anyone who hadn't been there. He wouldn't even talk to Vets of other foreign wars. But he and Ed had served together, and their bond was fierce.

"He had some tough moments," Ed said once, and nothing more.

We know only that Larch was at Pearl Harbor, and that sobering news gave us all enough sense to honor the yawning silence that followed the news and to ask no more questions, just as I never asked Ed about his Bronze Star a second time, after my first salvo met with his complete disregard.

At the time we needed Ed to give up driving, Larch still stood fairly straight, and his eyebrows were still bushy, not wispy from illness, and he had a wicked laugh—deep and sonorous, all of which was accentuated by those crazy eyebrows. He had unruly white hair that matched his brows, and he repeatedly tried to wrestle it into obedience, stroking it down into place. A futile effort.

Ed was taller than Larch and thicker, but he came with a little panache. Late in his life, he still had defined muscles in his arms. His hair had thinned but didn't go white until near the very end of his life, and he kept it trimmed and neat, a holdover from the Navy that never left. Just like the way he folded clothes and blankets. His eyes were quick, gray, like a cat's. His age surprised people, when he shared it, which was usually an accident, just like his friendship with Larch, which he once admitted arose only from circumstance and not a pleasant one. I could imagine them bonding all those years ago. It made me uncomfortable to consider what violence had cemented the friendship. Someone had saved someone, Sarah and I had decided. And then they had kept saving each other all their lives, if only from loneliness.

The morning I planned to speak to Ed, the Navy friends peeled off quickly, some taking their crullers with them. Sometimes, there were mornings when the tall tales gave way to memories that none of them wanted to discuss or perhaps to discuss around me, and that day a battle had been mentioned and suddenly the crowd began to thin. I understood. I had had a grandfather in the war, and he hadn't wanted to say much either. Soon it was just Ed and me and two fresh, hot cups of coffee gradually cooling while I gathered courage. But because it was just us, I needed to take my chance.

I clapped Ed on the shoulder and said loudly, "Ed."

He looked in my eyes, really looked at me hard, as though the tenor of my voice had changed. Maybe it had. Maybe it shook.

I dove in, lowering my voice. "Ed, nobody thinks it's safe for you to drive anymore. I know that stinks. It really, really stinks. But we love you, and we need you to pass over the keys."

He never looked away, and a long breath held between us. Then he sniffed and shrugged and wrestled his car keys out of his pants pocket and handed them over without a word. I slid them into my coat pocket. I wanted to pat his arm, say something, but I was too busy trying not to tremble. I'd thought the worst part would be telling him, but the worst part was sitting with him afterward in that long silence.

"How did you get this job?" he asked after a while, his voice even but gruff.

I told him the truth. Truth seemed essential. "They think you'll take it best from me."

Outside, the air was clear, the sky holding wisps of clouds, the names of which I had once known and couldn't remember. Cumulus?

"They're right," Ed said.

ED WASN'T A REAL TALL GUY. I was a little taller, but he had a bearing I lack, a command that had nothing to do with size. I still can't figure what gave him that kind of authority; I only know that I don't have it. It shows at the U when I'm teaching and lose the thread of my lecture and someone sighs or snickers, or when summoning my most authoritative voice to ask for silence when students chatter mid-class and instead of quieting, they lower their voices. But Ed had the ability to motivate people with a glance or a swift change in tone of voice. He was no saint, and yet he was. People trusted him, and he took care of them, so for him to sneak out of the house early in the morning only one week after our conversation and take his old Volvo off someplace, to sneak out of his own house, was almost unfathomable.

Almost.

That was my first thought as we sped down the highway to Sarah's parents' home that shiny spring, Saturday morning, after her mother called and informed us that Grandpa had taken the car and gone. One week.

Grandpa on the lam, I thought as I drove. Grandpa breaking free. Go for it, Ed, I thought, but even then I knew how wrong I was. He had one good eye and ears of stone. This was no joke.

Since Sarah and I had been summoned, we joined the family at the beat-up yellow table in her parents' kitchen, waiting for bad news. One thing about the Macmillan's, they've always worried together. They celebrate together, but they also gather in a family summit to face the worst, and always at their paint-chipped, bright yellow kitchen table. Even Glennie. She might not show for a birthday or any day, but say the word emergency, and she showed. That word was one she understood, her whole being primed for medical work at a pace.

"I swear to God he does what he wants," their mother said from the head of the table. And then: "He certainly hears what he wants. I bet he isn't even deaf."

At times like this, Sarah would giggle. I'd giggle. Not Glennie, who somehow equated such comments with blasphemy. Even when I finally entered the picture, that late in their lives, Sarah could appreciate the humor and not Glennie.

"He has always had a mind of his own," their mother said, and we fell quiet.

That Saturday, we lived under the terrible weight of long hours until Ed pulled in with the Volvo, him alive and it intact. With everyone else on the road also alive. Still, that night, I watched the ten o'clock news for hit and runs. He could hit something and not know. He'd nearly demolished the metal trash can behind Larch's doughnut shop a few weeks before, rushing to park so that he could chat with his Vet friends over food none of them should have been eating. It was the very event that had sparked the whole "take the keys" debacle.

"It's a trash can," Larch had said at the time, shrugging. He brought me out to the alley, quietly, away from the fellows, to show me Ed's car and the trash bin.

Larch owned who knew how many properties, and he didn't worry about details like trash cans. I got it: he had survived something horrible during World War Two, or maybe several devastations, and a trash can was nothing. I knew he wouldn't file with the insurance over garbage.

"But," Larch said, glancing up at me.

"I know," I said, nodding.

I said nothing to Ed as we parted that morning, but later, that evening, I told Sarah about it all, and she called her mom, and there was a debate about how to handle things, and they decided I would be the one to ask Ed to hand over his keys.

And so I had.

Who knew he had two sets?

WHEN THEY WERE GROWING UP, Grandpa would chatter to the girls about cars and the weather. He would explain football. But he never talked to them about boyfriends. Ever. Alcohol. Yes, he'd talk about drinking with them. Smoking. How to skin a fish. But never, ever boys. Growing tomatoes, the Republicans, life on a Navy vessel. He even told them a few jokes he knew from his time in the Navy that I thought, after hearing them myself, were pretty steep for young ears. But Ed never said a word about their men. Both Glennie and Sarah testify to this. He wanted no involvement in romance or heartbreak.

Except once.

I don't know what really happened because, of course, I wasn't there, but stories in Sarah's family are as important as blood, and I've heard tell many times about the day Grandpa finally spoke up. I'd always understood Ed; and he, me. We just clicked the way people sometimes do. I guess he felt, as an outsider looking in, that Sarah and I were botching up a good thing when, early in our relationship, we broke up, and I've always been grateful that this funny, sharp man was also a bold one when bold was required.

I ought to have expected his fearlessness. For all the stories we have, many are lost, many dying across the table at the doughnut shop, passing with the death of each Vet. I'd heard threads here and there about Ed's service, seen the medal on his dresser, but to my knowledge no one has ever heard the whole story about how he earned it. Only Larch knew.

"He doesn't want to relive it," Sarah said once. "Or maybe he feels the same way that Larch does, that you can't really understand if you weren't there."

"Was Larch there with him? They were together?"

Sarah bit her lip and shook her head. "You know, I'm not sure, but I think so."

"So he's keeping it to himself? Forever?" The thought was unimaginable to me, in this family of stories.

"Yes," Sarah said. "That story is just his."

"We can have a story of our own?" I asked. I was joking, but I wasn't. The thought of my own story, our own history, made me feel light.

But the point is that it shouldn't have been a shock to me that Ed would walk into the line of fire. And God knows, he certainly had.

"I liked Al," Ed apparently said to Sarah one day, sometime after our break-up.

She was driving him to the doughnut shop in her old Datsun.

At that time, Larch thought coffee shops were the new hot thing, and so he had converted his doughnut store in a newly chic part of town to emphasize coffee and added savories in addition to doughnuts, which he loved and would never take off the menu. Now, new moms rolled in with strollers and pretty packages from high-end neighborhood boutiques and presumably somewhere in the mess of bags, small children; gaggles of girlfriends met to indulge; and businessmen popped in, suave in their suits. The Vets and the doughnuts were the draw, the clutch of them at "their" table adding local color and a feeling of nostalgia. It should be noted that only they ever got the ten-cent doughnut Happy Hour. I had to pay full price, along with everyone else.

If someone in the group failed to appear on any Thursday, family members could expect a round of phone calls, some abrupt and gruff; others more tactful. Appearances any other day were welcome, a table was always in reserve, but Thursday was as important to this crowd as Sunday church services were to my mother's, and absences raised alarms.

When Grandpa showed up late that Thursday when Sarah drove him over, phones were already ringing throughout Minneapolis. The Vets called Sarah's mother, Glennie at school, her father at work.

Little did they know that everything was fine. The only problem was that Sarah had stopped the car. Grandpa spoke up about me during the drive because he knew they'd be alone. Sarah was the person who most often took him places, a gift of time and even of duty that I know he found deeply moving. He knew Glennie loved him, but seeing her was rare. Sarah made time, and he didn't want to embarrass her or create an awkward situation by talking to her in the house, where someone else might appear, or overhear. If he mentioned something in the doughnut shop, he knew all too well what would happen. I had a good rapport with the Thursday Vets. Artie and Pete, Craig and Mike, Leroy and Elmer, Alfred and John. Midwestern boys who had served and come back to the family farms, the small shops, the restaurants their parents owned. I'd shared many a good tale and far too many doughnuts with these men. They'd been asking Ed where I was lately and what had happened between Sarah and me. Artie had even asked for my phone number.

"He was a good guy, that Al. I really liked him, and I didn't like some of the other ones you brought home," Ed said. "Turn right here. There's construction on West 50th."

Sarah pulled over and remained silent. Ed narrowed his eyes and stared her down.

"You gotta hear me on this one, Sarah. He was a good guy. You need to try and fix this."

No reply, just a sinking of the shoulders, a shrinking into herself I've sadly grown to know. The weight of sadness, but also the readjustment of her frame, to gather herself up and try again, try whatever is required. She refused to start the car for how long? Who knows, but it was a while.

"Sometimes what it takes is a willingness to give in," Ed said.

"What what takes?" Sarah asked, sounding sharp, I imagine.

"Marriage."

"We weren't talking about getting married, Grandpa."

"Oh," he said. "Just plain oh."

Pause.

"Well, what the hell was it all about then?" he asked.

The doughnut-now-coffee shop was a white stucco building with large front windows and barren gas pumps out front. Larch kept them, just in case he needed to convert the place back to an actual gas station. Larch also owned a few bars in the less reputable neighborhoods of Minneapolis and St. Paul, in old buildings he meticulously maintained, in case the area ever bounced back. He insisted they'd been reputable when he'd bought them, which Ed doubted.

"He never was a good judge of character," Ed said. "It's why he chose me for a friend."

The joke was an old one, but each time she heard it, Sarah laughed or smiled. Not to do so would have been heartbreaking for both her and Ed. Sharing jokes, even the worn-out ones, was among their strongest bonds—the sense of shared history, almost their own vocabulary.

Sarah pulled around the pumps when, finally, they got to the shop, and Ed climbed slowly out, setting one leg on the pavement, then the other, inching himself forward, grabbing the door frame to lift himself out. No longer loose limbed, just looser tongued.

"All this for a doughnut and weak coffee," he said. "And to hear Larch tell more bad jokes."

At the door to the shop, Ed turned to wave. Larch was there, trying to hold the door open for him.

"He never was a good judge of character," Ed hollered, and Sarah started to smile at the joke and chuckle. "But he got one right. He thought the world of Al."

Ed was through the door and aiming for the counter by the time Sarah looked up, Larch right beside him, leaning toward him as if to confide but more than likely then, for support. Slowly Sarah pulled the car around the pumps and back out on to the road. She says she drove in a deep quiet, radio off. She drove for a long time, longer than she realized. At home, she made two calls, the first to me. She left me a message. She had thought carefully about what point she wished to make while driving and so her message was brief:

"Al, it's Sarah. On December 18th, I graduated."

I remember getting her voicemail, feeling a clutch in my chest. I played it over and over, feeling both relieved and terrified.

Then she called the doughnut shop. Missy answered. Sarah didn't know Missy, but whoever she was, she was kind enough to put down the phone and go tell Ed that Sarah said "Uncle." Before Missy made it back to the phone, Sarah heard a cheer erupt in the doughnut shop.

The Thursday Vets were all invited to the wedding. They sat in a row, wives we'd never met tucked beside them, and they cornered a table at the reception. Their cards were generally bawdy, their gifts all cash and far too generous, their alcohol consumption a sight to behold.

Shortly afterward, Artie died. I received a call from his son, a man I'd never met but had heard stories about, of course. He asked if I would serve as a pallbearer because I was an "honorary member" of the Thursday Vets Club. I've never been in a club. Often, my associations with them have been negative. But this was company I was proud to keep, and I said yes, I would be there. It was the least I could do.

I have been the pall bearer for seven of these fine men, Ed and Larch being the last two.

For those who knew them, it's no surprise that Larch kept the table open at the doughnut-now-coffee shop, no matter how busy it got. The table stayed spartan and clean, plenty of chairs pulled up. On it remains a small sign that reads "Reserved."

I once thanked Larch, for keeping the pressure on Ed to say something to Sarah. Almost everyone was still with us then, and Amelia was a bright new rose. Oh, the joy a baby brings. Larch held her every opportunity he was given. We were in the doughnut shop. That's all I remember, besides the conversation.

He shrugged. Shrugging was his language. One interpreted the exact meaning only from context.

"I didn't have the courage to call her," I told Larch.

Silence.

"I don't know if Sarah would have called me without Ed's encouragement," I added.

Larch shrugged again.

"Ed says you all chimed in. You all wanted her to call me, or me her. Artie was getting ready to send some spitfire down my phone line."

Larch laughed. "Artie would have."

"Thanks, Larch. I hear you're the one who moved Ed off the dime."

"You do whatever it takes," Larch said. "Especially for family."

"You'll let me know if you ever need anything?"

Larch slapped me on the back. "Always keep my seat at the table," he said.

I DROVE ED TO THE DOUGHNUT SHOP after Sarah and I were married. I had Tuesday and Thursday evening seminars so I had the time.

"You should just give me my keys back," Ed told me once, toward the end.

"You'd miss me."

"Ha!"

At the door, Larch was waiting for him.

"You two are an old married couple."

"Even better," Ed said. "We're friends."

I dropped Ed off right in front of the door that day. The pumps were still outside. Larch was bent but opening the door as much as he could. A crack. They disappeared inside together, and I paused. I parked the car with care and stepped quietly into the shop. They were the only two at the Vets table, side by side, hands around their ceramic cups, a plate of doughnuts between them. If I wiped away the wrinkles, I could see them. 1943. 1944. 1945. Doing whatever it took to survive, together.

How could I hold seats? I asked myself. How do you ever hold seats for men like these?

But I did. When the time came and Larch finally let go, passing on as the new century rolled in, and after I was informed that I now owned the doughnut shop, I pushed the reserve sign out to the most visible edge of the table the next Thursday and sat down heavily at the table opposite, remembering. Artie's bad jokes, Mike's dirty ones, the ragged whispers, hoarse voices. 1945. VE Day. The beaches.

"I was on those beaches," Artie once said.

And after he said it, we'd sat silently, imagining. Or remembering.

It was no surprise to any of us that Larch was the last to go. It broke my heart that with each passing, this lonely man became even lonelier, but I still came each Thursday morning, and he and I would talk for a while. I sit here now, across from their table, remembering them all. So really, in the end, I am the last one, and realizing that, I move myself over. I sit up a little straighter.

I understand how Sarah must feel, with each relative passing. It's hard to be the last one, the keeper of the stories, the memory. But my lord, what a gift.

Patchwork
Sarah
January 1996

I FOUND IT WHEN I WAS CLEANING out my grandmother's cedar chest, a small lock of hair, one curl, tucked into the pages of John's first epistle. I'd been looking for a bundle of old newspapers that my grandmother wanted me to see, but once I discovered the hair, I forgot about the papers. I knew whose hair it was. I recognized the yellow, almost golden color, my grandmother had described. It was Cecily's hair, Cecily, whose name had long ago been erased from the family tree.

The cedar chest was in what was once my grandparents' bedroom. For most of my life, they had lived on the lower level of my parents' house, in three adjoining rooms. I used to sit on their shag carpet floor and watch television, or hold my grandmother's hand and talk, each of us sunk into their old striped couch, shoulders touching. I thought I'd seen everything they owned in the long years of growing up. I thought, during the days we packed Grandma and Grandpa for the nursing home, I'd seen everything in the cedar chest.

I put the lid of the cedar chest down. A thin layer of dust lined the top, like the new, thin layer of silence that had filled the house since Grandma and Grandpa had left; like the old layer of silence, long undisturbed, that I had just discovered.

Cecily. Spitfire. Flame. Turner. "She turned," Grandma had said once, "like milk."

GRANDMA WAS WAITING FOR ME in the nursing home lobby. She sat on the blue flowered couch, feet crossed at her ankles, hands folded. She stared at the floor, and she didn't move unless she saw a blur of feet pass by, then she squinted at the passing shape. Her hair, newly permed and carefully arranged, covered her growing bald spot. She looked thin, and the wheelchair placed strategically within reach was a sure sign that she was feeling weak, unable to use her walker. Yet when she took my hand, her grip was strong.

"Did you find them?" she asked. There was a story behind the newspapers that she was going to tell me so that I could include it in the family history we were compiling.

"I found something else I wanted to talk about."

I pulled a plastic baggy from my purse and laid it carefully in Grandma's hands. Grandma pressed the plastic flat to see, then pulled the hair out and ran it between her fingers.

"I was surprised to find this," I said.

Grandma squinted at the hair, bent over it. "She was my sister," she said.

"I'd like to write about her," I said.

She shook her head. "No," she said, "not her."

61

"But she's—"

"She's nothing," Grandma said. She closed her hand around the curl of hair, tugged at her wheelchair with the other. "Cecily," she said, "is not family."

I avoided her gaze. In the lobby, the other scattered stuffed chairs were empty. Grandma swatted at my hand.

"Push me to the window," she said. "I'll watch you leave."

Surprised, I took her by the arm, lowered her slowly into the wheelchair. Grandma still had Cecily's hair, and I worried about what she would do with it, maybe flush it, but I didn't have the courage to ask. I pushed her to the window.

"I love you," I said, uncertain what my sudden dismissal might mean.

She tilted her head up to look at me, and she smiled. "Leave Cecily out," she said.

I gave her a kiss on the cheek and said nothing. I waited for the doors to open, marched out into the frigid air. I should have hurried to my car. Instead, I turned and looked back at her. She was holding that curl of hair up to the light.

CECILY MANNING Morris HUFFNER BOWES. The fifth of nine children, squashed between Jocelyn and Edward, both of whom died of diphtheria. Born in 1909, died in 1953. Left no will.

"That," my grandmother once said, "is a crock. She left plenty of will behind, just not the kind they were looking for."

Grandma talked about Cecily on rare occasions, on days when I traipsed home from school in thick snow, and dark came early, and we sat at the kitchen table reviewing the day. Maybe after a glass of wine, when Grandpa started telling stories, and Grandma would insist he had them wrong, and the stories got lost temporarily in the debate. Sometimes then, amidst the chaos, Cecily came through in a line.

I knew that Cecily had sinned, but I didn't know what could drive her apart from the family, make her what she had become, a whisper, a sideways glance, an interrupted line, never recovered.

In our attic, packed carefully into cardboard boxes with the baby clothes my mother hopes to pass on, is the women's potholder quilt. Each generation adds a row, or at least a square. My grandmother's square is now pale yellow. It's plain save for the careful red stitching that makes her name. Catherine Andersen.

The plainness of her square is striking in a patchwork quilt of names and symbols, favorite colors and long quotes. Whitman. Roosevelt. The Bible. Her name is all she needed to record. I was here, it seems to say, once a long time ago, and I was called Catherine.

I am Sarah, and I will not embroider my name for years. I will not embroider my name until I know who I am, can script with such confidence the identity I struggle to define, until I know, as easily, and with such simplicity, the way to be remembered.

Cecily knew. In the second to last row of the quilt is her square, all her names in succession, each one stitched in a different color. The names are all hers, and that she listed them, demanded to be remembered for who she was, is a trait I admire.

Cecily, I was told, flipped her long, gold hair once too often. She had shamed the family. She was a tramp. Cecily liked to watch football games with Grandpa, smoking cigarettes one after the other. She went through men just as fast, Grandma said. Cecily used to waltz into Grandma's house, swinging that hair, swinging those slim little hips. She had all the curves in all the right places and liked to show them off, to twist around on the sidewalk to see who might be watching her, to sashay into one of Grandpa's card games or football parties and take a seat.

After all the buildup, I'd expected more. A bank robber, a whore, a witch. But what I got was a woman with one hell of a libido. I didn't think she should have been run out of the family will, erased from the family tree. I thought she deserved a round of applause. Four men, and working on her fifth when she died. She deserved a medal, I thought, for being gutsy in an age when women were allowed nothing, certainly not sexuality.

But I came to these thoughts slowly, after I'd found her hair. Nothing about Cecily seemed shocking. After all, I lived with Al. And though I wasn't supposed to, I surreptitiously began to write Cecily into the family stories, giving her entire sections all her own because no one, it seemed, would share a story with her.

AT FIRST, THE STORIES WERE A BLESSING. Writing them down gave me a break from the endless, seemingly hopeless, task of mailing resumes and calling contacts. Hello, I'm Sarah Macmillan, and I recently left Pillsbury. Chose to leave Pillsbury. Told my boss he was irresponsible and stormed out the door of Pillsbury. Punched the doughboy and ran. Hello, I'm Sarah Macmillan, and my savings are almost gone. The stories became a lifeline, something else for me to think about, something more for Grandma than routine.

I had looked for work the first week of January, but in the second, I pushed my job files away and picked up a pen. The words came easily, like water, and I turned the page. I wrote one morning, then the next, and my job search slipped quietly into its own dark grave. I didn't ask myself why I was writing, or for whom, or for how long. I simply let the pages fill. I ate Cap'n Crunch. I paced the house with Alber in step, and together we etched the family history into something tangible. We wrote it down, each step a story, each story a life.

Grandma spent hours with my first stories. She settled in the lobby by the largest window she could find. She held each page in one hand, out to the light like a gift, and slowly passed her heavy magnifying glass over each word. Grandma asked for larger type, and I returned with the font so large that I felt like I'd written things on a billboard. For days, Grandma read as if possessed. The speed with which she read, for a woman who is legally blind, should have warned me. It didn't.

"The Cartwright women did not have big fannies," Grandma said, after finishing the first stories.

As a descendant of the Cartwrights herself, I thought this was going to be hard to contest.

"We have round fannies," she said. "Not big. Round."

Every story had five versions. She wanted hers.

AFTER GRANDMA'S REACTION TO MY FIRST STORIES, I drove out to see Mom. February loomed, and Grandma wanted more stories. I only had part of Cecily's. I needed advice.

Cecily wasn't easy to write about. The pictures of her that remained were black and white, hard to see. Beautiful hair, long. She was almost always smiling, almost always smoking. Her handwriting, in the few letters Grandma had saved, was thin, tight and scrunched. "Dear Cath," her early letters began. And then a later one, written from St. Louis in 1948, which began, "Catherine." Other than the quilt, the curl, and the photos, that was all of Cecily that remained.

Mom met me at the door in jeans and a maroon sweater, long hair pulled back in a braid, her gray streak twisting down her back. At the old yellow kitchen table, bare in spots where the paint had chipped, my mother finished the sentences Grandma used to break off.

When Mom was little, Cecily had swept through the door one night like she belonged, grabbed a bottle of beer from the refrigerator, and walked into the living room. Mom had followed her, lingering in the door, waiting for her hello. Cecily said nothing to Mom or Grandma, but she said a hello to each of the men in turn. Hello, Sammy. Joe. Ed. Then she took her seat at the card table, on Grandpa's lap.

Grandpa tried to laugh her off. The other men laughed, too, and Mom laughed. Grandma didn't. She marched into the living room with a bowl of peanuts and set the bowl down hard. Cecily stayed right where she was, sipping her beer, laughing. Grandma offered Cecily a chair, and Cecily said no thanks, she didn't need one. Grandpa tried to shoo her off. There was a silence then. One of the other men coughed; another lit a cigarette. Mom remembered that cigarette, the way the tip glowed when the man sucked in, the way the air seemed to fill, suddenly, with the smell. Then Grandpa pushed so hard, Mom said, that Cecily fell.

Twice more Cecily tried to settle where she should not have settled, at least twice more that Mom knew. The last time, Mom woke to

Grandma yelling. She walked into the kitchen. Grandma had Cecily by the hair, and Grandpa was trying to pull them apart. Grandma wouldn't let go.

"Did they have an affair?" I asked.

"He was so handsome," Mom said. "He really was. You've seen the pictures. He had that confidence that comes with good looks. He walked tall. He laughed easily. To Cecily, I think, he was the one. But he wouldn't have acted on it. She embarrassed him. I think he was truly ashamed of her."

There are turning points, turns of fortune, turns like Cecily's, when the heart withers, and the spirit sours, and the world moves on with less sympathy than it had before. My vision of the family changed. We were not as strong or as solid as I'd thought. We were not a fortress. We never had been. We'd only ever been human, individuals whose foibles were magnified by size.

"Think about the difference between a quilt and a history," my mother said as I left. "The quilt makes it look like Cecily married all those men."

I TIMED MY NEXT VISIT to the nursing home carefully, spotted Grandma at her current events lecture, and sneaked down the hall to Grandpa. He was sitting in bed, gray hair combed away from his forehead, Twins cap on. He was contemplating a chess board.

"What is that?" he asked, pointing at the black king. His hand shook. His finger, knotted with arthritis, curled like a talon.

"It's the king," I yelled.

"Oh," Grandpa said, not hearing.

I lifted the piece, put it into his palm, and rolled it around. "King," I said again, this time into his ear.

"I'm losing against myself." He said, then he laughed. "King," he said and nodded.

"I want to talk to you," I said, and Grandpa, magically, turned his head toward me. "About Cecily."

He set the king down. "Move it someplace good for me. Don't tell me where."

"Cecily," I said again, placing the king in a free square, having no idea what the rules of chess allowed.

Grandpa sniffed. He was still looking at his chess board. He squinted, looking for the king. "Can't do that," he said, pointing to it.

I sighed, handed back the piece. Not even he would talk about her, or so it seemed.

"She rooted for the Packers," Grandpa said, "just to be contrary." He held his elbow to steady his arm and plopped the king down on an appropriate square. The board shook. "She was a party girl. You know the type." Grandpa scrunched up his nose. "Nobody likes a girl like that. Why do you want to know about her?"

"Nobody liked her," I said, trying to keep my words at a minimum. The fewer my words, the better chance he had of hearing me.

"Nobody liked her," he agreed. "Except your grandmother." He laughed. "They were always close, those two. She'd never tell you that, but it was true. Grandma defended Cecily early on, but the rest of the family. Well." Grandpa laughed. "Your grandmother never forgave Cecily."

"Never forgave her for what?"

"Sarah," he said, "she was a hussy." He sounded sad, as though he wished Cecily hadn't been.

"Did you like her?" I asked.

Grandpa didn't respond. He leaned back and rubbed his eyes. "When I play with your Al, he beats me every darn time," he said. " 'Course he can see. Makes a difference."

"Did you like Cecily, Grandpa?" I asked, tapping his arm, making him look at me.

Grandpa stared at me blankly. He knew, must have known, what I was asking. "She was a hard girl to like," he said.

Grandpa readjusted his hat, and I brushed an imaginary hair off his shoulder, just to touch him.

"Tell your Al to sneak in some scotch," Grandpa said as I left. He patted me on the back, winked, gave me the OK sign with his fingers. "Maybe if he gets drunk, he'll lose."

I stopped to look at Grandma in current events. She was sitting in the front row, directly in front of the speaker.

"You do not abandon family," Grandma had often said, "no matter what."

But Cecily had abandoned family every time she appeared at a card game. Later she bought a one-way bus ticket to St. Louis. It wasn't until I talked to Mom that I understood. All the names Cecily took were never hers, just the name of the man of the moment. She was all these and more.

"She was free," Grandma often said.

But that wasn't true. Cecily wasn't free She had exacted a price. She nearly cost Grandpa a marriage, and she cost herself a family.

Kirsten had taken TO CALLING ME REGULARLY with any problems, since I was the family member most easily reached.

"I'm busy looking for work," I had said the first day she'd called, the day I had gotten up at my normal time, dressed for success in my pajamas, and stayed in bed. Kirsten had ignored me, which was probably just as well. Then she began to command me. I better do this, and I better do that.

"You better get over here," she said after I had dropped off new stories for Grandma to read, including Cecily's. "Your grandmother has a few words for you."

"I can't come over until later."

She said, "I am not living with this all day."

That cemented it.

"I'll be there at five," I said.

Grandma was furious when I arrived, finally, at seven. She sat on the blue couch in the lobby and watched who came, who went. She wore her best sweat suit, a teal blue. In her lap lay the family history, the pages neatly tied around the middle with rubber bands.

"You've been avoiding me," she said the minute I swept through the door. She, who said she couldn't see well enough to watch television, had no trouble sighting me then.

"I have not been avoiding you."

"Yes, you have. Kirsten called you this morning. I know. I was sitting right there." She pointed her finger at me, punctuating her sentence with jabs in the air.

I sat down in an overstuffed chair opposite the couch. My grandmother squinted at me, and my heart beat faster.

She pulled out a sheaf of pages. "You wrote about Cecily," she said. She handed them to me.

"What are you doing?"

"Taking her back out."

I saw the way this could go, the bitterness, the awful words that could fly between us and never be recovered. I had only described Cecily's childhood, and then Manning; the absence of the marriage everyone expected, and the sudden, unexpected appearance of Morris. I said, "What do you want to do, write her out after 1948?"

And that was where we left the family history, right where it was, in 1948, the year Cecily left as well, calling herself Cecily Morris.

"I don't want you to change it when I'm gone," Grandma said, voice trembling.

"I would never do that."

"You said you would never write about Cecily either, but you did," Grandma snapped.

"I won't change the history," I said.

"You think you know what it was like to have sister like her back then? Grandma pursed her lips. "Well, you don't."

"I have an idea," I said. "I talked to Grandpa. And Mom."

Grandma stiffened. "That was my business to tell."

"What does it matter?"

"It matters to me," Grandma said. "I don't want that known. Do you understand?"

"You, who said never to abandon family."

Grandma stood up slowly, gripping her walker. She lifted her chin. She said, "I am the vine and my Father is the gardener. He cuts off every branch in me that bears no fruit, while every branch that does bear fruit, he trims clean so that it can be even more fruitful. John 15."

I knew we had come to a new place, she and I. I had Cecily's pages in my hand, and I grabbed my coat. I stood. My reply was brief. "Anyone who claims to be in the light but hates his brother is still in the darkness. John's first epistle."

My grandmother never lowered her head, nor did she turn away. She said, "Get out."

I knew, as I breezed out the door, that she was still there, watching me leave.

She yelled after me. Her voice carried through the open doors, which eased shut, to allow slow moving people time to walk through them. "You cannot write what you want," she yelled. "It's not just your story." Her voice had a strength then that I had not heard for weeks, a power that made it rise and crack.

Who could lay claim to the past? That was what we were arguing about, who would control the way we were remembered. We had not thought of what we were doing. We had not practiced the kinds of verbal reconciliation that we'd need. That came later, slowly, like the snow that winter.

FEBRUARY ROLLED IN WITH A STORM. The snow came, and it hung in the air like a bad mood. We settled into the fight, as stubborn as the snow, as unwilling to budge. Each day, Al carved a path from the back door to the sidewalk, and each day the snow covered it. Each day, I waited for Grandma to call, and she for me, and so we sat, miles apart, stories away, fuming over what was only ever ours to share. The snow trickled down, settling like dust.

I recognized then, in the hushed world of the snowstorm, that I was writing my way to my square of the quilt, taking my slow place among the women I was only then learning to know. Even Grandma herself. I'd never realized before how entirely separate she was from me. I had only ever seen her as my grandmother, and yet when I thought of the quilt, I couldn't imagine what quote she might have considered, what symbol. A flag? A garden hoe? The sea? I'd lived with her most of my life, but I could never have sewn her square if she had asked.

But she knew how to embroider Cecily's. She knew the two names after Morris, knew the way Cecily wanted to be remembered, and only Grandma would have stitched them on, pulled the patchwork that was Cecily into place.

That was the easy part to write. The part that was both anger and forgiveness, love and hate.

In early February, the snow slowed, and then stopped, and I cleared through it, headlights on. At the nursing home, the nurses had pasted little red hearts on every door. I paused at the nurse's station, staring at the hearts along the hallway.

Kirsten put her hands on her hips. "What did you write this time?"

"Nothing incendiary," I said.

Kirsten looked skeptical, but I knew what was in the envelope. The part about Grandma. I wrote her as I saw her, as a woman, not as a relation. I wrote about her as if I were reporting, and she stepped off the page for me, became something I had only glimpsed before. Whole.

Kirsten took a deep breath. She said, "You need a job."

"Will you tell her I'm here?" I wouldn't go see Grandma until I had a sense of what my reception would be.

Kirsten checked her watch. "Let me give Mortimer his pill."

I was sitting in the nursing home hallway when the light over 129 flickered, then again, on the board at the empty nurse's station. I hurried down the hall. Grandma lay in bed, eyes closed. I touched her shoulder, and she didn't open her eyes, she simply took my hand. That was all she wanted.

When she opened her eyes later, she stared at me for a while, but she held on.

"Who will apologize first?" I asked.

My grandmother stared at me. "How dare you quote the Bible to me." She sat up slowly. "I raised you to have opinions," she said, "but I did not raise you to disagree with me."

I laughed.

"I am apologizing first," she said.

My grandmother read her section while I was there. She tilted her lamp down over the pages, and when her eyes got tired, I read to her. We leaned into each other, shoulder to shoulder, out of habit. I described her first job at the five and dime; described how Cecily, whom she had so often defended, turned on her; described the salvaging of one lock of hair. I said that love had an amazing capacity to endure.

Grandma did not speak for a long time, and when she did, she said little, as though she had run out of words. She said, "You stuck to the facts."

I nodded.

Grandma looked at me. She picked up my hand, uncannily like hers. "You give me more credit than I deserve."

I remember a rush of feeling, that sudden relief and sadness, a sadness I had not expected and could not contain. I remember Grandpa, hand out, shaking, reaching for the pages. I remember Grandma opening her dresser drawer and pointing to the curl.

"Do you trust me to keep it?" she asked, and I nodded.

"I trust you, too," Grandma said. She stared at the clock. "What time is it?" she asked.

"Six o'clock."

"Time for current events," she said. I handed her her walker.

"You better write Cecily yourself," Grandma said. She spoke at the turn, when she would go left to the lobby and the assembled rows of chairs, and I would go to the right, to a side entrance, to the parking lot, and home.

"What?"

"I don't want to write anymore," Grandma said.

"I won't write this myself."

My GRANDMOTHER TURNED and rattled down the hall with her walker.

"Don't ever turn your back on me," I said. My voice carried, and Grandma turned, her face expressionless. Farther down the hall, I saw a nurse poke her head out of a bedroom, another take a tentative step our way, then pause.

My grandmother raised her hand, palm flat against the air as if she was pushing open a door. Then her hand twisted, moved in the air, like she was waving or tossing something off. The gesture was my benediction. She said, "You tell them yourself. Tell them all. But do us justice, or I'll haunt you." Then my grandmother laughed. She turned and aimed for the lobby. Then she stopped, turned one last time and said, "I could do it, you know," but she smiled when she spoke, and as I watched her go, I nodded, having no doubt that she would haunt me all my life.

Beginnings
Sarah
February 1996

OUTSIDE IN THE PARKING LOT, Al is circling for a space in my rumbling Datsun. It's squat and faded blue, but that little car reliably growls us around the Twin Cities, its only complaint a high-pitched whine when we press the gas pedal to the floor, as we did on the way here. But we made it, the car squealing us down the highway in the icy grip of near dawn.

Al dropped me off at the door because the message he received was garbled, my mother in a panic. I fled the car, jacket flapping in the wind, the dim gray sky lit with one wide, beautiful rosy slash. Grandma is that slash of red in our otherwise quiet family—that sudden, unexpected color. She is our fire. And she is why we are gathering.

I know this waiting room too well, and I'm sick of the buzzing fluorescents, the whish of the revolving door, the pale gray walls. I'm sick of the same magazines from months ago, so thoroughly thumbed that the corners crinkle upwards. I'm even sick of the same night-weary nurses who know me by name. These lovely women and one man who patiently, kindly, assist my family. Saints. I am sick of saints.

The doors hiss, and I feel a thread of chilly air as someone comes inside, hear voices that are not my family's. Subdued sobs. A stretcher rattling down the hall. I don't even turn to look. I am beyond curiosity, beyond worry, beyond weary. I am on rote, clutching my notes so that when the nurse returns, I am planted where she can't miss me, right at the front desk, just in case she's new. Planted so I can recite the information like a prayer and pass over my wrinkled paperwork: medications, doctor's names and beeper numbers, nursing home. Social worker. Grandpa's name. My name. My phone number.

My coat is itchy, the wool cuffs longer than the pajama top I have on underneath, and I absentmindedly scratch, like my grandmother now does, all the time. Scabs on her scalp, as insidious as moss, everywhere.

Shows you. That's what'd she'd tell me, if she could. She, who would never go to the grocery store in her pajamas. Because that's where I was when Al found me this morning. At Red Owl in my PJs, thinking no one would ever know. I rushed out of Red Owl holding a tomato.

Shows you. It's only recently that she has added sharpness and bite to what she says, and I know that means our real Catherine is disappearing, becoming what age and pain remake her. Carving her a new face, creating a new spitting vocabulary.

Once, she would have giggled about the PJs. She might even have thought it breezily risqué.

"Sarah." A nod, an apologetic smile. It's Estelle, her slender frame tucking itself into the dark chair at the intake desk, her bobbed brown hair stuck in place with hairspray.

"Estelle." I nod back.

"Just you with her this time?"

I shake my head. My parents are still on their way, having farther to come. Al is coming through the door any minute. He phoned Glennie, too. Where is she? I think, pulling at my coat collar. Away. My little sister is always away. And I am always the one who makes it to the hospital before anyone else. The one with the lists of medicines and doctors' names taped in her frayed, thin wallet. The unemployed one. The available one. The one who is the mathematician, counting who was there, who was not, who I can rely on.

Right now, I can count on Estelle.

I wish I could count on Glennie. I sometimes wonder where things begin, if the reason I am the strong one is because I did not get the pretty face; if because I am the oldest, I assumed responsibility, letting her off the hook. Does she now believe I'll take care of everything?

At nearly twenty-one, Glennie has a will of her own, a single-mindedness that nine times out of ten puts me to shame. But it's single-mindedness like a laser, aimed toward one goal. I am often in doubt. I fear change but am never surprised by it. Glennie is. She is as shocked by a swift change of seasons as she is by turns of events. She's not, I tell her repeatedly, in tune with the world. She has shut herself away in a laboratory with a pile of MCAT prep books. She has shut herself off, and that is dangerous.

"I have to concentrate," she replies. Always the same answer.

I press. "Don't you want a boyfriend? Sex? A good meal now and again? Don't you want more than this?"

She doesn't answer. She's a bundle of nerves and tensions. MCAT; high scores; the cost of applications.

You will regret this, I tell her. There is more to the heart than what you can name; there is more in the blood than you can label.

The waiting room falls quiet. No conversation, TV silent, and then, as if in apology, sounds race forward. A siren coming from the distance, the smack of a hand shoving open the door in the hallway behind me. A phone trilling. The hum of voices. But for one whole breath, the Emergency room was silent, and I wonder who in that breath left us, and who in that breath arrived.

It's still early morning, and somewhere on the other side of Minneapolis my sister is waking in a strange bed, or maybe it's not so strange really.

"She's at Ted's," her roommate said when I called again, from the hospital.

Who? I thought, but what I said was, "I need you to take a message." My voice had sounded faint. Only a few feet away, in the depths of the Emergency room, someone was trying to beat life back into my grandmother. I thought about Ted. Whoever Ted was. I thought about Glennie's heart, beating faster and faster.

The roommate was hardly agreeable, but when she heard the message, she wished me well, said she'd pin the note to the front door so that Glennie couldn't miss it, but I knew Glennie could. She could pound up the steps, already listing what to study for the day. Fumble with the key. Look down.

I had called from the pay phone tucked down a thin strip of hallway off the waiting room, part of the old familiar. The patterned tile, the row of vending machines, the bank of phones. The waiting room was half-lit, as was the sky. I knew Glennie wouldn't get to the hospital for hours, if she got here at all.

I wonder now when Glennie's secret relationship began. Last night after lab? A week ago at MCAT prep? I wonder what Ted did or said that made her lift her eyes from the page. We are all full of secrets. Glennie, with the new lover nobody knows. Grandma, who stopped taking her Coumadin. Me.

Over the PA system, a call goes out for Dr. Jones, please. Dr. Jones to Peds. Down the way, Al paces, creating stepping patterns along the multi-colored tile. He is dancing in his own heavy-footed way, his feet thumping with each step, his belly hanging down over his trousers. But he is graceful, too, swinging his arms out delicately, turning on the tips of his toes, repeating the pattern, balancing the heavy with the light.

My father is leaning against the wall, head bowed, hands shoved in his pockets, his briefcase at his feet. He stares absently at the tops of his shoes, then reaches down and rubs a scuff from the toe, the whole bulk of him, belly and broad shoulders and gray beard, focused, like Al, on something small, something easily controlled. My mother waits by the double doors. A nurse tries to get her to sit and she refuses, bluntly.

"You might get your nose whacked," the nurse says.

My mother doesn't respond. She stares, arms crossed, through the small window in one door, then flips her braid and steps back, but not too far.

This is most of us, gathered together in a place none of us wants to be. I still have my coupons in my coat pocket, remnants, like my father's briefcase, which was already in hand when their phone began ringing, when Jack called. Jack from the nursing home. A night shift aide whom we have never met. At the nursing home, Jack still sits beside Grandpa's bed, though his shift is long over. I imagine they have run out of conversation now and are waiting, just like us.

I don't know why, sitting here for the second time this month alone, they keep us in the dark. There ought to be a way to let us know how things are going, what's happening. There ought to be someone who can pull my mother away and calm her down, have sympathy for the way she cranes her head every time the double doors swing open.

Glennie will not believe at first that Grandma stopped taking her Coumadin intentionally, not until she sees the small cache of pills stowed neatly in Grandma's dresser drawer, which Jack found when he hurriedly opened her drawer, looking for her glasses case. The pills rolled with the force of his pull, like an avalanche. But Glennie has hardly visited. The news would be less surprising if she'd been over, seen how irritable Grandma is.

"I can't hear you," Grandma had started saying, waving her hand in front of her face. "I can't hear you, didn't you hear me? Why are you talking when I can't hear you?"

Pressing the button above the bed. Needing to be sedated. Sitting in her wheelchair with her hand out, hoping someone will take it. I hope, in a way, that she has succeeded, that she will slip away on this cold spring morning and never have to sit again with her hand out, like a beggar. Then I hate myself, in the same way Glennie will hate herself when she realizes how her absences have cut her off, made her unaware, oblivious. I want to protect Glennie from that, from her own absences, from the guilt. Nobody anticipated this.

A thin noise breaks into the silence. My mother is crying, and something in me sinks, like a deep breath, except that I don't feel like I'm breathing. A nurse is talking to her, holding open a double door, half in the lobby, half out.

My father moves with a speed I didn't know he could attain. Al moves with a speed I didn't know he could attain. But Al rushes toward me, hand extended. He wraps his arm around me, and we walk toward the doors together, because we have decided to always be together now, and we will, he said, take each other slowly down whatever road we face.

I WAS IN THE GROCERY STORE, rummaging through the tomato bin like my grandmother used to do, poking tomatoes to test their firmness. It was early, around six, a time I liked to shop. Shopping then got me out of bed, prevented me from lounging around in my pajamas pretending to look for a job. I cut coupons, stuck them in an envelope, and off I went, morning after morning, to shop with what our adjusted daily budget allowed for daily bread.

An old lady was muttering to herself by the mushrooms. She eyed the price and shook her head. She looked wide given the layers she'd wrapped around herself. Black wool coat, heavy plaid scarf. She looked like she could really whack that price sign and send it spinning. She did not look frail like my grandmother.

"Prices are too high," the lady said, catching my eye.

I'd nodded. The tomatoes, I remember clearly, lacked a certain luster, but I found one that would work well enough in a dinner salad, and I had it in my hand when a car horn started honking.

There are times when I get gut feelings, when I pick up the phone already knowing who is calling, already knowing, in a sense, what I will hear. Maybe there is nothing special about this, maybe it happens to everyone, but I knew then to step away from the bin, to walk outside.

Al was climbing out of my Datsun, fumbling with the seat belt, which had wrapped around his arm. "Get in."

He had on a blue Oxford shirt and a pair of dingy old jeans. No coat. He'd put his sneakers on without socks. I looked down the road at our house, a small, white two story with a brown lawn that dipped, dramatically, before reaching the sidewalk.

"Sarah," Al said, finally free of the seat belt yet climbing back inside. "Get in."

He started the car, leaned over and threw open my door. I slid into the seat and let the door close with a click. I still had that tomato, and I held it carefully, like it was china.

"Who is it?" I asked.

"Your grandmother," he said, and off we went, careening out of the Red Owl parking lot, heading east.

"What happened?"

Al signaled his turn, and we sped onto the highway. "She had a heart attack."

I thought a prayer. I sent it to Grandma, with beams of energy and light that I imagined I had, thoughts of power and fight and strength.

Take that, I thought, and that. Power strength defiance anger. Make your anger keep you alive.

Tomatoes are good in salads, with salt, and with cheese and onion. In the summer, a salami and cheese and tomato make a good meal. In winter, tomatoes are good with cheese and onion and hot soup. As for sauces, any. I listed things off in my mind. I spelled the word tomato backward and forward. We drove.

MY GRANDMOTHER HAD, IN THE LAST WEEK, DECIDED TO START PAINTING. She said, "I can hardly see. I'll probably create masterpieces."

I stopped by one afternoon and found her, eyes closed, running a paint brush over a canvas. She was ensconced in the dining room, surrounded by tubes of paint and newspaper, the day's *Star Tribune*. Someone had tied a bib around her, and the bib was flecked with red and orange. She didn't hear me. I watched her paint line after line, then I said her name, and she stopped and said, "What color next?"

I paused to consider the canvas, a series of stripes, some overlapping, some broken off.

Grandma snorted. "None? Is that what you're trying to tell me?" She fumbled among the tubes, squirted blue onto her brush, ignoring the way the paint plopped onto her hand. "No color? Don't paint?"

"Take that," she said, dipping her paint brush into a jar of water, making the jar shake and tilt. Then, a bright blue streak, right across the canvas, again and again.

"Grandma," I said.

She didn't hear.

"Grandma," I said again, louder that time, and she still didn't hear. I selected a color, orange, and handed her the tube.

"Who's that?" she asked.

I took her clean hand. "Sarah," I said, and I ran her hand over my engagement ring.

"Sarah," she said, sighing, "there is somebody else in this room."

My grandmother has not died. She is, in fact, furious that we think so. She has awakened, and with a vengeance.

She sees us and says, voice hoarse, "What's going on?"

"Devil didn't want you, huh?" Al asks, tweaking her toes.

I give him a glance that would send anyone to hell, but Al only winks at me. Grandma hasn't heard, and she would have laughed if she had, because Al said it. Al gets away with what no one else can, third helpings, breaking a china plate, swearing if the Vikings lose. Not even Dad has these privileges, though Dad is close. Even Grandpa can't, as he says, make a mouse-sized fart around Grandma without the roof coming down.

She is awake, and she is ornery, and my mother is weeping.

"Take me home," Grandma says. She's frowning now, glancing from one to the other. "Get me home," she says, with a little less strength, and finally, "Where's Ed?"

At the mention of his name, Al disappears to call, carefully closing behind him the blue curtain surrounding the bed. Who knows at this point what Grandpa will understand, what he will hear? The night Grandma woke screaming, not so long ago, he understood her raving, apparently whispered for God to take her, if she'd have to live like this. Who knows what he hopes for her now. Hope is different, he has said, when you get this age. Kirsten told me what the night aide told her: that the night Grandma raved, unable to separate her nightmare from the world, it was Grandpa watching from his bed for whom the night aide had sympathy, the way Grandpa tried, despite the feet of distance, to soothe her with his voice. With whispers of love, traveling from the night to the day, from one pale and weary person to another.

Grandma sighs deeply and closes her eyes. My mother has stopped crying now, and she stares off into the distance. Her hair has fallen loose from her braid. My father guides her from the bed, rocks her back and forth, his voice a soft murmur. My mother's shoulders sag.

A nurse pulls the blue curtain open in two efficient tugs, then closes them in one brisk motion. She is an older woman, pale, her make-up only adding to the fatigue evident in the darkness around her eyes, in the heaviness of her movements. She glances quickly at my grandmother, then at my parents, then me. "She's awake?"

I nod.

The nurse busies herself with taking Grandma's pulse, something Glennie will one day being doing. Glennie will know the components of blood. She will be able to resuscitate a stopped heart. She will be Dr. Macmillan, and for that privilege she will have made sacrifices.

Grandma seems to be listening to the nurse, to the thin rustle of her stiff white skirt, the whooshing sound of her shoes. How she could hear anything, I don't know, but I watch her eyes move under her lids, and I know she is paying attention, at least trying to hear. I go to her and hold her hand. The nurse touches Grandma's shoulder, and Grandma squeezes my hand.

"Are you feeling better, Catherine?" the nurse asks loudly.

Grandma nods.

A male nurse joins the first, towing a stretcher behind him, letting it swing wide when he opens the curtains. He has chest hair poking up under his uniform, and I think about that, focus on that, think about Ted. Wonder if he has chest hair. Wonder if Glennie likes that. Wonder why I'm wondering.

When the nurses lift her, Grandma's release is a reluctant one. Grandma does not look heavy. She looks like wet laundry, like a sheet, hanging down a little in the middle, loose and light on the ends.

From a place inside myself I do not recognize, comes my voice. "Be careful with her."

The woman looks offended, and my voice, just a rush of words, a thin stream of air, suddenly settles into something stronger. "She's afraid," I say quietly. The nurse's eyes meet mine, and she nods.

"What's happening?" Dad's voice is calm.

"We have to run a few tests," the woman says, trying to smile.

I follow them from the room.

"The doctor wants a few tests," the woman repeats as they go. "She's okay. She's alright."

I watch the nurse move, try to peek around her wide, swinging hips to see Grandma's white head. Through another set of double doors, and they are gone.

"What doctor?" I ask.

LETTING GO IS IMPOSSIBLE, I have decided. You never really let go, you just accept that what you had is gone. There is a difference. In his lectures at the U, Al is careful, patient. He tells his students all the things religion can be and in the end, they define it for themselves.

I have never been good with death, never easy, never unafraid. I am haunted by the renewals and cycles that will always leave me turning, looking for the person who is not there.

"What doctor?" I ask dad, looking back over my shoulder.

He shrugs. He looks confused. "I don't know. Maybe Kline called in some tests."

Kline, the elusive doctor, the one on his way from his new home in Eden Prairie. Once farmland. Like out where my friend Brenda lives. They are filling in the spaces.

"What's going on?" I ask.

"It must be the right thing," Dad says.

"Well, they ought to tell us what's happening. We have a right to know."

"They don't have time to tell us anything," Dad says softly.

He's right. I let my arms uncross then. I wonder where the hell I lost my tomato. I think about seeds and new gardens, cycles and changing seasons, the ways in which all my life I have fought for moments to not move forward. I have heard that those who fight live the longest, and so I know we will be together for a while in one capacity or another. I think of Grandpa praying for Grandma and think capacity may not be enough. It's going to happen. Maybe not here, not now, not for a long time, but death will come, silently, and spirit away what I love, turn my world into a new world. This isn't acceptance. It is recognition, it is resignation. Because I could never accept the loss, or forgive it really.

Glennie bursts down the hallway, blonde hair flying, a flash. She looks like she will rush past us, and I turn, because I am the strong one, and hold out my arms.

LATER, WHEN GRANDMA IS SETTLED IN A PRIVATE ROOM, and we are waiting for results from tests we cannot name, I walk into the hallway and down the stairs. My feet feel heavy, and yet I walk down quickly, through the double doors of the emergency entrance that open for me alone, since no one else is coming or going. I unzip my coat.

Someone asked me once why I loved Minnesota. I said I didn't love the place; I loved the cold. The cold is numbing. I stand with my coat thrown open, hat off, hands exposed, hoping the cold will burn into me, freeze whatever strength I have left.

I need to get out of the room, away from Glennie and my mother. Glennie, arriving in sweats much too large for her, sits stunned in Grandma's room, a silent, bony woman tucked away in the corner, biting her nails. My mother noticed the sweats, said, "Where did you get those? Those are cute." But she didn't notice that the logo was wrong, or the school name. Macalester College.

After Glennie had arrived, I pulled her away. We stood outside the double doors, back in the lobby, which was empty. I told her that nobody had had any idea. I told her about the Coumadin, how Jack said that at first, he thought the pills were candy.

"I was at Ted's," she said.

I began to tell her that everyone needed relationships, that I was happy for her, but the look on her face stopped me. Her look was apologetic.

"I'm not as busy as you think."

Funny thing about the cold. It makes a person feel oddly warm, the way frost bite tingles and burns, for instance. Now out here alone, I spread my arms and point my toes, touch delicately the hard ground, and turn. I have a secret. I have a secret growing in my belly like a whisper, then a song. I am a woman, and I know. I am superstitious, uncertain, and I cannot look my grandmother in the eye. What dies continues on. I have a dread and a joy. I have a check and balance. I turn.

Al appears in the doorway, face flushed, breathing heavily. He rests his hands on his hips. I don't want to know what has happened. I want a moment of stillness, of quiet.

Back upstairs, a doctor is messing with Grandma's wrist, taking her pulse, again. His hands shake. Grandma eyeballs him and says nothing. He smiles at us when he's done, but the smile is too cheery for the occasion, and I instantly distrust him. He's too young, too new at this, I think, to be honest from the get-go. I demand honest from the get-go. I don't have time for false cheer. I don't have the patience.

"May I speak to you in the hallway?" he says to my father.

I catch his eye and raise an eyebrow.

"The whole family," the doctor says, stuttering slightly.

Mom and Dad squeeze out the door together, but Glennie doesn't move. She avoids my glance. Something in me hardens. It is the I-told-you-so, ready for use.

Finally she says, "I should have gone over more."

Between us, in the middle of the room, Grandma sleeps quietly, her head turned to one side, mouth open. I'm reminded of how it is with sisters in this family, how we get so close we breathe each other's air. Glennie looks at me. She waits, and as angry as I am, I know there is no time for either self-indulgence or I-told-you-sos.

"So go over now," I say.

Al pokes his head in the door and says softly, "We're waiting." He jingles the loose change in his pockets. He doesn't smile.

I walk into the hallway after Glennie, who rubs her hands together over and over. We stand in a semi-circle around the tall pale man with the wispy mustache who is our temporary doctor, since Doctor Kline has somehow not yet managed to arrive from Eden Prairie. I cross my arms and listen. Add, subtract, multiply, divide, I think. Carry over. Carry on.

The Keeper Of Secrets
Sarah
October, 1996

My grandmother was a keeper of secrets. During her last few days, semi-coherent, she told them all, let loose the accumulated small and large betrayals in whispers, the secrets hissing out of her like a tire losing air. She lay in her bed muttering, and we collected the secrets like we collect shells on the beach. Some secrets we understood; others were as mysterious to us as the various old black and white family photos of people we couldn't name, tucked in her photo albums. The secrets spilled out of her quickly, unspooled.

"Thank God she never worked for the CIA," Al said to me in a low voice.

We learned many things, most benign; a few, not. We learned that she had cheated on high school math tests. Twice. We learned that she had cribbed her baked bean recipe from someone named Carol, a friend from Sunday School class, no less. An old neighbor shoplifted from Dayton's and B. Dalton and surprisingly got caught with the blouses, not the books. Their former minister helped himself to the communion wine. And we learned that she had corresponded with Cecily after their last argument, long after we thought they'd last been in touch.

"So much for the famous family recipe for baked beans," Mom said, trying to laugh.

The beans? What about the auntie who sat on her dad's lap? "Why didn't she tell anyone that she wrote to Cecily?" I asked.

Mom shrugged. "Maybe the letters were all bad."

Even as we spoke, Grandma whispered and tossed and turned, wrestled with her confessions until she was free of them. Mom rubbed her arm. She listened, even tried to answer, anything to soothe. I clamped my mouth shut except to tell Grandma I loved her. There were no other words to offer a person in torment.

I was awash in hormones, blotchy-faced and lacking sleep. Grandma had lived long enough to meet her first grandchild, but I kept my sweet baby home under the keen eye of my college friend, Ann, since I hadn't been able to reach Glennie. There were germs in nursing homes. Grief. All of it catchable.

"You can't catch grief," Ann had said to me sternly. She had always been matter of fact, precise, and tough, and she had combined her skills to become an accountant, in the end, leaving dance behind. She worked from home in an insanely clean office.

But I believed being around grief would unsettle Amelia, at best, and so Ann marched over and cared for my baby like I imagined a soldier might, guarding against every sniffle, armed with books and extra diapers, keeping a tight schedule. I drove home to feed Amelia and to relieve Ann, and then hurried back to the nursing home. Al stayed with my grandfather, being his favorite. The days were long and overwhelming but few, and knowing the days would be few was both a relief and made me feel guilty.

"Don't," said Ann. "No guilt. You don't want her to suffer. And all these secrets mean she was, is."

Thank God for Ann, who had marched through her life with every surety and had not blinked. Her confidence gave me permission to release my guilt, let it unwind out and away from me.

On her last day, Grandma interrupted herself to ask for Grandpa. The staff got him out of bed and settled him in a chair beside her, so he could hold her hand. Grandpa hadn't heard her whispers and now, loudly, he recited his own, forgetting we were there. Walking the shoreline at Lake Harriet. Taking her to a Rotary dinner. Ice cream someplace, when he dropped his cone on the sidewalk. Their first kiss. I thought she was listening because she canted her head toward his voice, let her own still. Grandpa patted her hand as he spoke and smoothed back her hair. Late that afternoon, when she struggled to breathe, he said in a whisper that was a roar, Goodbye for now, sweet Cathy and with his blessing, she passed peacefully, silently. At ease.

After she was gone, we settled my agitated Grandpa by asking Al to sit with him, and Al did, pulling a chair right up to the headboard and doing whatever was required. Holding hands, sharing memories, letting him cry. At one point, Al pulled out a flask, and I opened my mouth to speak, but Mom stopped me, her hand resting on my arm, her eyes clear but flat and without expression.

Al stayed with my grandfather while they removed my grandmother's body, which he would not leave, and until Grandpa fell asleep that night. I stayed with my mother, helping her manage the paperwork and the battery of tasks that she now needed to complete. My dad arrived late from critical work appointments, stepping in so I could relieve Al, a hug our only communication as we passed in the doorframe.

"She's okay now, Mom," I said, before I headed back down to the room. "She's probably up there trying to organize the angels."

Mom didn't laugh or even look at me. In the poor light, her cheekbones showed, and the deepening lines in her forehead, which suddenly wrinkled. "She was the keeper of the stories," Mom said. "Just more than we knew."

ABOUT A WEEK LATER, after we thought the crisis had passed and as grief settled into our bones, just when we thought we would be okay for a while, the phone rang, sending me tearing through the streets toward the nursing home. I pulled into the parking lot fast, with a squeal of my tires, and stopped hard in the nearest empty spot. The weather was turning, and against the gray sky the nursing home looked sad and hard up. The last of the fall flowers drooped along the walkway, listing against a new harsh wind. A flyer taped to the front door flapped wildly.

For a moment, I paused to collect myself. I had left Amelia with Ann, again, and Ann was now at my house, punching numbers into a calculator, spreadsheets lined up in columns across my kitchen table while Amelia slept in her bassinet. Ann, who was determined to start her own business. She would probably take over the world.

What thanks I could mumble to her as I sped out the door were likely incomprehensible. I couldn't remember when I had last slept well. I couldn't remember when I had last combed my hair.

The nurses from the afternoon shift were leaving, but they hardly picked up their pace as they traversed the lot, indifferent to the wind. They waved each other good-bye, each gesture riddled with fatigue. I knew them all. I knew Sally was getting divorced, and that Jane's daughter won the statewide spelling bee, and that Herman, who is from Africa, hated the cold.

A slow, hesitant rain began, the drops falling heavily on the car roof. Herman drove by in his beat-up second-hand Ford, cigarette hanging dangerously from his lips. Then Sally. Then Jane, a look on her face of hard concentration, a quick, dark glance at the sky.

I shivered, climbed out of my car, and ran through the parking lot with my coat unzipped and my hood bouncing against my back. In the main lobby, my glasses fogged, and my breathing was harsh, and I knew where I was mostly by sound: the front desk receptionist transferred a call to two; an old man asked another about a mutual friend; a metal cart whined by, attended by a blur of white and the smell of cheap aftershave. But I kept on walking, as sure of my footing as anything.

I heard the thin slap of cards and knew that Mary was nearby, playing Old Maid with a volunteer, the only game she could play because those were the only cards large enough for her to see. As my glasses cleared I saw her, all spirit and fire, dressed in a brightly colored blouse, wearing a too bright red lipstick, her hair carefully coiffed. I waved, and she lifted a hand, and I sailed past, down the brown carpeted hallway, through the pungent, sharp smell of urine, past the day room, where the television blared news to a sleeping audience, and on down a root hallway, a hallway like a limb or branch, a peace offering, to the very end.

In his room, Grandpa was sound asleep. Whatever had required my urgent arrival, quelled.

Kirsten appeared, from where I had no idea. "He was fighting with the staff, trying to pull out his IV, so we sedated him."

"Sedated him? What IV?"

"Doctors' orders. He won't eat."

"When did this start? Does Mom know?"

"She's on her way."

I thumped down heavily in Grandma's old chair and looked carefully at my Grandpa, whose mouth was wide open and whose stuffed cat was peeking out from beneath his folded hands. I had hit my breaking point. I put my head in my hands. And I sobbed.

I DON'T THINK ANYONE wants to be the one who is left behind, and certainly my grandfather never expected it. In the first days after her funeral, a tidy, brief affair with only family and some of the nursing home staff, I visited when I could. But after the IV debacle, I went over every day. Grandpa stayed in his room as much as possible. He wouldn't talk to other residents. He didn't even turn on his lights, and so I had to flip them on when I arrived. He wouldn't play checkers with me or reminisce. He looked at my pictures of Amelia, but he said little. When Al dropped by, Grandpa tried to chat, but he soon wore out, gave up.

That evening, I called my mother. "He's trying to follow her."

"I know."

"What are we going to do?"

I drank a glass of wine while she and I talked. I didn't intend to, but I had the drink in my hand when I dialed, and over the course of what was a short conversation, the wine disappeared, a waste of breast milk.

I walked in circles around the periphery of the living room as we spoke, unable to be still, whispering, as if our conversation was a conspiracy. Al was asleep on the couch, snoring softly, his old fuzzy bear paw slippers sticking out over the armrest. He didn't stir.

"We're talking about bringing him home."

"Home? Mom, you can't lift him. You can't do what the nurses can do."

"I know. But you see, he's my dad," mom said, voice breaking.

I listened as she cried and when she quieted, I told her I was sure that she'd do the right thing.

I had no idea what that was. None of us did.

But Glennie visited him the next day and did the one thing no one else had thought to do. She asked him.

GRANDPA RETURNED TO THE HOUSE but not to the bottom floor. He moved into my old room. He didn't like it—the flowery curtains, the pale pink walls.

"I never liked it either," I told him. "I wanted yellow."

"Why didn't you say?" he asked, roaring.

I shrugged. Why didn't any of us say half the things we should have? Like I'm sorry?

A home health nurse came every day, and Larch came over to visit every Wednesday, with doughnuts. Larch made all the difference to our lives then. Even Al couldn't reach Grandpa the way Larch could. Grandpa and Larch had navigated unspeakable things, and we ought to have known that only Larch could get him through this one.

Larch brought the pastries, but I am sure he also smuggled in a secret stash of Scotch. He used his connections to haul over some new furniture. My room became a mix of Grandpa's things and mine. Navy memorabilia amidst flower curtains. A huge lounge chair that lifted itself to spit Grandpa out stood next to my pictures from graduation, which were now in community with prints of naval battle ships. And Larch talked to him. About the war. About meeting Grandma. About what all his pals at the doughnut shop had to say. About my new sparkling baby. In the end, Grandpa tried to live for Amelia, whom I brought to visit him each morning, and to whom he read an entire large print Patrick O'Brien novel.

"Rest," he'd say to me. "We have a whole series to get through in here."

Grandpa held Amelia and read to her until she fell asleep, and then while she softly snored. If Larch came over, Larch held her, too. Her first months of life seemed to save Grandpa's, and she grew in a soil I never expected, soil made up of battle stories and bawdy stories, crullers and Oban. She did not absorb their grief. They became a trio, and I settled at the yellow kitchen table, exhausted and needing respite, listening, catching words, lyrics, and sometimes even laughter; and I thought she was enough, Amelia.

I'd thought a lot about what to do with Grandma's secrets, about what adding them to the family history might mean, but I was unsettled by how I'd learned them all.

"Would anything really change if you put it all in?" Al asked, potato chip in hand, feet up on the recliner, one evening after returning from a long day at the university. Faculty meetings and teaching and office hours.

I sat on the arm of my own chair, unable to fully relax. "Maybe knowing that she wrote to Cecily is important, makes her seem like a better person."

"I don't think secrets are good things. Not secrets like those. I'd add them in," Al said, rifling in the potato chip bag. "Let them out and let the family think what they want."

"I don't even know who Pastor Ahrens is."

"Well, you might spare him." Al stared thoughtfully at his next chip. "Can I ask you a favor, though? Don't be like her. Don't get bitter about Glennie."

"Bitter?" He could not be right. I was not like my grandmother.

But I was.

Later that night, I added Grandma's secrets into the text, the ones about us, because they were part of us, and one morning when I dropped Amelia off with Grandpa, I told him. About Grandma letting loose, about the family history.

He looked out at his paintings of battleships. Amelia watched him, waiting for her story. I waited, watching him, to learn the fate of ours. Mom came into the room behind me, and there we were, four generations.

"Oh, Sarahstina," Grandpa said. "Cecily was harmless, really. I don't remember the pastor or the neighbor with the stolen stuff. Do you want everyone to remember?"

"It's part of who we are, what shaped us."

Grandpa looked down at Amelia. "Do you want to know about the thieving neighbor?" Then he pointed at me, punching the air. "If you're going to tell it all, tell it all, but I have some things to add."

I hadn't thought of asking him to share. He had topics that were off-limits. Whole years that were off-limits.

"I will tell Amelia," he said, "and you write it down."

He began slowly that morning, describing his childhood on a small family farm in southern Minnesota, and muttered into November, which was his last, unfolding his own life and threading it with Grandma's. He talked about everything but the war.

"It's too hard to talk about," he said.

"Will you at least tell me how you earned the medal?"

He shook his head. "Some wounds," he said, "never heal."

For a while, I remembered his voice that morning, gruff where Grandma's had been soft, loud where hers had been sibilant. But eventually I lost the sound memory. That morning, Amelia cried, and I went out to the living room to feed her, and Grandpa got a phone call from Larch, whom he could not hear, and the radio announcer noted the time. I held Amelia close and listened to the music filter out into the morning, to Grandpa's conversation.

"I miss her so much," he was telling Larch. "Sometimes, when I'm alone, I just sit here and cry."

His own secrets, spilling into the morning, in that last bitter season. I held my daughter with tears running down my face, and when she was fed and burped and happy and snoring in her travel bed, I went back into my grandfather's room and told him what I had heard, and we sat together with all the secrets out in the ugly open.

"I'm kind of shocked she passed off those baked beans as hers," I said finally, trying to be funny, which I realized had been my mom's goal at the nursing home, to ease the pain.

Grandpa laughed. "Oh, she'd told me. She told me everything."

"So you are the keeper of secrets?"

"I guess." He laughed again.

"What happened to the letters between her and Cecily?"

"Oh, I think she threw them out, but you brought her home in that family history. I think your Grandma was glad about that."

"But that was close enough?"

Grandpa smiled.

"Nothing takes away the loss, you know," he said, putting his hand on mine. "Take care of Al."

I looked at my grandpa sharply then, but he gave my hand a good squeeze, as if to show his strength, as if to imply he was staying a while.

"I won't add the stuff about the thieving neighbor," I said.

Grandpa nodded. "Let them be."

"Just us."

"Just us."

Salvage
Al
May 1998

THE SKY WAS BLACK, as if someone had wiped away the clouds and wavering sunlight, and all the small sounds that usually piggy-backed on the breeze—their neighbor, Mark, swearing over his power mower, or a thin hum of jazz coming from Howard and Norda's place, something Al thought was probably hip, but which he was old enough now to be slightly past enjoying. Wiped away the familiar and replaced it with what felt like midnight. Yet it was the middle of the day, a Saturday afternoon. The world had gone dark and the trees stood still as fence posts and the birds had stopped chirping. Nature seemed to be holding its breath and in that silence, in that moment of warning, Al glanced at the neighborhood beneath that sky, before the tornado came—-at the empty yards, greener than he'd ever seen them against the black and heavy sky, lit by a strange, eerie light.

Sarah and Amelia were huddled in the laundry room, tucked under the old oak worktable with a battery-powered radio. He was supposed to be grabbing the lockbox, but here he was instead, out on the porch, watching the sky for the funnel. In the lockbox, tucked behind the deed to the house and their passports and their wills and their mortgage was a small silver chain, given to him by his mother. He had no idea whose chain it was, just that she loved it. And he had no idea why he was thinking of it now, as he turned back into his house to save it.

HE HAD BEEN A POPULAR BOY, but the one who bore an onslaught of name-calling and insult due to his size, the one to whom people would address the most hurtful remark and then ask to dinner. "It was just a joke, Al." Al accepted every invitation. He liked people and always had, even those who seemed to see him in only one role, one world. One shape. He was tagged to be a lineman the first day he walked into high school by a senior quarterback named Joey Falvino, who saw Al in the halls and said he needed "more beef on the line." For the sake of harmony, Al went along with the crueler friends as well as the kind. He hardly spoke to them now, though. They had scattered to different colleges and then spread like seeds into various communities, in search of sundry dreams. But here, unexpectedly, he had met people he could rely on. Mark. Howard. Especially Anil. Here, he had made friends.

Aside from accepting more shit than he should have, Al hadn't ever been able to name what seemed abnormal about his childhood until he invited Sarah to visit his parents in Chicago, and she named the mildly disturbing and elusive quality of his youth: silence.

"I've never known a home so quiet," she had said as they drove away. "It's as though something tragic has happened to your parents and they can't speak, but you don't know what it is, and you feel like you can't ask, so the silence just hangs there."

And she was right. There was a melancholy in his folks' house that seemed to cling to everything, and a seriousness. He had never been able to pinpoint what it was about his childhood that seemed so aggravating, but absence is sometimes hard to define. People spend lifetimes searching for things in their lives that they can't quite voice. Al searched for noise and passion and enthusiasm. He searched for connection. He searched for people who would close the distance. It was as though he and his parents had lived in a dream, and they couldn't speak through the haze. Their voices were eaten, absorbed, tossed away; and they knew no other language to bridge the divide.

AL COULDN'T SEE THE TORNADO, but the stillness suddenly made him uncomfortable. He closed and locked the front door, out of habit. Were his neighbors all safe? He worried about where his in-laws were, if they were tucked into their laundry room, hunched over the radio, pets in accompaniment. He hoped Glennie was at the hospital, which had to be as safe as a fortress.

And that's when he realized he had no idea where the cat was.

He and Alber had always been together. Alber was the size of a small dog. And imperious. His name was Alber because the t got left off his name on the tags and so they adapted. Al called out to him and there was no reply. But the cat never did come when he was called or even deign to throw a glance his way.

Al hurried into the living room, eyed a pile of couch cushions, and continued on into each room. Room after room. In his study, he grabbed the lockbox out of the closet and without thinking, his fishing pole. He used it like a walking stick to get through the rooms a second time, just as Sarah's voice came as though through water from the downstairs, a voice small sounding and pleading.

"I'm looking for Alber," he said, and he knew his voice sounded worried, that he had bellowed, and the bellow had probably carried in it some large fear, because within moments, there Alber was, round and furry and looking bored but in plain view.

The only time the cat did respond was in a time of crisis. It was his house, after all. And if the people were in pain, he'd bestow upon them his rotund, benign, and stoic presence.

"We have to go downstairs," Al said, swiftly picking up Alber and lugging him and the lockbox and the fishing pole toward the door. In that instant, he thought he saw himself very clearly: a man of some height, sensitive and a bit lumpy, who liked to fish because it was a sedentary sport, and who loved his cat. Happily married and a proud father. A professor. A man who kept a lockbox and who even had a will, though there wasn't much to go around. He had willed Amelia his fishing pole. A child should have something a parent loved, if the parent passes. And there he was at the crest of the door when he saw the funnel through the window, a dark, burrowing, wild spread of air. And he bellowed again, the wind rising to steal his voice. He bellowed and charged downstairs, letting go of the pole on the way but holding the cat and the lockbox so tightly he thought he would cry. He yelled instructions. To get under the table, to cover their heads, to hold onto one another, though for the life of him he had no idea what that could do, except sweep them away in one fell swoop. But he wasn't thinking clearly now, and holding on sounded right. He was crawling under the table on his knees with no free hand to give him additional speed, cat howling, Sarah reaching for him, Amelia screaming, when the tornado hit and tried to steal his world.

In the aftermath, they thanked whatever higher powers they believed in for the old oak table, which meant they had one another. For the lockbox and the cat. For Sarah's particularities, one of which was to insure themselves against every eventuality, including tornadoes. They could not have absorbed personal loss or financial blows. Not then. So even though the house sustained damage, they felt ebullient, charged, resilient. They felt, in whispers, even ecstatic, though the feeling faded, and quickly, in light of what chance had created. Families with no homes and financial fears, huge fears; the devastating losses that harden a soul, allow bitterness to filter in and run through a body like blood.

Nobody died, and yet the neighborhood was never the same. It divided into the devastated and the fortunate; the east end of the street and the west; and neighbors looked at each other differently afterward. It was a small change, one that registered only if you'd known people prior. The division was visible in an extra sigh, or a quick glance filled with sadness or anger or envy. Green looks, Al called them. Green looks everywhere casting a sickly pall over everything.

Lots of green looks, he said, coming home one day after helping the Lundgrens salvage what they could.

The Lundgrens were empty nesters at the opposite end of their street, in a cluster of houses that had been nearly wiped away, as opposed to their end, where the damage was more manageable. Their houses could be fixed. The Lundgren's had no house at all.

Al was quiet while helping others to dig for the stray mementos that might ease the strain. Photo albums and favorite blouses, still wearable and wasn't that a miracle?, crystal from a wedding and maybe, here or there, intact furniture. He dug through heaps of wood, watching for nails, sweating through the lifting. (He was always asked to lift. Garbage, bags of leaves, construction jobs in the summer, moving boxes. Al lifted his way through the world). And he lifted then, while Sarah listened, leaning into this woman or that, or that child, or this man, head tilted to better hear. Listened to the loss spiral out of them and into the earth, where she said to him later that she hoped it would be buried and not sown.

He found a photo album, a framed picture that needed new glass but was undamaged, a book or two, books he imagined had been more decorative than meaningful. He found a decent chair. He uncovered broken records and unwound tapes and waterlogged CDs. Drenched beds. Lives sagging from the weight. Not real lives, just all the accumulated bits that define a home, sometimes even a person. And he'd hand items over quietly, as quietly as he could, so that his presence didn't intrude any more than it had to in the salvaging of these neighbors' lives. There was something about the process that made him so grateful he couldn't speak, as though he had suddenly become superstitious. Made silence seem like reverence. Made him think of his parents. Made him realize, for the first time, all the things silence could and could not be. That silence had a life of its own. Made him, standing the in the rubble of the

Lundgren's house, feel that a small flame had tickled him; that he saw differently now.

INSIDE THE LOCKBOX WERE PAPERS—titles to the two cars, insurance documents, the deed to the house, medical information, their will. There was a set of keys, to unlock what he didn't know, and a pair of beautiful old pearl earrings. There was some extra cash. His mother's chain. Inside the house, in the kitchen, they found Amelia's dollhouse—the one intact house in the neighborhood, his father-in-law had said dryly, later. And his fishing pole, miraculously, almost symbolically, standing against the doorjamb where he'd thrown in it his mad dash downstairs.

Many of their neighbors rode away that day in blankets provided by the local Red Cross, in a truck that carried them like refugees. The Lundgrens, a crumpled, beaten bunch; Andy Millet looking steadfastly ahead, his wife sitting with head bowed beside him. They did not wave at the clutch of neighbors from the east end of the road who had gathered to watch them leave: Howard and Norda. Anil and his entire family, every last child. Mark and even Marshall, who barked a farewell, which devolved into a steady whine as the truck disappeared.

"Where do they go?" Anil asked.

"A shelter somewhere," Howard said quietly. He still wore his pressed pants and loafers from work, but he had dirt across his LaCoste.

"I heard they opened up the high school, but they won't take pets," Mark said, who like them, had a damaged roof. "I need a place for the night. Can anyone take me and Marsh?"

Mark looked at Al, and Al shook his head. Mark with his giant pillow of a dog looked a bit like the animal all of a sudden, barefoot, long hair in a tangled wave.

"We're heading to my in-laws...We don't even know if they are okay. The phone lines are down."

Mark looked away. He didn't reply. Al felt shaky and ill. "Maybe I can call Sarah's sister?"

But Mark was already walking away with Anil, who would take care of them, whose house with all its children was still standing brightly, solid, unaltered.

Al and Sarah drove away in Sarah's aging Datsun, sputtering through the wasted area that once was an old neighborhood in Minneapolis, out to the suburbs, where an old man watered his lawn and a small boy teetered along the sidewalk on a new shiny bike with training wheels. Where summer still held its glorious sway, save for the last house on the block, on the corner of Sherman and Oak, where they found her parents dialing, dialing, dialing and white with fear.

"My God," her mother said, grabbing Amelia, stone-faced, touching them each in turn, just as the tinny, annoying sound of the phone ringing came to them through the day. Where the air hung heavy, and the smell of freshly cut lawns pervaded. Al thought it smelled nice, and he couldn't quite believe how twenty minutes could so separate worlds and lives and dreams.

"The house has a hole in it," Sarah said. "The house has a hole."

And that was where they started over, snug in the kitchen of his in-law's house. He had a scotch and felt ten times better than he normally did drinking scotch until he realized, in a vapor, that he was stone cold drunk; that the alcohol had seeped into every slowly relaxing pore in his body.

The phone rang. Rang and rang. Glennie calling from God knew where because truly only God ever did know where Glennie ever was. She'd phone in, but no one ever reached her at home. Yet she called, absolutely hysterical, having driven to the far border of their neighborhood, down by the Lundgren's, only to be held back by rescue personnel.

"There was nothing there," she told her mother. "It was flattened."

Sarah looked at Al and whispered, "Held back?"

Al shrugged. It was an emergency. Of course Glennie would show, wouldn't she?

"Is she coming over?" But no, no Glennie wasn't. She was back at work now. Sarah frowned and looked hard at a family photo on the wall, and Al felt a shiver.

The phone rang and rang, his parents the next time. Frantic.

Frantic? He knew his parents well, he thought, and he had never known them to be frantic, only stoic. He thought the scotch was a wonderful thing and went to the phone.

He told his father. "We're okay," he said. "And we have the cat." It seemed critical to him that they had even saved the family pet.

"The cat?" his father said, sounding deflated.

There was a long pause and Al thought, how ironic. But his father coughed then and said something.

"What?" Al said.

And his father answered, "We love you."

"Yes," Al said, having never heard it before that he could remember. "We love you, too."

Sarah looked up.

Al hung up the phone. He looked at Sarah and said, "Are we in shock?"

THE KEY WAS TO A SAFETY DEPOSIT BOX, Sarah told him. The earrings had been her grandmother's, when she was young, and were quite valuable. The cash from the lockbox was minimal—what one would need to get someplace safe, Sarah said later, that she tucked away one day when they were flush.

"What's in the safe deposit box?" he asked.

Sarah didn't remember.

They let her parents drive them to the bank, where they waited politely and took their turn and opened the box. It was empty.

"Why do we have this?" Al asked.

Sarah looked at him. "I guess I got it just in case."

Al nodded.

They left quietly.

"Well?" his father-in-law asked.

"Just stuff for peace of mind," Al said.

He looked out the window at the bright day.

THE NEXT MORNING, Al drove back to the house. He saw Mark next door, kicking at the ground and talking to a police officer. Al kicked the ground, too, and then grabbed a few things they might need from the house, under the scrutiny of another police officer. Al was quiet, picking through their lives, as quiet as he'd been picking through his neighbor's.

"You have tornadoes on your insurance?" said the police officer, and Al nodded yes.

The policeman nodded then, too. "I think you might be the only one."

"My wife," said Al. He shook his head. "I wouldn't have done it."

"Makes you think," the other man said.

"Makes you thankful," Al replied.

He had hole in his roof, he thought. He felt that he had hole in his brain, too, as if he were still in a vapor of some kind, and he wondered how he'd feel when he finally touched down. There was a tarp over the hole. Al didn't know who had put it there. He squinted into the bright aftermath. He was still inside the storm, under the table, head into Alber, free arm around his family, listening to a wind he had never heard before, like the vengeance of God, roaring through his house and trying to lift it, shuddering, from the foundations.

The policeman touched him on the shoulder. "You ready?"

Al nodded.

"Let's go," the man said. "Everybody in your family okay?"

Al nodded.

The policeman looked at him then.

"Take care of yourself," he said, and Al nodded again, tried to say thank you, but couldn't get the words out.

Al stared at Mark for a minute, and as if sensing his presence, Mark looked up, paused, and then slowly lifted his arm. And that became the most central memory of all the memories that remained: Mark waving to him over the rubble and waste, that old familiar hello salvaged as well.

About Amelia, For Amelia, Who Is Asking About Herself

Sarah

1999, remembering 1996

I KNEW. Maybe a week, maybe more than one, but the days held me in a trance, a leadenness. Well before the day I finally pushed open the brown office door at the doctor's office, I knew. In the early mornings when I woke, warm with sleep, and turned to curl up along Al's back; in the welcome sun through the windows, when even the light seemed different, as if promising change, a tilt in my world; in the closed, small, examining room, with the framed farm print on the far wall; in anyplace, the feeling clung.

Yet somehow, I was surprised when my gynecologist said the word. Pregnant. My gynecologist in her white coat, with her name on a small pin attached to the pocket.

I don't remember being happy or excited. I remember only the quiet, as she waited for whatever reaction I was going to have, and

I stared at the farm print hanging on her white wall and wondered where she found it, if she'd bought it at one of those huge art auctions they advertised on late night TV, the ones held in the Marriott down on 495.

If someone had told me that at age twenty-four, I would be married and pregnant, I would have worried, not because I feared the prospect, but because I didn't. Something appealed. I liked the hum of a garden, the slant of morning sun on the counter as I cut tomatoes for a new recipe. But I wanted more, too. Something for myself, that something all my friends were busy chasing in corporate jobs and teaching jobs and across the mountains of the Alps.

I never would have found it—myself or the work—had it not been for Amelia. Some things, as my grandmother says, shock a person into understanding. Amelia was that shock for me. A giant, unexpected, six-pound three-ounce shock. A shock like an earth tremor for a woman who had been on the pill so long that pregnancy seemed a distant dream. In one month, I missed twice, lazily taking the pills at breakfast, unconcerned that twelve or more hours had passed. I'd been on the pill so long, how could my body make any assumptions?

"The pill can fail," my gynecologist said. She was a severe woman. Tall, angular, with straight brown hair that accentuated her high cheekbones. Ellen Norquist. El, she liked to be called, and it suited her, the shortness of it, the snap. "I'm sorry about this, Sarah, but it does happen."

Thanks, El, I thought. Thanks a load. Thanks for your calm, blunt statement of facts. Thanks, by the way, for forgetting, to congratulate me. Like my life was over. Like the mistake had to be remedied. No,

I thought. The mistake has to be born. The happy, glorious, hopefully tow-headed, heart-tugging mistake.

"It's good news, El," I said.

"Well, then congratulations!" Her voice lifted.

I didn't envy her her job. I didn't even envy her that she had one while I still muddled through an endless job search. She passed me a few handouts, suggested prenatal vitamins, and then I was back at the front desk, booking my next appointment. I stood in the parking lot before getting in the car, trying to breathe. I glanced at El's handouts about books to read and foods to avoid and the importance of safe exercise and then my eyes locked on her looping cursive on the top of one sheet. A date. September 9th.

When Al came home, he took off his down jacket, slammed down the soggy paper, and grumbled about the bus being late. I waited until he grumbled himself into a seated position, until I had his eye, and I chose my words carefully.

"I have great news," I said, and he smiled, instantly. I love Al for many reasons, but this is one, the way he can absorb light and reverse himself out of a bad mood.

I said, "I'm pregnant." He smiled the same smile, until his smile faded, then lit up again, softer, surprised, in awe. It was a smile of wonder.

His was the first celebration of you. He danced, more graceful than any ballerina, around the kitchen in his socks, arms out, like he had wanted this all the time, all his life, and been waiting.

I danced later. I remember the day. I danced the first day I woke up and felt fuller, ran my hand down my stomach and felt a roundness, felt like I could touch you.

But at first, I couldn't tell anyone other than Al about you.

"What's the big secret?" he said, not looking at me, looking at my flat stomach instead. It had taken me years to have flat stomach, but he was looking at it as though it would begin sprouting before his very eyes.

"I think I want it secret for a while."

Al shook his head. "I want to tell the whole world."

And he did. He began his lecture the following morning, one on God, by announcing the imminent birth of his first-ever child.

My mother called me later that afternoon. Gloria Johansson's son was in Al's class. Al didn't make the connection.

"Swenson, Johansson, Nelson," Al said later. "This is Minnesota. How was I supposed to know?"

My mother was hurt. She wanted to know why I hadn't told her, and I tried to explain, but my father grabbed the phone away to say congratulations, sounding giddy. In the afterglow of his joy, I called Glennie. She wasn't home. Voice high, I trilled a message, saying, "You're going to be an Auntie!" She took forever to call back. What would it take to matter to her? I had begun to ask myself. Who did matter to her? Finally, I reached out to my grandmother, who had not called and who said, "I told them to leave you alone. I understand, even if they don't. Some things a person needs to adjust to herself before she tells other people."

I felt grateful for her defense. Then she said, "When are you due?" And I told her September 9th, and my grandmother repeated the date to herself several times, a mantra, and I knew what the mantra meant. It meant she had something new to live for, and she was determined, despite her health, to make it, and I wondered if to keep her alive all I had to do was continue to reproduce.

My grandfather, she said, was absolutely thrilled. And even though he was stuck back in bed again for his belly, he had somehow spread the word throughout the nursing home, and aged people, as she called the other nursing home residents, had begun to trickle into the room. They wanted to hear all the news. There was so little good news.

IT WAS GRANDPA WHO NAMED YOU. On a rainy day when the bare trees were oddly beautiful in their ragged, raw simplicity, when they looked only like bone and yet were filled with grace, and we still had a middle name to choose. On a day Grandma sat with her new friend, Edith, who wasn't well, nodding to us as we passed Edith's room, nodding as if to say, Shhhh, it's okay. On that day in the halogen-lighted room, in that quick breath of time we had before Grandma at least popped in for a quick hug before returning to soothe Edith, he named you. His voice all gravel and hope, he whispered only: Amelia Catherine.

Al and I agreed.

Tears, from this Navy veteran of two world wars.

"What did you do?" Grandma asked when she appeared and saw him crying. "What did you say?" She rushed over to him. "Ed," she said, patting him on the back. "Eddy."

"Catherine," Al said, getting only that far, touching her on the arm.

"Did something happen?" she asked, her face crumpling.

"He's fine. Everything is fine. Amelia's middle name will be

Catherine." My voice sounded loud. Perhaps it was.

Grandma looked at me, then Al, and then her eyes widened.

"He asked," Al added, "and we agreed that it was the perfect name."

Grandma continued to pat Grandpa's back, then she bent and kissed him on the head. "It's okay, Eddy," she whispered. "Thank you, Eddy."

Grandpa was overjoyed, but when I walked into the nursing home each week, it was Grandma holding sway in their room, like a queen holding court; and if I looked carefully, surreptitiously, under her mattress, in the drawer of her nightstand, in the nooks and crannies of the room, I found no stash of Coumadin. She was taking her pills again.

"Breast milk," Kirsten would tell me, every time I saw her, as if I needed reminding. My pregnancy provided hours of conversation. "I say breast milk."

And my grandfather, bed bound, would shake his head if he was around and try to get Kirsten to leave her ministrations or at least be quiet. "I don't need to keep hearing about breasts," he'd say.

As my stomach rounded, they began to touch it. Kirsten. Edith, who I went to visit. Mary Smith from 201, who came down and made friends when she heard the news. Swaddling. How to treat hemorrhoids, if I got them. The ways to deal with nausea, as I bent over Grandma and Grandpa's toilet, with them all clucking behind me, Grandma frantically pressing the button for the nurse's aides.

The day our labor began, I was waddling along the nursing home hallway to say hello and stopped flat. I'd been trying to visit more often, especially since, when the baby came, I wouldn't visit as much while I got used to things. The nurse's aide, Jack, now working days, found me with my back pressed against the wall and who knows what look on my face. He was gangly, and his face was covered with acne scars, and he was patient and kind. Jack lifted my arm, slung it around his shoulder, walked me slowly back down the hall to a chair at the nurse's station at the end of the hall.

"Let's make a few phone calls," he said. He who was all of what, eighteen? Nineteen? Out of high school and drifting, taking the only job he could get and doing his best. He settled me in a chair, and then his age showed. "So who do I call?" he asked, eyes wide.

I HAD NO FEAR TO KEEP MY VISION NARROW. I felt only that explosive confidence of knowing I was in the right place, that I was happy with my life and hoping, as Jack made his way to the phone, that all would go well. Go well, go well, go well, I thought, over and over.

Grandma reached me first. She held my hand. "I'm right here, Sarahstina. Try to breathe. You will both be fine. We all love you."

We all love you, we all love you, we all love.

It's important to know how one's story begins, especially in our family. Stories connect us; words are our banners and flags. We have no crest. We have the twining of our chapters.

Your name came to me in a dream. In the dream, I was gardening in the front yard, planting flowers by the front door, and a child came tearing across the lawn as I planted, pulling a balloon behind her. The balloon dragged, kicked up little spits of mowed grass with each lonely bump on the ground. My daughter was tow-headed. She was two, maybe three, her arms and legs still carrying the plumpness of babyhood. As she headed out of the yard, straight toward the road, a car turned the corner heading our way, and I fumbled but stood and yelled for the child to stop. Screamed. The name I screamed was Amelia. When I woke up, blurry from a bad night's rest and still round with you, I had a strange feeling, the sense that I had known you for much longer, that one day you would run through one my gardens hauling a kite behind you, and that I would be speechless, the kite all my dreams for you, dreams you handled roughly, oblivious, because you were determined to have your own.

You think, Amelia, that you are one hell of a kid. You are. But you are also one of a long, long line of stinkers. Wait 'til you know more about your great-grandmother. You'll look at pictures of her white hair and her thick wrinkles and the unseeing eyes, like they had clouds behind them, and they did, and you'll think she couldn't have been much, because she wasn't at the end. She was still a force to be reckoned with. She saw. Do not be misled.

Your arrival was met with a round of apple juice, served in plastic cups, at precisely two p.m. central time, in Grace Nursing Home, Minneapolis, Minnesota. They posted a sign, congratulating Ed and Catherine on the birth of their first great-grandchild. A sign was unnecessary. Grandma had slowly, painfully, made Kirsten wheel her way down the hall, knocking on doors.

And you. Well. When it was okay to take you there for a visit, you were met with a cheer. Friends lined the hallway, wheeled themselves down to meet you. Edith, better now, first in line, Mary right behind, and Judith Renfield's niece, standing in for Judith, who couldn't leave her bed. Kirsten. Jack. Grandma, wheelchair smack dab at the front of the hall, Grandma held you first, and I have never seen her more beautiful. She was more alive than she had been in years. She was glowing.

Kirsten wheeled Grandpa into the hall. How, I'll never know. But she made sure he was in the doorway of their room as we three came down the hall so that he wouldn't miss a thing. Remember this, little girl: small kindnesses can deliver worlds of good.

And it was Grandpa who added you to the family Bible in his slanted, block capital letters because cursive was too hard, drawing a thin shaky new line to the tree and with great determination writing in your name. Amelia Catherine, b. September 12, 1996.

WOMEN CALL, DROP BY, bring with them scraps of fabric, elaborate designs, dreams and fantasies of what a dress will make them. Brides are the worst. They expect perfection. What they want most is the fairy tale. Still, pins in my mouth, I hold fabric up to the faces, page through glossy fashion magazines. I try. I remember: we all have dreams.

"Your hands," my grandmother said once, "are your gift."

My hands are like her hands; she, too, sewed. She, too, according to my mother, made clothes the other girls envied.

"It's because I know how to make figures look nice," Grandma said "All shapes, all sizes. I know where to tuck and pin. I know when tucking and pinning won't do."

She sat with me several afternoons, helping me through my first few dresses. In the bright morning light, her rough, knotted hands sliding over the fabric, we would plan. She would touch the fabric, get a feel for the grain, and I would describe the body shape, and she would adjust the pattern in her head. We talked about personalities, too, because customer service matters and once I even called Larch for advice. He had so many businesses, he had to have a few tips.

"Oh, people," he said. "People are the worst."

On occasion, Al came home from school to find my mother carefully cutting along chalked lines; to find my grandmother sipping tea. Even my father came, later in the evening, because, as he said, his house was empty. We'd cluster around the bolts of fabric, the machine, squeezed together.

"Be clear," Grandma always said. "With sewing, always be clear. A seamstress can only do so much."

And I am clear. If anything, I am clearer than I need to be. I cannot give you breasts, I told one woman, but I can make what you have look fuller. I can't take an inch off you, I told another, softly, kindly. I try to be tactful, to choose my words carefully, make my point. These women, who want so much to look like other people, I gently remind are only themselves. And I have never lost a customer.

What a glory when we like who we are, I told one customer.

"How did you start sewing?" customers ask, each in turn, as I scribble measurements on a piece of paper, file the measurements in manila folders which bear their names.

"I couldn't afford to buy maternity clothes for myself or clothes for my baby," I say. "My husband was in graduate school; I was unemployed."

Unemployed, with COBRA fees eating us into debt. But making the clothes had sparked something.

Every woman in my family has made her mark with needle and thread, if only once, on our family women's quilt. For me, the sound of the sewing machine, the sun warm and bright across the cloth, the way the cloth moves briskly under the needle, falling in short tugs to my feet, these things ease me. It took time for me to understand, and a little more time to appreciate, that this is my best life.

What one always hopes for one's children is that they are better people, my grandmother used to say.

I had thought she meant something other, until I became pregnant. I had thought she wanted us to rise and shine, to achieve wonderful things, but I know now that what she wanted was for us was far simpler: not to inherit her faults, or Mom's and Dad's. We do, though. We can't help but. We can't help but bring a little of our parents' spirits along with the blood they give us. But we also bring along surprises. We sew when we were supposed to be in marketing. We marry unexpectedly. We become ourselves.

Heroes and Other Extinct Species
Anil and Al
2000

IN THE COOL, DIM BASEMENT that smelled faintly of mildew (hadn't they cleared that up? He thought they had), Anil waited, arms crossed, for his one role in their ritual. As the tiny train rounded the tracks and aimed for the station, he reached a delicate finger to the right of the miniature town and hit the button that made the train toot. Anil smiled. This was his favorite part, hearing the whistle blow, and the only part of the drama that Al ever relinquished. But it was the best part, too, hearing the three high blasts from their engine as it aimed toward their faux New England town. It reminded him of his youth, when he'd daydreamed about where his studies might take him, away from his pressuring father, who wanted him to be a doctor, to a smaller, quieter city than New Delhi, which he'd yearned to leave. It reminded Anil of the things he had always hoped for in life: a satisfying job, a happy family, a pleasant place to live, good friends. He especially hoped for these things now, in this foreign place that seemed like it would never quite accept him or give him ease. His hopes are why he came here, half-way around the world, to a land best known for snow and ice and freezing temperatures.

The train stopped at the tracks in front of the miniature people grouped on the platform, who were frozen in waves and grins and happy homecomings.

For a moment, there was silence. Then Al asked, "One more time?" and Anil nodded.

Al was large and had a paunch, but he was fast on his feet, oddly lithe. He reset the switch, and off the train went, away from the station into a small section of woods. On it went, winding its way forward across the broad raised platform that took up a sizable portion of the room. This was what Anil hoped for more than anything himself, to move forward. It was, for different reasons, what Al hoped for also. Hoped rather than wanted because they had each reached a point in their lives where hoping seemed safest and least likely to disappoint. In this and much else, they were unlikely allies, Anil thought. The doughy religion professor with the easy laugh and open face, and the reed-thin Indian theoretical physics professor, always with a stain on his cuffs, who liked people but half the time got his vocabulary mixed up and so never quite connected. Until Al. Al understood his accent and funny ways of speaking. But then Al was as much in need of friendship as was Anil.

Anil sometimes wondered if Al should have aimed higher, tried for jobs at the top programs, but Al was content where he was, and wasn't that a gift nowadays? Al had one book under him, an insightful if slim volume on interpretations of Christianity in America as it turned toward a new century. "Just a small book," Al called it. He never gave himself enough credit, in Anil's opinion.

Sometimes they had long talks about university politics or about faith and science while working on the trains. It was easy to tackle big subjects while distracted by toys. Or in a car. Anything but face to face. Anil wished he'd known this when he was younger, when he'd told his father that he would not become a doctor. He would have taken his father outside at night, told him while pointing at the stars left to see through the lights of the city. Anil loved the stars. He would have studied astronomy, but he didn't want to dissect the beauty of it all, to ruin it. He liked the wonder he felt. He liked the awe. Anil glanced at his cuffs now. In the background, the train huffed quietly up a makeshift hill. And there it was, right there: syrup on his right shirt cuff from helping Aditi with the children at breakfast. He didn't want to check his left.

They wasted hours down here, Al and Anil. Their kids grew bored with the repetition and drifted away, or wanted to make the trains crash, which neither Anil nor Al would ever allow. Their wives shrugged the amusement away, saying boys will be boys. Yet Al and Anil still trooped down here, more frequently of late. Without interruption, for these brief hours, Anil and Al earned a respite from the grief and sadness lurking upstairs and in the neighborhood as a whole, like air. They avoided household chores and grading. They let their thoughts drift. Beers in hand, sometimes Scotch, they stood together in Al's cool basement, regardless of season, and watched a toy train chug its way to a make-believe, cheery small town.

IT BEGAN HERE, AL WOULD THINK as he stepped into the garage each morning and hit the button to raise the door. His heart would race, and his stomach would turn, though lately that had abated. He'd bend down and peek outside as the garage door rose.

Early last October, Al had waited patiently in the dark as the garage door hummed upward. He was dressed in his typical Saturday morning attire, an untucked chamois shirt, sweatpants, and his favorite pair of down-in-the-heel house shoes with the Gopher logo stitched onto the toes. He'd run his hands through his hair and let his gaze drift over the assorted lumps and shadows. A rusting station wagon that he had once revived and would again. Hulking dim shapes that he knew were boxes of Christmas ornaments. Squeezed between the Volvo and the wall, he caught sight of the exercise bike and sighed.

A breeze came in as the garage door climbed, came in tinged with cold, that first breath of winter. God, was he thankful for winter. The best and the worst in his life routinely came with it, but somehow, he always remembered the best as something bright and fulfilling and hopeful, and the worst as something he had powerfully endured. He'd always been susceptible to stories, especially adventure tales where the heroes survived, even triumphed, over glaring personal foibles. During bad winters, he'd imagined himself strong. He'd believed he could inspire, even when heartbroken. He'd plowed through bad winters with the heart of a lion.

Al had survived the winter of wonder and worry, when Amelia arrived just as Sarah's grandparents were failing; the winter his mother had decided to visit them for two weeks; and the winter they were frozen in for days. Summer seemed mildly disconcerting in comparison. Al seemed to sleepwalk through it. He simply could not bear the heat. He had no tolerance for temperature. Or much for temper. Maybe because he was raised in such chilly silence.

Some people just ought to divorce, he thought. Sometimes splitting up saves the world.

The garage door creaked through its final curve and then there was the October morning, gray and cool, holding a promise of snow. At the end of the drive, fluttering in the rising wind, was the morning slew of bad news, and Al walked to it out of obligation. He was a hopeful sort. He was an optimist. But he was also a man of routine. In the morning, he read the paper. In the evening, he watched the news. His father had done these things, and the rituals gave him comfort. It was the only language he and his father had shared: news commentary.

Half-way down the drive, he glanced over at the Morone's, a few doors down, across the street. Timmy was curled in the driveway, as though he had fallen asleep there.

"Timmy?" Al had said, sounding tentative.

Timmy was a red-haired, freckled, slightly unkempt boy. Maybe eight, maybe nine. A weed, he was so thin. He was usually going someplace, yelling, rounding up a gang for this or that. He had more energy than clothes (or fences) could contain and so he was usually without one piece of clothing or another. One day a shoe, the other his t-shirt. He lost mittens and caps with regularity. If Timmy wasn't on the move (or talking), then Al could be certain hell had frozen over.

Now, in the cool morning, Al rushed over to the boy, his breath catching, heart pounding. God, he thought, I need to get in shape, but even then, he knew his gasping came from fear. Living, choking fear. The boy's ribs peeked out where his t-shirt had slid up his torso, and then there, by his head, a dark puddle that made Al gag. Al stumbled, scanned the neighborhood, something rising in his heart. He reeled and looked back toward his garage, but Sarah hadn't followed him outside and nor, for once, thank God, had Amelia, who was Al's shadow, a trailing four-year-old dragon, as full of energy as Timmy once had been. A spitfire. She considered Timmy a kindred spirit.

Al reached down and checked for Timmy's pulse even though he knew there wouldn't be one. Somehow, he felt he owed Timmy that caution, perhaps respect. The boy's skin was cold, and Al shivered and pulled his hand away. He was breathing hard. Was he panting? He tried to pull himself together as he hurried over to the Morone's front door and rang the bell. When Joyce first greeted him, Al could only spread his hands, wordless. He let her have all the words. For the life of him, he could think of nothing to say. He couldn't even think.

Later, it would come back to him, how the wind had swept in like a whisper as the garage door rose, how it had spread in him a sense of peace and relief, that cool air reviving memories, the good and the bad, memories of how strong he thought he was. He supposed he was strong in some way, but now he'd had more than his share of burdens. That's what he thought, anyway. He believed he could take no more.

TIMMY MORONE HAD OWNED A USED 10-SPEED BICYCLE that he pretended was a rocket, something that could, with supersonic speed, take him away from Magnolia Street and Minneapolis to anyplace more magical. Or so he'd told Al one day the summer before, when his bike chain had broken and he had asked Al to help him fix it. It was a hot, muggy day and the last thing Al cared to do was anything that involved movement or effort.

"I can go anywhere, "Timmy had said. "It's like my own private rocket, but it's not a rocket. I just like to think it is."

Al was inspecting the bike and chain. "That's great, Timmy."

"Tim."

Al looked up at him. "Tim. Of course."

Al eyeballed the loose chain. He had no idea how to fix one, but he understood why Tim had asked him. Glancing over at Tim's house, which was down from Norda and Howard's, even Al was intimidated. The curtains were drawn in every window, and his father's Chevy was parked cock-eyed in the driveway. Again. It was eight in the morning on a Saturday, and Al knew that Tom Morone had been out 'til the wee hours. No wonder Timmy rang their doorbell, Al thought. Where else could a kid go?

Al fiddled with the chain.

"Your dad asleep?"

"Yes."

"Mom, too?"

Timmy nodded.

Al reattached the bike chain, feeling a wave of relief and pride pass through him.

"How are things, Tim?" he asked, trying to sound casual. "Joining any sports teams?"

Tim shrugged. He avoided Al's gaze. "I'm cycling all the way to St.

132

Paul today," he said.

Al nodded. "Long ride," he said. "Better bring some water. Want to borrow a water bottle?"

"Do you want to come?"

Al laughed. "Tim, I'd make it about a block and collapse. But let me get you that water bottle."

Tim sped off after a quick thank you, fake laughing as loudly as he could about Al collapsing in a block, the plastic Gophers water bottle and a hastily packed bag lunch strapped awkwardly to his bike. Al walked back into the house repeating the boy's name change in his mind, hoping it would stick, just like he did every new term when students swept into his lecture hall. He hardly listened to their answers to his questions during the first week of classes because he was staring intently at their faces and trying to implant last names in his memory. Swenson. Nelson. Jones. Johanssen. Students thought he was intimidating when he did this, or so he'd heard. Little did they know.

The next time Tim rang the doorbell, he had popped his chain again. He had on a Twins cap, backwards, torn jeans, and a dirty white t-shirt with faded writing. Al noticed the water bottle, dented in one corner, still attached limply to the back of the bike.

"My chain broke again. Would you fix it for me?"

Tim had dropped by right in the middle of a breakfast. Al was sure his hair was sticking straight up. There was little enough of it left, and it seemed what was left had decided to stand guard. Al paused, and then he knew he couldn't say no. "Sure, let me help with that. Where are you off to today?"

Tim shrugged.

Al reattached the chain slowly, glancing up, as he always seemed to do, at the forbidding exterior of Tim's house. No car in the drive today.

"Your Dad already out today?"

Tim pretended he didn't hear.

Al nodded at him. "Got the chain fixed. Need some water? Have you eaten?"

Tim had his shoulders hunched, his gaze on his driveway, and Al remembered moments like these, moments when all you wanted to do was get away and at the same time all you wanted to do was have somebody nice cut you a break.

"Wait here," Al said.

Tim didn't follow past the front door, and when Al reemerged with a bag lunch, Tim grabbed it and disappeared. No thank you, no look back, just pedaling the hell out of his bike, escaping everything. Al stared after him, then looked over at Tim's house. He felt mildly irritated. Where was the kid's father? Couldn't he ever get it together? What about Joyce, for Christ's sake? Where was she? But then Al felt terrible. It wasn't Tim's fault. He clearly didn't have anyone he could count on. What trouble was it for Al to fix a bike chain and give the kid a PB&J?

And so it began, the bike chain drop-bys as Sarah called them. Tim appeared nearly every weekend. Theirs was an uneasy alliance. As long as Al didn't ask Tim about his family or anything that touched on family. Or Halloween plans, or birthday plans. Or friends. Just the bike and sports and maybe school. Maybe. Even that subject could be dangerous for reasons Al couldn't surmise.

"What happens in the fall, or God, the winter?" Al asked Sarah one night over dinner. "He's not going to be able to get out of that house to cycle anywhere."

Sarah eyed Al, glancing at Amelia as a warning.

"I don't know." Her voice was soft. "I wish there was something we could do."

"We'd have to know more about what was happening over there first," Al said.

"Does he ever say anything at all?"

"Never." Al thought back over the last few weekends. "No, not a thing that sticks out anyway."

"Do you ever notice marks on him?"

He shook his head no. No marks. Not the physical kind.

"He's just lonely and maybe scared," Al said. Feelings he had once known too well, though for different reasons.

The next few times Tim rang the doorbell, it wasn't early, as though he had radar and knew to wait until after breakfast. He seemed to have a sense of people, or perhaps, of boundaries. Al imagined that living with Thomas Morone gave a kid a pretty good temper meter. How many nights had he and Sarah looked at each other across the table or bed as voices rose down there or a car squealed into their drive during the wee hours?

"I hope he doesn't go through the garage one night," Sarah had whispered once.

And they'd giggled.

But that was before they were feeding Tim breakfast or lunch or something every weekend. Tim would wait on the steps until he thought it was safe to ring the bell, and now sometimes he simply stayed in their yard and played with Amelia rather than cycle away. The weather was cooling toward autumn, the heat slipping away from the days.

"You have to wonder about Joyce," Sarah said one morning. "She looks normal enough. Hair cut in a cute bob, nice jeans and sports tees with the ¾ sleeves. She looks like everybody else." Then she paused. "Actually," Sarah had said, "she looks better than everybody else. You know with Tom somehow that something's wrong. He never looks quite clean, and he avoids your eyes when speaking with you. But Joyce seems normal. Where is she in all this?"

That, Al felt, he knew perfectly well. He recognized in Joyce the behavior he associated with his mother—the standing-up-straight in spite of it all. With his mother, it had been grief, he suspected, based on a comment or two from his dad. But with Joyce, who knew?

Al watched out the window as Tim helped Amelia down the slide. "It's like we're raising him."

Sarah nodded. "And how do you turn a child away? You can't. But this can't go on, us watching him more and more. We're going to have to say something."

"I know," Al said. "It just worries me. For him. I think it might come back to haunt him."

Sarah turned suddenly then, her face pinched, and there was the face, older now, that had captured him in the library reference line all those years ago. The reddish hair. The deep blue eyes and perfect eyebrows. The thin, delicate lips. He loved her now as he had then. No, that wasn't true. He loved her differently. The past was always with you, wasn't it? There was no doe-eyed innocence anymore. They had had their troubles. But here was the woman he loved, in all her glory and in all her humanness. He knew she felt the same. They loved each other differently, but perhaps better now, perhaps in a more real way. In a way that allowed people their faults and differences and grief.

Outside, Amelia wanted another turn on the slide.

"Give me a chance now, Lia," Tim said clearly. They could hear him through the glass. But Amelia was racing to the slide and climbing, chubby legs pumping.

Tim acquiesced. "Okay," they heard him say. "But then I get a turn."

DURING HIS CHILDHOOD, Al thought very little about escaping his home. He'd sensed that what was wrong with his family wasn't something to rebel against but rather to endure. His mother's fragility, carefully re-shaped into an immaculate appearance, a long to do list, and a perfectly kept home, managed to satisfy most people. Adele was not well-liked, but admired. People found her cool, distant.

It's all a lie, Al had wanted to say, because he knew what people thought about her, even as a child. Brittle, officious, cold. She's sad, he'd wanted to scream. He knew it, though not why. He wanted to shout: she's held together by string. Give her half a chance.

But people aren't good about giving each other chances, not really. At least not in Al's experience. He remembered keenly the few attempts his mother made to socialize, how surprised people were, how quickly she retreated when rebuffed. And she was rebuffed. She was awkward, she made people uncomfortable. Friendships didn't last. She didn't have the rhythm for them.

How she'd fallen in love and created a home, he'd never fully understood. Adele put on her smart clothes and sharp shoes and walked out into each day with her grief in tow, or whatever it was, her father lockstep with her. As Al grew older, he noticed the way his parents worked the evenings away, or, once home, lingered in different rooms; how little they shared but meals and school appointments. The quiet, the busyness, the cool nature of the house slowly made strange sense. But he never knew the exact cause. It became one of the central concerns of his life.

His whole life, Al had been his mother's anchor, his job to hold her fast to earth, to rise above the unspoken. This was still his role in a family life of silence and unanswered questions, for whom ritual and faith had proven the final trinity. Three tiers, three lines, holding his father and mother up like sails: ritual, faith, child.

IF THERE WAS ONE THING ABOUT AL people noticed, it was how easy-going he was. Al laughed easily. He made casual friends easily. He was easy to be around. He was easy on people. Very forgiving. Because he taught religion. That's what they said. He's a religion professor so he'll either be hell to know or he'll be the salt of the earth. People thought Al was the salt of the earth. He was reliable. They couldn't remember seeing him angry, until the Morone boy (was that his name? The one who was everywhere, all the time? What do you call that? ADD?) died, right there in his own driveway. Then Al seemed to change, and maybe it was in him all the time, that growing sadness. He had certainly had his share. He had certainly borne more than most.

That's what people said, and Al knew it. He knew well who he was, and in navigating the minefields of all too frequent neighborhood picnics and potlucks, he caught the whispers and snippets of conversation about himself. The neighborhood gathered often around the holidays, and that November, earnest and over-eager Mark Johanssen had decided that gathering was all the more important. Al understood, they all did, and so they dutifully met at Mark's home for a potluck. Al donned his Twins cap and a pair of baggy khakis. He wore the nice blue sweater Sarah had given him last Christmas. Trying to look presentable, even sharp. Trying to be his old self, but he wasn't.

Thomas Morone, pissed on Aquavit of all things, had hit his own boy and been too drunk to know. Hit his own boy as that child raced out of the house to ask him to stay home that evening. And where had Joyce been? In the bedroom with the TV blaring so she could cry and not be heard. Didn't come out all night. Timmy was used to taking care of himself by now. Al couldn't forget Tim's thin back, those ribs, the blood. The tiny pulse that was not there.

At the potluck, Al piled his plate with lasagna, potato chips, various colorful salads (except the ones with beans). He complimented each dish. But instead of playing games with the kids, or chatting with the other dads, Al moved away and walked out into the yard, his excuse that somebody needed to pay attention to Marshall, Mark's aged golden retriever and every neighbor's friend. He plopped himself down on the front step. The evening was cool but not cold. There was no snow, and he and Marshall sat in companionable silence, Marshall occasionally leaning over for an ear scratch. Once, Anil came out to chat. Anil was a good friend, but he was also an unnervingly perceptive man with whom Al could no longer bear to converse. Anil saw too easily through

Al's bluff. Perhaps they all did, but only Anil was bearable. They had grown close, and Anil knew Al's limits. After a quick, tactful inquiry, he would nod and depart. Which is just what he did. Others lingered in Al's silence until they found excuses to leave.

Sometimes Al understood the concern. He had taken Tim's death hard, perhaps too hard, since Tim wasn't his son. But mostly he felt his neighbors were fulfilling a need for drama. Sarah deftly deflected polite inquiries by reminding people that Al had cared for Timmy, and vice versa. She had said this very thing in his presence that evening. Al had then taken this opportunity to escape. He didn't want to be there, and he didn't have any energy for Mark, nice guy though he was. Out in the dark, with the streetlights on and houses glowing with holiday decorations, Al felt a calm come over him. Marshall moved closer, and they leaned on each other, letting the party go on without them.

"It's nice being away from it all, isn't it, Marshall? I always thought you'd want to be inside with us."

Marshall looked at Al.

"It's the Newsome kids, isn't it? Enough to drive anyone away." It was a lame joke, offered to a dog, but Al laughed anyway.

Then, Al said quietly, "I think it's true, Marshall. I think I've changed."

THE GARAGE DOOR OPENING THEREAFTER WAS HELL. Al never waited to see it open fully before he ducked his head under and peeked out. A superstition now, a real loss of faith. Faith in what, he wasn't sure. But loss of trust in something. Maybe even God, who was not someone Al had ever professed to know. That's what had led him to study religion. Al wanted to believe in goodness, and even more, in redemption. Maybe even in a better life next time, since his mother's current one was so broken. So he looked first in one book, and then the next, and then he had looked in so many places and read so many books, it seemed he knew enough to share his questions. He still had those questions, and he grew over the years less and less interested in answers, until Timmy Morone. Timmy Morone changed everything. He changed hearts.

At Mark's Thanksgiving potluck, the murmur was all Timmy Morone. What a loss, how sad, what a shame. The words from some sounded shallow, but from many, not. There was some sense of community failure. Some sense of a secret. Some sense that someone (who? Who could have made him listen?) should have reined in Tom Morone long ago.

You cannot stop a train wreck, Sarah had said, her voice sounding cold, even to Al. He'd come back in the house, Marshall in tow. It was too cold for Marshall outside now, with the temperature beginning to fall. Or so Al said, and everyone let it pass.

Sarah's comment stopped conversation. The circle of friends shifted their feet, looked away. She shrugged. "What could we have said to Tom that would have made a difference? What could we have done?" Her voice was thin, defensive.

"Tried," Al said gently. "We could have tried." And then he bent down and scratched Marshall's ears, avoiding his wife's face. But a husband can't avoid these situations, leave his wife stranded, and so Al looked up and met her gaze. Her hair pulled back, the soft wave around her ears. Those deep blue eyes. The new creases around her mouth. He looked at the woman he loved.

Sarah nodded, something in her seeming to deflate. She wasn't perfect, nor was he, but she was always strong enough to be honest. So was he.

"You're right," she said. "We should have at least called the police. We waited too long."

"You can't second guess, and this wasn't your fault," Mark said, in an obvious attempt at changing the subject, adding, "Come on, Marshall, why don't you go downstairs."

But Marshall wouldn't go until Al went with him, and Al spent the rest of evening in the basement, where he was happy enough to be. His solace for grief was in less complicated things. Like beer. And dogs. And trains. And punching bags.

AL HAD, IN RECENT YEARS, organized his basement to suit his father's old train collection, a relic passed down through the generations and only selectively augmented. Now, with Timmy Morone gone, Al looked at the collection with a certain sadness. He would have loved to show the collection to the neighborhood kids, a motley but generally good crew of mostly Scandinavian kids with a smattering of rather too bright Indian children. Too bright for Al, who adored questions and yet was always startled by theirs, by their wisdom. But in America in its fresh century, a neighbor couldn't invite kids into the yard let alone the house.

So, at first, Al showed the trains only to Amelia, who was reverent and awestruck, as he'd hoped she'd be. Al knew that had she dismissed the trains, a small part of him would have remained hurt forever. They were the sparkling part of his own childhood, a rare bright happy spot.

Here, his father had lost all reserve and rigidity, was prone to babbling. Here, his face lit up like a moon. Al remembered his father's descriptions of the trains. He remembered the animation in his father's voice. Later, Anil brought his brood down a few times, but in the end, the people who most loved the trains were them, the dads.

With the potluck still humming, Anil came down to Mark's basement, his light weight still making the old steps creak, his steps tentative. Al couldn't imagine the noise he'd made in comparison. Anil said nothing, this bone-thin Indian man who could only have been chilled in the cool interior. All his clothes were baggy. Unlike Al's which were under tremendous pressure, Al thought, all the time. Marshall glanced up at Anil but didn't move. He didn't need to. This was his domain.

Anil was the progenitor of some of the polite and too bright children who occasionally unnerved Al during block parties or cook outs.

For a while they were silent, Al remembering the first time he had chatted with Anil at a block party years ago. Al had said, "In my basement, I have a train set. A collection."

Anil had raised an eyebrow. "This is a hobby?"

Al heard no judgment in Anil's voice, only a need for clarification.

Al had laughed and said, "It's an act of faith."

Anil had nodded. "Yes," he said, as though they'd decided something together.

"I appreciate your coming down, Anil. Checking on me. But I'm okay," Al said, looking up at him now.

Anil nodded. He glanced around the basement, patted Marshall on the head, and returned to the party without a word. But he set a beer bottle down before he left.

Late that evening, Al went downstairs to his own basement and flicked on the light. He sat on the last step, in the cold, and scanned the landscape his father had created and he'd augmented: the mini-trees, the tiny people waving on the platform, the sleek trains. A happy bright community where everything looked green and fresh.

THE DAY OF THE FUNERAL, Al chose a bright tie. It took him a while. He looked through every tie he owned. He looked slowly and chose a red solid, something he'd flung over the tie rack one night after a long day of telling students that no, there were not any right answers in his class. For right answers, they should have signed up for chemistry. This was religion 101. This was the class where they asked questions all semester. They could also look to history for answers, as long as they realized who was writing the questions and who else had decided already what the answers were. That course would lead them, he had said, back to religion 101, where he hoped they would be happy to make his re-acquaintance. Then he pointed to a new sign he had posted: no grumps or whiners allowed. Grumps and whiners should be in sociology.

Shortly thereafter the departmental secretary had slipped him a note saying that sign needed to come down, per the chair. Al asked which chair: his or sociology? She was not amused.

Al had climbed on a chair in the middle of this lecture, still talking, and ripped the sign off the wall.

That was the night he told Sarah he was pissed. Vaguely eruptive. Unsettled. And he had flung his dependable tie over the rack and stormed downstairs without another word.

It was a long hour or so before she came to him and said that with all due respect, she felt he was more than angry, that he was grieving, deeply. It was the first time he'd realized how close rage and grief came.

Al had a full class this semester, despite his rather rocky beginning. He had 50 freshmen and sophomores considering religion 101 important to their academic careers. 50 young adults who had withstood his tirade on the importance of questions; enjoyed his sign and subsequent reprimand; and now, apparently, according to buzz he'd heard in the hallway, expected a great class, something really different, where there would be a lot of eye-opening discussion. This was not the semester to be wordless. But something had fallen silent in him after finding Timmy Morone. Something had simply stopped. He struggled through his lectures. He heard his own voice droning on and on and could barely stand to listen himself.

A few faces disappeared. A few more. Al felt he owed them something better. He wasn't one to get personal with students but the day of the funeral, the day he floundered choosing a tie and opted for the red solid, he announced that he would be leaving early for a child's funeral.

"His name was Timmy Morone, and he was about nine. His father ran over him one night because he didn't see Timmy there. Nobody really understands what happened. I suppose in a sense it doesn't matter. But I am telling you this because you get to sneak out early today and go enjoy some of this nice fall weather. And I'm telling you this because it has been a hard few weeks, and I appreciate your patience. A little boy I thought a lot of has died, and I am heartbroken."

The class dutifully lowered their heads and left with as little noise as Al had heard in years, their eyes cast down to avoid his, and Al slunk out, too, embarrassed by his blunt honesty. He made it through the door, felt eased, but colored when he remembered what he'd said. Heartbroken.

At the funeral, Al wept, alone, because Sarah had stayed home with Amelia. Later, at the Morone house, he stayed to help wrap up the leftovers, wash the dishes, sweep up the specks of leaves in the front hall. Sarah opened the front door as he walked home, her beautiful auburny-brown hair blown back because the wind had risen again. She looked somber, her face pale. She reached out to hug Al as he stepped inside. Before he closed the door, he couldn't help but look back over his shoulder, toward the Morone's.

So, he thought. This is how our new winter begins.

LATER, HE WOULD BEGIN TO WORRY, when everybody else seemed to re-adjust and Al still felt bent, off kilter. He avoided looking at the Morone house. He felt guilty. Guilt for avoiding them, for disliking them now. For letting Timmy down. And hadn't he, in some way, let Timmy down? Al could imagine the thin line between grief and madness, could see it, see how easy it would be for a person to lose all sense of direction. Which may explain the walking, how it started. At least then, if only then, he knew where he was going.

Toward the end of term, Al began to take longer walks. On Saturdays, Al often awoke to the scraping sound of aged Paddy Reece making his way down to the little park about half a mile away. He was more reliable than the Post Office. Whatever the weather or world event, Paddy, though 80, didn't let anything but his determination dictate his personal schedule. Al was sure this is why Paddy had survived two world wars and his wife. If Paddy could do it, why not Al? Maybe he could walk part way to the university, hop a bus for the rest. Al could only benefit. It was part of a new regime, not simply for fitness but to clear his head.

The morning was cool, with a feathery snow, and he buttoned his coat against the day and slid his feet into his shoes, worn down in the back from his constant effort to force his feet inside. Al grabbed his cracked leather briefcase, the straps groaning with the hearty lift, and headed out the front door. He left wisps like wings trailing from each footprint when he lifted his boot. Like Nike, he thought.

On the way past Mark's house, he stopped to wave at Marshall in the window.

Al hadn't gone far when a car stopped, a rusted Honda Civic in desperate need of a new muffler. It could only be Anil. The neighborhood knew the car, a throaty intrusion both morning and evening, but somehow not a bother. How could it be? With Anil waving as he passed, all smiles, hollering hellos over the din. Who else even bothered to say hello, let alone wave?

It took a while in the cold, but finally the window came unstuck and Anil rolled it down.

"My friend, do you need a ride?" he asked.

"I'm trying to get some exercise," Al said.

"You have exercised enough. It is too cold for more exercise."

Al looked down the block, saw his trail of footprints. He had walked half a block, but he knew Anil would insist and he'd end up standing in the cold, politely arguing but arguing, nonetheless.

"Thank you," Al said, as he climbed in the car. For all its problems, the heater still worked.

"Your car is not working?"

"No, my car is working fine. I just thought I could use some exercise." Al paused. He had always felt implicitly that Anil was someone to trust, perhaps because he never pried. "And I thought I could use the time to clear my head a bit," Al confessed.

Anil nodded. In the mild roar due to the muffler, gestures proved easier than words.

Anil was a dignified rather quiet man, tall and slight with tapered fingers. Al noticed his fingers because they seemed so delicate, so opposite of himself. Now that Al looked more closely, he noticed the way the sleeves puffed away from Anil's arms, his bony wrists and baggy eyes. He noticed, and wished he hadn't, the brown stain on Anil's cuff.

Well, he thought, we're all weary. I'm sure he sees past my size to my fatigue, my ancient briefcase, my jacket with the frayed cuff. My fraying heart.

"You are thinking about the Morone boy."

"Timmy. Though he was beginning to call himself Tim."

"You must know," Anil said, "that we are all feeling the same thing. We all knew about the father drinking."

"It doesn't make a difference really, does it?"

Anil shrugged. "Maybe."

"I can't get over it," Al said.

Anil looked at him then, on the downshift. They had hit a patch of street laced with ice and coasted. Then Anil brought the car back under control.

"We're all bothered because he was a boy. Just a boy. And he was on his own quite a bit, wasn't he? Racing around gathering kids up for games. Always in the center, but always creating that center."

This hit Al in the gut, and he looked out his window. He'd never thought of Timmy that way, struggling to build connections where none existed. Yet it was obvious, and understanding all this made him feel even worse. Maybe Timmy messed up his own bike chain. This was not a soothing conversation. It was turning in to its own version of Purgatory. Circle Ten: fathers trying to console themselves across language barriers.

"I want them to leave," Al said suddenly, shocked at himself. This was a new impulse, banishment, and yet he felt it keenly, was disturbed by the sight of Joyce at the Red Owl, driving away from the house, at any car parked in their driveway.

Anil didn't reply. He stared straight ahead into the breezy snow. When he did reply, finally, after a lengthy pause, his response was unexpected. "We all have to find our own God," he said.

"Pardon me?"

"I said, we all need to find our own God." Anil had by now turned in to faculty parking. "It is the premise of what you teach, in essence. It is the premise of what I teach, too, perhaps. We must ask and answer our own questions. We must find our own God."

The sudden quiet when Anil turned off the car made the silence shocking.

"I think tomorrow I'll walk," Al said, and Anil laughed.

"No clearing of the mind?"

"Far from it."

Anil heaved himself against his door, forcing it open.

"Anil, you need a new car."

"Not in the budget," he replied matter-of-factly. Then, "I leave promptly at five. I will meet you back here."

"Thank you," Al said, watching Anil walk briskly to his office, the thin figure like the line of a young tree against the gray sky. Al trudged after him, their buildings being in the same direction.

The campus seemed oddly subdued, only the stray student here, the University bus there. Al reached his office early, aware of the calm in the halls, the hush. He sat down, still bundled in his coat, and wrote at the top of his calendar: "We all must find our own God." And he stared at it until a colleague arrived, Sue, new from the East Coast, with the sharp lines around her eyes and mouth that showed her to be older than she looked, someone who had survived a few things. Al, with the softness of extra flesh, thought he would never have those lines, only ever the posture. Upright. Chin high. Eyes locked on the horizon. Like Sue, who nodded a brisk hello. Like his mother, as she marched through their spacious Cape Codder, goal in mind, direction clearly marked. Like Glennie.

"Direction, Al. Just choose a path," his mother had said, over and over, as he had pondered first colleges, then a major. "Someday," she had said, "you have to have the courage to choose."

Al could think of only one choice he had ever made, really. Sarah. He had chosen Sarah with all his heart, and all that came with it: children, home, new family, new grief, holidays and traditions, and occasionally being forced on a diet. But with Sarah, there would always be a candle lighting the window, there would always be that door opening for him as he came toward the door.

"Are you okay?" Sue had stopped before his desk. She was brisk, but not unkind.

"Fine, thank you. I was just thinking about something my neighbor said to me this morning."

"What was it?"

"That we must all choose our own God."

"Not very profound." Sue's eyes narrowed, as though suddenly Al was suspect. The religion professor asking such banal questions? Were his exams multiple choice?

"But isn't it?" Al asked her.

Sue sighed. "I think it sounds like a self-help book kind of question. I don't find it compelling."

Sue was just like his mother. She bathed in lacquer every morning: immaculate outfit, shiny, silky hair. Tough. A smile cracked the carefully put together face. The kind of person, and he was ashamed he thought this, one could never imagine in bed. Or at least, imagine being very much fun in bed.

Al returned her shrug. "I think it's thought-provoking."

Al thought he understood her perspective. He had often thought faith was for the weak, in the past. Yet it was, in its own wonderful way, a sign of strength. To release your woe to God was to have the strength to let go of it, the strength to trust rather than to hold on to it tightly, savor it, keep licking the wound. It was what gave someone the breath, the hope, the break needed to get back on their feet and walk forward to new possibilities, or at least, past the pain. It was a beautiful kind of strength, and he who had once thought he could take no more realized that he could indeed take more when it wasn't his to carry alone.

Al moved away from his desk then, having noted the time. He gave her one of her own nods, then paused at the door.

"Do you like it here?"

The question seemed to surprise her. She blinked. "Where?"

"Here, at the university. Here, in Minnesota. Here."

Sue stared at him. "No," she said, shaking her head. It was the most animated he had seen her. Even her hair managed to shake free of her hair spray. "No, not at all."

"You don't have to stay."

"Leaving isn't an option at the moment."

Al nodded. "That's too bad," he said. "It stinks being stuck." Sometimes, he thought, you have to have the courage to choose.

In religion 101, a slim boy named Emil, a freshman, asked Al what he personally believed. The question came up almost every semester. Al eyed the solid 35 who had stayed with him and answered as he always had, though he wanted to add something new this time. He wasn't sure what.

"What I believe has to remain private, because of the nature of teaching today. It's my job to lead a dialogue that isn't suffused with any sense of persuasion."

Emil nodded. Several in the class nodded. They understood. These were dangerous questions, ones that led in this new world to lawsuits. These were the situations where academic dialogue became stupid with fear.

Al cleared his throat. He felt himself on a precipice, lightheaded. "The point is, though," he began, voice wavering, "that we all have to be clear with ourselves, don't we?"

Al wasn't sure where he was going with this but couldn't stop himself. "The point of asking questions is to clarify or deepen our inquiry, the point of study is to educate, to understand. We study to understand our world, and ourselves. We ask questions to define who and what we are and believe."

Someone squirmed and in the old lecture hall, one of the last, the sound seemed loud.

"You didn't know religion mattered so much, did you?" Al smiled. "You thought you were just meeting a requirement. It's that business degree that matters, huh? Well, part of being in business is being ethical."

Al stopped. He flipped open his lesson plan, where he noted there was no mention of ethics or business degrees. He knew where he was going now, and he felt his throat close. He was talking about accountability. He was talking about his own. Anil was right. They had known. Each and every one of them. And they had pretended not to, buried the knowledge in politesse. But everybody had known that little boy, racing like he had wings, was increasingly desperate and God help them, they had quietly, uniformly, turned away from making the necessary phone call.

And here was the sad thing: Al finally had something to talk to his mother about. They finally shared common ground. He of the Questions would finally ask a new one: how did she do it? How did she dress each day in her handsome outfits, comb her hair, make him toast? How did she glue the pieces of herself back together?

In this, he felt somewhat removed from Sarah, who had the strength of oxen in her blood. She had endured deep pain and loss, and yet there never seemed in her any flagging of self, only energy. She was still there, burning bright. And Amelia had that, too, that presence. While Al felt he could melt away in a moment's notice, missed only by them and Anil, who would wait while the world ended in his battered old car before turning on to the main road too quickly and missing his friend.

At five o'clock precisely Al was waiting by Anil's car, as Anil sat inside trying with great patience to start it. The car was not cooperating, and Al was just about to suggest they walk—how bad could it be?—when Sue approached, head down, car keys out.

"Please could we have a jump start?" Anil asked, pouncing before Al did.

And so it was that they trundled home in Anil's car, Sue in the back seat, because her car now would not start. Sue was frowning.

"I will come get you in the morning," Anil told Sue.

"Thank you."

"Do you have a mechanic?"

"No. I'll just call the dealer."

"I recommend you call my friend Ralph," Anil said helpfully. "He will fix your car, and he will not cheat you. I know, you see, because he is always at work on mine."

IN THE SUMMER EVENINGS, despite the mosquitoes, Al liked to sit on the front porch with a beer and watch the cars go by. Sarah often joined him, having sat with her grandfather for much of her childhood in much the same way. That was how she learned so much about cars. Her grandfather would eye models as they passed—Buicks, Fords, foreign makes—and describe their failings and strengths.

"I could have worked in a dealership," she had said once, "except I would have been as honest about each car as he was."

On summer nights, when Amelia was in bed, they snuck outside and sat together, hardly talking. It was something that had healed their marriage when healing was needed, spending this quiet time together. A time that allowed conversation if they wanted but eventually became a time of companionship and calm. A time that helped smooth over the tensions and losses that had pockmarked their first years together.

But in the middle of winter, there was no way to sit on the porch, and only so many times Anil could come over and talk trains. In the end, it was the most unlikely of things that brought Al back: his father called.

"How are the trains?" he asked.

"The same," Al replied. "I haven't added anything new since your last visit."

"Did you ever get to show them to that boy?"

"No, Dad, I didn't." Al's voice sounded rough.

"You tried to help, Al. You tried, and from what Sarah says, you guys were getting ready to call the authorities."

Al nodded, and into the pause that was his silence, his father spoke again.

"I don't know if there are ever any heroes in situations like these, Al, even when someone does call, you know? Please, please remember you tried to help the poor kid. Please focus on that."

"Okay."

"Grief can be tricky, Al," his father went on. "Your mom suffered a loss before I met her. But I guess you know that."

This was it. The Great Unspoken. "What loss?"

"She was engaged to another fellow before me. He was driving them to the movies, and he wrecked."

Al is silent, absorbing this news, which would have been easy to share on so many other occasions. Why now?

"I love her," his father says. "Did you ever know that? Do you understand?"

Al paused, and his father went on.

"Sometimes grief scars a person. She does love us, you know. She's just not good at showing it. That's what happens when you're afraid of losing people. Sometimes you just can't love them good enough."

And that was where they left it, right there, at the mention of love.

Al let the world come back to him then: the memories, the bird-song, the fact of that now empty house down the street, with a stain on the driveway and a For Sale sign, finally, on the lawn. He let the world come back to him and said goodbye to his father, the conversation being too tender and the vocabulary too new for further exploration right then.

Al remembered his mother, how she looked when she was going someplace—any place—her straight back, her long strides, head down. Plowing ahead despite her memories and fears. Like how Glennie walked.

Al took a deep breath, stood, and made himself look at Timmy's house. Who would ever buy it? Who would want to live with that history, those ghosts? Out the other window, Amelia played alone on her swing set and slide. She continued to ask for Timmy.

"He's gone," Al told her gently, each time she asked. He

explained about heaven and the stars and goodbyes and feeling sad, as best he could.

"Timmy was my brother," Amelia told Al.

And Al would explain that no, he had only been a dear friend.

No, she insisted. He was her brother.

And Al tried to explain blood lines and parenting, which made him feel ridiculous.

No, Amelia replied, giving him her full-hearted smile. He was my brother, Daddy. In my heart.

Geographies of the Heart
Sarah
2002, recalling late November 1996

THE NIGHT OUR GRANDFATHER DIED was a night without stars, the snow falling in endless repeat, first veiling the moon, the constellations, then the sharp edges of buildings – our whole world. Toward the end, when my grandfather seemed only to be lingering of his own will, I stood outside the main entrance of the hospital, looking for headlights; stunned by the deep and unsettling quiet of Minneapolis under snow and then by the long keening wail of a siren inching toward Emergency, the neon lights there obscured by snow and ice and hope.

It was a night of mourning, and the mourning had come early. Grandpa had slipped beyond us at dusk, the rattle of his breathing slowly losing energy and force, the night lengthening and darkening with each diminished breath. Upstairs, my family huddled in his cramped room or took turns pacing the hall outside, each footstep measured like a heartbeat and almost as constant. We leaned against one another, against the pressure of what was coming as slowly and stealthily as that snow, wild in the wind outside yet silent. We leaned past dusk into nighttime, and as the night went on, we listened to his struggling breaths and held our own. In the end he gasped.

Before he died, I took the elevator down to the lobby and phoned my sister. It was the third time that day I'd tried to reach her. She wasn't home, as usual. Still, I listened for her answer, and I watched the main entrance, hoping to see her slide through the doors, riding in on the edge of this latest snowstorm in a blossom of white, a brief rush of cold. It was late then, and while she could have gotten to the hospital earlier, I doubted she would make it now, and I wondered where she was. She had known how fast Grandpa was deteriorating. She had known, just as I had, to be ready for the phone to ring. And so I called, one last time.

This was during the first week of November. I had not talked to Glennie in weeks. For the length of the fall, she had remained noticeably absent, despite calls for company, for help with the baby. Despite our obvious, looming loss. I was twenty-four then, and she was twenty-one. She was finishing her second to last semester at the U, and she had recently begun calling at odd hours, when I wasn't home, and leaving messages like telegrams. *Am fine. Talk soon. Kiss Amelia. Hi to Al.* She shrank into a line, all bone and tumbling gold hair, and devoted herself with religious intensity to school.

At the start of the semester she had spent her free evenings drafting lengthy essays for medical school applications. In her brief appearances, over coffee down by the university, at our house for dinner, she always wore the same Gopher sweatshirt and a pair of running tights.

She chewed her nails. She looked paler than I thought was possible, the rich yellow of her hair making her skin look alabaster, the fineness of her bones growing more prominent. I had tried to talk to her, me leaking with milk that stained my blouses, me with the warmth and curves Amelia had given me, but Glennie's answers were perfunctory, her gaze drifting elsewhere. She was waiting, she said, to hear; and so it seemed she could not listen. I thought of all this that night at the hospital, staring out from the phone cubby into the white of the storm. But I thought she would come, in one last show of love. In the end.

I waited a long time with that phone receiver in my hand, listening to the flat, buzzing ring. The phone rang so long that the operator finally cut in and asked if I was all right. Her voice had startled me. I thought she was Glennie. I said, "It's Sarah. You better come now."

When I hung up the phone and walked outside into that silent new world, searching for sight of her car, I reminded myself that she would have phoned if she'd been stranded. We would know. The quiet, interrupted in fits and starts by a siren, then a howl of wind, was broken finally by the ambulance itself, pressing against the wind; against the onslaught of snow. And then again, that deep quiet filled the night. I waited until the cold sent me back inside. And when I turned back to the elevators alone, I turned like others in my family had turned before me, some like milk, others like fall leaves, a little more sour, or ready to crumble at the touch. I turned and something twisted in me when I did.

That winter, there were constant reminders of Grandpa's passing with the holidays to background his absence, with Glennie's strange new behavior to accentuate all the change. When I was growing up, we had all lived in one house, the generations piled in layers, like the number of floors: three. Every time I went over to Mom and Dad's, the downstairs where grandparents had lived was silent and gaping, and I realized again how much he'd marked my growing up, how I'd lived less by a clock than by his rituals: his alarm clock sounding into the early morning and waking me where I slept upstairs, or the chinking sound of the beer cap falling onto the kitchen counter at five o'clock, when he pulled a chair onto the front porch and watched cars drive by. I'd often joined him, and he would tell me what I was seeing: a house finch, cumulus clouds, an '84 Ford. I had grown up fingering the yellowed newspapers that had announced D-Day and Kennedy's assassination. I had watched the ritual picking of the cucumber yield and their slow progression into sweet pickles, Grandma patiently stirring, Grandpa quick to swear if he sliced a finger, which he'd wag at me. I understood references to the point system and knew old Navy jokes that no small child should know. I learned when to fold in a poker game. Every room held a slim memory, like a sleeve.

During Grandpa's last FEW WEEKS I kept an old list in my wallet of what medicines he took and for what ailments, out of habit and just in case. I kept a separate old list of doctors' names and beeper numbers. And toward the end, when the world reeled in that endless snow, I kept vigil, shooting straight up in bed each late night the phone rang, or not even sleeping at all but staring out the window, watching the next storm ride in.

I made two emergency trips to the hospital that winter, once in the early afternoon, when Mom had taken a break and gone home, and once on Halloween, at dawn, when my car was the only one that started, coughing and spitting into the morning with all the reluctance I felt. The exhaust rose behind the car like a premonition.

His doctor had told us that Grandpa's systems would slow and then stop one by one, as if someone were systematically going through a house and shutting off all the lights. I still haven't gotten over that image. And that last cold October morning, with my Honda sputtering in the cold, with Amelia snug in her car seat and smiling against what seemed to me a gray and dismal day, I wondered what was stopping now for Grandpa, what system had finally come to rest.

At the hospital I'd handed over the soft, worn lists and watched as a nurse unfolded them and scanned the names and numbers. Yes, she told me, we have this information. I let my thoughts drift to Glennie, who had left another breathy message on my machine the night before. Her voice had sounded tentative. *Really busy. Can't talk. Call me.* I had instead stumbled to bed, guilty for not calling but swept with a fatigue deeper and more rooted than any I'd ever known. Now there I was in the hospital, wondering where she was and what the hell was wrong. I wondered if she was okay. But of course she wasn't, and I knew it.

The nurse called the doctor, her voice low; and when she knew her answers, and I knew Grandpa would be all right, when I had sat with him for a minute and fixed his hair and covered his feet with a blanket; after I had called my mother and she had calmed down; after this I lifted my cooing and beautiful daughter higher on my hip and marched us both over to the row of pay phones to call the sister who was narrowing. Herself, her heart. And mine.

I left Glennie a message. About fatigue and Grandpa and the baby. My voice was sharp. I demanded to know what the hell was wrong. I was holding Amelia in the crook of one arm, and she crowed into the receiver, leaving an aria for her aunt, who barely seemed to have words left, or the energy to speak them. We Macmillan women, thin-skinned from an overabundance of snow and sadness, let words lodge like icicles inside us. We froze.

What the hell, I had said into the receiver.

Glennie later told me she'd needed a break that winter, but a break from what I've never fully known. Never once did she make it to the hospital before Grandpa died. She did not help sort through his things. She called Mom and Dad, leaving messages in the same tele-graphed language, which heaped one worry upon another, and she arrived at the funeral looking disheveled and as bitten as her nails. And this is where it begins, rising like a blister over the same worn spot. One might imagine we are too old for old grievances, that we have moved beyond. But how do you move past an absence like hers without taking notice?

Distance doesn't always make the heart grow fonder. Sometimes, I've learned, it makes the heart grow harder. But I called. Finally. It had been years since Glennie and I had really talked. Our conversa-tions usually circled the controversial and relied on the secure, though even then I had a tendency for the quick jab, the sarcastic remark. She'd come by and have dinner, maybe linger over a drink at some brief happy hour, but I didn't know the details of her days or what she thought about the M.D. now that she had it, after all those years of fight. I didn't know her anymore, or she me; and so I took a look at my calendar one morning, saw my thirtieth birthday approaching, and decided to give myself a gift. I'd take her on a mini-vacation. Pull her out of her hospital, away from her milieu and away from mine, and on neutral territory we'd try to connect again, not with who we were or what we'd shared in the past, but with who we had become.

I'd laugh if I felt like laughing: she was still impossible to reach. I had to leave a message. So I did, a staccato, stammering message that made me feel a sliver of recognition, like a shiver. I said: *It's me. Your sister. Please call.*

I HADN'T PLANNED ANYTHING EXTRAVAGANT. A bed and breakfast, a three-day weekend, maybe a little more wine than usual. I planned only for us to get away, as if that effort alone overtaxed my imagination.

I arrived at her hospital late in the afternoon. It was hot for April, steaming even, and I kept the station wagon running and aimed every vent in my direction, let the tepid air bother loose a strand of hair. A fistful of daffodils bloomed at the base of the flagpole, and every once in a while the flag lifted with the breeze and a ripple passed over the clutch of blooms. I let my head fall back against the seat. I closed my eyes.

Her hospital, which is what I have always called it for no clear reason, was in Minneapolis; her apartment nearby, within a stone's throw, as my grandfather might have said. The drive from our house was short, but we didn't make the route often, Al, Amelia and I. We dropped by on holidays. Remembered her birthday. We had per-fected--I had required that we perfect--the brief, cheery visit. The fifteen-minute family.

The station wagon was a relic from the 1970s that Al had magically, and with great love, revived over the course of spring semester. Early on Saturday mornings, when his only company was an occasional house finch or the low rush of a passing car, or occasionally a curious Amelia drawn by the clanking and crashing and frequent string of curses, Al backed the wagon out of the garage and tinkered, got his mind away from papers and books and students, from the heavy questions which defined his profession.

Al had never looked like a religion professor, rounded as he was, and with his white-blond hair. He looked like an athletic coach, a man who could cheer his team on to great feats. And he did. Each semester, he cheered on the students who refused to work or read, who called his assignments too hard because, in effect, they did not want to think. He had graded the first round of papers that spring with a sagging spirit of optimism. Then, halfway through the semester, with a stack of miserable midterms dominating the dining-room table, he found the car. I think it came from a junkyard, but it may have come from Larch, who still ran a bar downtown then and seemed to accumulate all sorts of strays. Suddenly the car appeared in the driveway, rusted, with two flat rear tires and a caved-in driver's side panel. And Al beamed. He thought it was wonderful.

The station wagon had fake paneling on the sides and a rich blue accent and when I drove it, the car hummed like it was happy to be back on the road. *I* was happy to be back on the road, packed for a vacation.

"There ought to be room," I had said to Al that morning, "for Glennie and me to grow apart and come back together again. There ought to be a little room for fluctuations."

But I was really saying that I hoped there was. She may be the OBGYN, and I the mother, but we came from the same places, the same hopes. We had to understand a little of one another, enough at least to share new ground. We were sisters, after all.

And that's what I kept thinking as she tumbled through the hospital doors, wriggling out of her white coat as she walked, each footstep efficient and clipped. She looked like a race walker as she came toward me, elbows jutting into the air. She climbed in, loosening the bun that held her hair and like her it tumbled, hair that I've always loved.

"We're off!" she said, raising her hands and laughing, her laugh flickering, light, resonating throughout the car.

For a moment, I stared at her, uncertain, but then I nodded.

Yes, we were off.

This was it.

Finally, despite all distractions, despite even ourselves, we were going.

I REMEMBER THE ODDEST THINGS about the winter Grandpa died. I remember in detail how the sun looked coming into the kitchen early one morning, falling in a lazy, generous beam, and how quiet the kitchen was. Al was asleep, Amelia was asleep, and I sat alone with a cup of peppermint tea, relishing the solitude. But a great deal else is only an impression. The hospital is a blur of white, as are the roads I traveled to and from; even Amelia learning to roll and chirping her first word (car) are memories crushed like flowers against the pages of a long, dense book, one that rivals for attention, one that demands.

But I remember Glennie.

Downstairs, curled on our sagging leather couch, exhausted from the semester, she slept through most of Christmas and we did not wake her. Al played pinball softly on Grandpa's old machine, but even when the bells and whistles clanked and sang, even when he hooted in victory, Glennie slept on, like a bear in hibernation, like the princess poisoned.

I watched her sleeping once. I placed my hand in front of her face until her breath moved softly against my skin, and I stayed to make sure her breathing remained even. Maybe this is the root of all trouble in my family, or in me: fear. I checked to make sure Glennie was still alive, drove the silent winter roads to Grandpa consumed by dread; she stayed away, then after the new year stood at the mailbox in the dead of winter, half-covered in an ill-fitting down jacket, waiting for her grades. All As, but not a glimmer of relief in her eye, just a look harder and more determined, as if she were doing calculations in her head. And I believe that she was. She was figuring her chances, the percentages, her possible acceptances. She hit it on the head, too. So dispassionate, so objective. She looked at herself like a pool of admissions counselors would and knew what to expect.

But what had she lost that winter to do it? Always, like a rumor, something insidious and whispery inside my heart: what had she let go of to become so cool?

In the car, Glennie rolls down her window and lets her head fall back against the seat.

"God," she says. "What a day. I kept thinking that all I had to do was to get through it, and then I'd be on the road."

"Me, too."

Glennie looks at me. "This will be fun," she says, and I am grateful for her effort, her small offering.

"Yes," I say, pressing my foot on the gas.

Somewhere outside of Minneapolis we break down. I should have known to take the Honda, I guess, but the large floating-boat feel of the station wagon appealed. The space appealed. And Al was so proud of it.

It is sweltering and dry on the highway, and gusts of warm air balloon toward us, gently rocking the car. My shirt is cool against my back, and I imagine what I look like: sweat rings darkening the under-arms of my white blouse, my hair pulled back but falling in wisps, and wetly, around my face; the lines around my eyes and mouth, the tired look to my gaze. The day is slipping away, near dusk, and neither of us know a thing about repairing cars.

It doesn't take long to find a gas station, since we'd just passed a ramp heading into a small town. The attendant, an older man with gray hair and a deeply lined face, agrees to give us a lift back in his tow truck, where he says he'll hazard a guess. He drives us back onto the highway, back into the dry, slow wind, and toward the station wagon, which suddenly looks not much different to me than when I'd first seen it. I think of Al's careful attention, as careful as his commentary on papers, as thoughtful and pre-cise, and I don't want it to fail, I don't want him to know.

"It's nothing," the old man says, and his voice is a whisper, dry like the wind, and as hot against my face.

He tows us back to his shop, and we sit thigh to thigh in the front seat, arm to arm, bumping down the ramp and into town. He smells of oil and dust, and Glennie smells of soap, something sharp that reminds me of spring. I know I'll remember that distinctly, that fresh smell off her in the heat.

Glennie and I walk through the highway underpass while the man works, shirtless, his back the sandy brown of a construction worker's and as smooth and muscular as a young man's. We steer ourselves past graffiti, around pop cans and stray plastic bags, past cigarette butts and random, sad purple flowers and walk the cracked sidewalk into downtown Belton, a pocket of shops nestled up against the highway.

Our choices are a steak house and fast food. We choose the steak house. We are our father's daughters, after all, raised on summer cookouts and the juicy first bite of steak; raised on the smell of it cooking. Inside, we slide our trays along the grooved countertop, craning our necks to see the menu. The restaurant is empty, save for the young chef finishing the last of his cigarette and a girl who piles droopy lettuce into a container for the salad bar. We choose a table in the center, under an air vent.

Glennie is hungry, but I've never known her to be less. Hunger is in her. She is starving or famished but always thin, always a reed.

"Dad used to cook the best steaks," she says.

I glance at her. On the tip of my tongue are the familiar old words, the bad habit: *he still does*, but I check myself and perhaps she senses this because she looks at me while she swallows, and there we are, face to face with it, the same old tension.

I lift my coffee cup and take a long, slow, easy sip, letting the liquid fill me with something close to strength and security.

"Have you been over to Mom and Dad's lately?" she asks.

"I was there last night."

"How are things?"

"Things are fine. Things are good."

And it's true, or true enough. She ought to know that Mom complained of stiffness in her hands, of stiffness settling in her everywhere, as though she is filling with cement, but I tell Glennie things are fine and hope it spares the two of us something.

Glennie watches me. I nod, suddenly hesitant to give voice to my lie again. I hold my coffee cup in front of my face, look out the window at the highway, at the brightness of the day slowly receding.

"Mom's enjoying her garden," I say.

"It won't always be."

"What?"

"It won't always be fine," Glennie says.

I look at her over the rim of my coffee cup. I hadn't expected this, and I stare at her for a moment, then set down my cup. We have decisions coming. We have more farewells. But those were far off, and what seems more relevant to me is that we do not have each other.

"That isn't what we need to talk about," I say suddenly. "That's not what this weekend is about."

Glennie says, "Isn't it?"

On that cold night, when Minnesota blessed us with temperatures warm enough for snow and we gathered without Glennie to say goodbye to my grandfather, I let go of a tradition, of what I understood a family to be. The snow came down and piled itself softly as though to cushion the blows.

The hospital had a machine that cleared Grandpa's lungs, but he had waved it away the last time he'd had strength, and now we were down to it, as he might have said.

"We're all here," Dad had told him, squeezing his hand. "All here."

Al leaned out the door and asked for a nurse, and Nancy came in, her footsteps hushed against our breathing, her movements swift. Nancy, who had over the weeks taken a place among us. She gave him a painkiller, or maybe that's what I'd like to think, the memory of his breathing, of the fluid in his lungs, too much to bear without the slim memory of relief, true or not.

I don't remember Nancy leaving, only that when we filtered into the hall late that night she was there, arms spread outward, as if she could hold us all. Only that we listened to the rattle of his breathing, whispering him onward, whispering our love, until all we heard was ourselves.

I didn't ask Glennie why she never came to the hospital that night, nor did she volunteer, and I said only one thing to her when she finally did appear the next morning, rushing into the hospital restaurant. Dad and Al had left to call Larch, who even at his age, and in that snow, was already waiting in the lobby, waiting while they called him at home. Mom had gone to the ladies' room, and there were Glennie and I seated at a small table, staring at each other. She asked if he'd gone peacefully, and I wanted to break her in half. I was grieving, and afraid: of her, whom I no longer knew; of her pencil-thin wrists; of how supremely angry I was.

I looked at her and said, "Don't."

Al said maybe she couldn't handle what touched her family, but I've never agreed. How much would it have required of her to appear, even briefly? At any ceremony, at any ritual, there were always six of us, then seven and eight with Al and Amelia, and I could not believe, am slow to forgive, that my grandfather died without the full measure of support he was due; that one small voice did not join our chorus on the only day it mattered.

"What if she just isn't as strong as you?" Al asks.

The question passes into each new year despite my efforts to forgive, despite my best intentions. I know what he's wondering. Does she sometimes question me, too? But I question only Glennie. Not her competence. Not her brains. But her compassion, which I believe is essential to love.

This year, though, as the subject made its way to the surface once again, Al asked a different question. It was a Saturday. I'd dropped Amelia off at a friend's house and returned home with an armload of groceries and some grievance. A bad driver ahead of me, a surly grocery clerk. I don't remember, only that the irritation arose and transformed itself and grew and suddenly I was back in that hospital again, and Glennie was not.

"For God's sake," Al finally said, quietly, as he peered into the engine of his rusted renovation. "Sarah, what the hell is this really about?"

He turned to me, away from the car, accepted in silence the pop I had brought out to him.

"Family," I replied. "Values and commitment and family and love. It's about how we were raised. It's about a way of life. It's about her not being there. For any of us. And certainly not for me."

And there it was, in all its bald and ugly and broken self: *I* had needed her that night. *I* was tired of holding up, holding together, holding hands. I needed her, and she was not there, and she did not come to us, like we had hoped. She fled somewhere else, to someone else for comfort, and left me waiting, standing at the phone bank in the hospital lobby, alone.

I blinked at Al, who turned back to the car, his gaze out to the road.

"You're letting bitterness eat you alive," he said.

THE COOL AIR IN THE RESTAURANT lowers a degree or two, and the background music abruptly switches to classical halfway through a whining and overdone love song.

I pause. "How are things with you?"

Glennie shrugs. "The same," she says. "People come to the hospital, and I try to help them, and sometimes I succeed."

I don't want to ask about failure. I can imagine what her feelings are. But I do want to know how she defines loss. At one time she'd confided, then at least gave the semblance of it, passing on news of boyfriends and school fears and snippets of dreams. But sitting there across from her, the two of us alone for the first time in years, I know she squirrels most of her life away; that we have broken apart, like continents, leaving a gaping ocean between us. She would not tell me what loss was, and I would not ask.

"Amelia shot up three inches this year," I say.

Glennie smiles. "She's going to be a tall one. One day you'll be looking in her eyes."

I laugh, but the laugh is short and high. I think, someday we all have to look each other in the eye, and I say what I've wanted to say for years.

173

"I've always been angry that you were never there." My voice sounds soft and even, but Glennie looks away, shakes her head.

"How much would it have taken out of you to be there for just a minute?" I ask, the question pressing forward with the weight of years.

"People aren't always perfect." She sounds worn at the edges, her answer running over my question.

"Were you eating at all?"

Glennie shoots me a glance, and her face, her jaw, seem rigid. The question goes unanswered.

"Where were you?"

She's staring out the window at the thin line of cars snaking along the highway, slowly for some odd reason, as if dusk is treacherous. And maybe it is. Dusk brought us to this place, where I no longer count on her, or she on me; where our roots fill different pots, and we reach for different light.

"He didn't know I wasn't there," she says, "so why do you care so much?"

I can't answer. Something inside me has suddenly ripped open.

Glennie pulls her gaze away from the road and back to me. "Just because I wasn't there doesn't mean I wasn't grieving. I was."

Forget the peaceful landscape, forget the quiet bed and breakfast where we could drink wine to take the edge off. It is now, over steaks and coffee. It's here. I'm suddenly too tired to get angry. "Why couldn't you come, just for a little? Why couldn't you just say goodbye?"

I wait. I'm not good at waiting.

"I didn't want to be there," she says finally, leaning forward, her face close to mine. I smell the steak sauce on her breath, watch the lines shaping around her mouth, lines that I know are not laugh lines. I never look away.

"I'll never want to be there. For anyone."

"Then why are you even bringing up the subject of Mom and Dad?"

Glennie takes a deep breath, one that she seems to have been gathering for years. "I don't want to see the people I care about … I don't want to remember them that way."

"It's not about you." My voice sounds sharp and tight, and I blush instantly because it is all about her and me and only ever has been. I suddenly can't believe who we've become.

And then she says, "I was there. In my apartment."

She's looking straight at me. It takes a minute for her meaning to sink in, and then it does.

"I'm sorry," I tell her. And I am. For both of us. For the ways we allow fear to preside. But she let me down, let us all down. She abandoned something I loved, and that makes me even sorrier.

Glennie squints her eyes. "Do you think you're the better person?"

I look at her, whose hands welcome lives, the thin fingers delicately guiding, then putting back into place what has ripped away; whose precision and care is renown.

"I think you should have been there," I tell her. "But mostly I think we're both selfish as hell and that Grandpa wouldn't like either one of us."

We sit quietly for a while and the restaurant fills in, and we are an island in the middle, sinking in spongy seats, seated at a hard plastic table, remembering.

I want to ask about hunger, about how she starved herself down to a nub in college, how she made it through medical school at all.

I want to tell her that I have never been prouder of her than the day the provost slipped the mantle over her gown and pronounced her name, enunciated each syllable: Dr. Carys Glenn Macmillan. We rose in our seats in one loud roar, all of us, even Larch. I want to breathe into our afternoon something like a prayer for her, something like a hymn for me.

"I'll need you there," I say, my voice trailing off.

And then, as the truth drifts out into the hot and steaming day, our pick-up time for the car already past, my sister says, "Do you ever forgive?"

I look up at her sharply, ready to answer until I see her expression, the way her eyes search mine, as though I'm unknown to her; until I realize that she has told me what loss is. I don't like her very much, even though I love her, and I wonder what size I've made her feel over the years, how much a person like me can wear another down, or send a scar straight into the marrow, to stay. I wonder how much she likes me.

We're from the same place, but we have different geographies of the heart.

I stare at her narrow frame with that hair like a prize and think: she consumed herself that winter, allowed herself to be consumed. She left us on the edge of her world, left my grandfather outside it, left simply and for good a part of her heart in the frozen landscape of that endless, relentless winter.

But so did I.

The restaurant is filling in, a family tucking into salads, not a word spoken, their attention focused on their bowls. An old man sits alone, his eyes rheumy and faraway, like Glennie's now, again. Like every-thing, suddenly. Faraway and hard to see.

I take a deep breath. "I'm going to go. I am going to go to this bed and breakfast."

Nothing in her expression changes, and so I force myself. Rise above. God, I'm sick of her. Mostly, though, I'm sick of myself.

"Are you coming?" I ask.

I wait. She turns toward me again and before I can let her say no, before I can bear up under the force of whatever her expression reveals, I take my chance. I know it is our last. I say, "Come."

We walk out into the hot day in step but grimly so. The day is dim, and the glow is almost gone, one last streak of light in the horizon. We walk under the highway, past the garbage and the empty coke cans and the scrawled messages of violence and love, and I know I will never forget the heat, though the day has cooled; I will never forget walking with her back to the small gas station, with its one pump and that old man behind the counter, who let us go with only a wave.

We climb into the car and thread our way back through the side streets to the ramp, and we shoot off, our red taillights disappearing into the open dark of the road. We don't sing any old songs we know; don't tell each other stories; don't relive what past there is to share. We go forward against some great falling crush. The ride is long, and we ride in a kind of relief, glad for the movement because movement feels like hope, driving toward the reconciliation beyond us, but there, like a beacon, or a constellation.

Taking Root
Al
2002

AL HAD THE PORCH LIGHT ON against the dark. In this old neighborhood, streetlights were few and far between, with just enough illumination to spare accidents and discourage some trouble, but tonight he wanted more, as a comfort to himself, and as a guide.

This late, the neighborhood was quiet, just the occasional breeze whispering through the solemn row of Russian olives at the bottom of his sloping lawn, down near the sidewalk. The sound eased him, seemed to shhh away his worries. He had expected more sound this evening, the lilt of voices in a passing conversation or, in this neighborhood, the thud and backfire of anybody's car. But as Sunday rolled into Monday, it did so with a whisper.

Next to him, Al heard Marshall's collar jingle as he shifted weight in his sleep. Marshall was an old dog. He wasn't even Al and Sarah's old dog, but here he was, as always, right beside Al. Marshall was a beautiful golden retriever with a flourish of a tail and large brown, rheumy eyes, and he was besotted with Al for reasons no one fully understood. Their next door neighbor, Mark, took the betrayal with good grace. Al felt grateful. Mildly anxious, but grateful. He knew, and he knew that Marshall knew, how much he needed one solid, reliable friend. Maybe loneliness was recognizable. Maybe it had a scent.

They were an odd collection, this clutch of neighbors. Mark, who shared Marshall with Al and Sarah and their one small child, only one; Howard and Norda across the street, serial hosts; and Anil, who lived next door to Howard and Norda and who seemed to have enough children for them all, enough to bust the seams of his house. It was clear the seams of Anil's budget were straining. Wasn't it Meira who had appeared the other day in a parka a size or two too small? Al tried, as circumstance allowed, to slip small kindnesses Anil's way, little gestures he hoped nobody noticed. Occasionally Al and Sarah watched the children, helped with rides, shared meals. But for all the kindnesses among them—hell, he and Mark even shared a dog— there was a reserve, a thin line. In this age of confession, they kept much to themselves.

The glow from the streetlights caught Howard's rusting bucket of a Chevy across the street, not to be outdone by Mark's dented bucket of a Tempo next door, and farther down the road, Anil's Volvo. They had a bet running, the whole block, on which would go first. Even Howard, Mark, and Anil had weighed in. Al had voted for Mark's Tempo. He knew that Howard had recently reworked the Chevy's engine. And Anil. Poor Anil. He would keep that Volvo running if only with prayer. He had nothing to spare for additional expenses.

Sometime soon, out from the pitch-black night, would come

Sarah's Volkswagen. They had been gone a week, his girls. Al couldn't quite sit still now. Any minute, there would be that familiar throaty thrum, that flash of headlights, and then, finally, there would be his wife and young daughter, who knew how tired, who knew how transformed, but home nonetheless because this was home, this ancient house and the property line of Russian olives, with the old dog that was not theirs, and Al.

His heart was entirely theirs.

In this neighborhood of unreliable cars and steady, hopeful hearts. In this city known for its winters, in the middle of the plains, in the heart of the country. In this gentle summer soon to slip into the cool of fall. Here in some kind of broken-down glory, they had taken root, and thrived. Mostly.

Now Al rose and stood at the porch rail, tapping his fingers, and finally, with a low groan, Marshall joined him standing, and they waited together in the long, long night for the beginning, for sight of those headlights. For the welcoming home.

LEAVING WAS SARAH'S IDEA. Leaving, she had made clear, in no way meant that she was leaving forever, or even unhappy. She was only tired and in a rut. She wanted to get away. She would have preferred to leave Amelia with Al and go off somewhere by herself, even to someplace like a monastery. Instead, Sarah chose a quiet New Mexico town, a small, sleepy place where she and Amelia could linger on the cheap and have some adventures, shop in the cozy downtown, have some lunches out, take hikes in the low, long hills. Be left alone and tourist free.

Al understood. He felt a bit panicked, but he did understand. The panic came from her clear assertion, her looking away as she said it, that she didn't know when they would be back.

"Are you thinking two weeks?" he had laughed nervously. "Or two months?"

Sarah had shrugged, her hair falling behind her bony shoulders. Sarah had always carried enough weight to look strong. But now here was Sarah getting tiny, and after all their years of worrying about Glennie, now Al worried for Sarah. He worried for his bright-eyed Amelia. He almost said, "Leave her here," but he knew Amelia would be confused, and he knew, too, that without Amelia Sarah would lose an anchor. Her focus.

"Take what time you need," Al had said. "I'll have Marshall," he added with a laugh, and at this last, Sarah had tipped her head and squinted at him, smiling slightly.

"This scares me to death, Sarah," he finally said.

That was when she said it wasn't over. It wasn't about them. It was some restlessness in her that she needed to put to rest, a fatigue. Al let it go. Despite the dissipating tension, pressing her for information or details felt dangerous. They were standing in the kitchen in the buttery glow of morning, the sun warming the yellow walls just as they'd planned when, newly married, they had chosen this home. Chosen it for this room and what light they could imagine. They knew the center of their world would be their kitchen. Six years now, and one rambunctious six-year-old later, here they stood.

"Part of it is the miscarriage," Sarah had said.

Al watched her, saw her face twitch. He could not know her grief. He knew part of it, but he did not know how it felt for that beautiful hope to slide, then wrestle its way out of her. Let it go naturally, the doctor had said, and they had all agreed. Natural sounded good, preferable. But Al had been angry ever since. Had he known it was a lengthy process. Had he known what pain Sarah would feel, that she'd be keening, rocking on the bedroom floor at one point and grasping his hands, he would have suggested exploring alternatives. She had needed a gentler passing. They both had. They had choked out a farewell to the baby that late haunted night and far later, when they had had the strength, they had planted a small tree for the heart they would never know. A silver maple. Something strong and proud. Not like the Russian olives, with their gray green leaves and sad bending branches.

That terrible night as he had held her and whispered careful soft assurances, Sarah had said to him. "I bet in heaven I'll see some tiny angel and will know its face."

Al hadn't shared her hope in this future reunion. He wasn't religious. But the idea took root once she left on her road trip with Amelia, and he began to think that perhaps there was a heaven and that up there, in the back row, the tiniest voice in the choir was his child, singing and laughing and waiting. It was silly. "Absolutely silly," he told himself, each time the thought crossed his mind, but the thought stayed with him, a solace. He thought often about his child. He wondered if it had been a boy or girl. He wondered why the baby hadn't made it. He wondered why he couldn't quite escape the sharp grip of grief. It was always there, a thin, sliver of cold; a splinter. Something hair thin, like a small crack, something pointed that caught in him and created a widespread ache. Sometimes, Al had to stop and catch his breath.

JUST AFTER SARAH AND AMELIA HAD LEFT, waving from their windows as the Volkswagen turned the corner and disappeared, Al took his coffee out on the porch. It, too, was a Sunday. The morning was cool, one of those late summer days that presaged fall. Al was ready. It was football season, and down the block he watched as Anil's oldest son, Sujay, gathered his gear and plonked it in the back of Anil's clunker.

"You have Sunday practice?" Al asked as they made their loud, slow progress down the street.

Their Volvo needed a new muffler, and the engine whirred as though going 15 miles an hour was straining all systems. Anil replied, but it was impossible to hear him over the noise.

Al waved them on and sat waiting for two things, a direction and the arrival of Marshall, who even now, having had a romp at the dog park with Mark, was making his way briskly up the cracked and heaving sidewalk toward Al, nose high. In the morning, first thing, Marshall had all the energy of a puppy.

"I've never had that, ever," thought Al.

Marshall settled himself on the porch after getting a vigorous head rub and hearty greeting, the combination of which seemed key to his having a successful day and quite enough to ensure one, as long as Al then stayed nearby.

Across the street, the detritus of Howard and Norda's last late gathering lay gathered neatly by the garage. A stack of empty glass bottles in a variety of shapes and colors and a compacted though bulging dark green garbage sack.

What Al had not expected was to see a dapper looking Howard

step out of the house and come across the lawn toward him. For a long moment, he couldn't speak, his thoughts gathering only slowly across the idea that he was not dapper. And not even fully awake.

"Al," said Howard. He looked a little gray, and Al felt secretly relieved to know Howard was human, and that he, Al, scruffy-faced with a significant paunch and a thatch of unruly hair sprouting from his head, was just one of the guys. Sort of.

"Hi, Howard."

How Howard and Norda maintained any semblance of a decent life, he had no idea, not with the racket they made each night, the parties. He imagined that at some point, they would crash, unable to keep up the pace. Parties and work and parties again. Crazy and reckless as they were, they had good hearts. Howard wouldn't blink before speeding across the street if he thought Al and Sarah needed him. Nor would Norda.

Tomorrow morning, as Al gathered his briefcase, student papers, and his coat, he'd venture out to lecture looking every bit his age, and like a sad, worn out shoe: soft, weathered, maybe lovable. And there would be Norda in her sleek suit and high heels, and Howard in his brand name casuals, and off they'd go in Norda's little roadster, coffee in hand, smiles on their faces, looking polished. They probably even smelled good up close, of a simple, fresh soap. They were a magazine cover. An ad.

If Howard and Norda were a manicured, landscaped yard, then Al and Sarah were an unmowed lawn. Slightly ruffled, wearing clothes with stains. They were also parents, something Al doubted that Howard and Norda could ever be and perhaps did not want. But what did he know? If he had learned anything recently, it was that one never knew another person's heart, not really. He had not known Sarah yearned for another child. He had not known how broken-hearted he'd feel at their loss, or how alone, in this place where there was no one to talk to save for Sarah, who barely had any words left herself, grief having somehow stolen her vocabulary. How often had she opened her mouth, then shook her head, unable to express herself?

But here was Howard, in pressed brown pants, his t-shirt unwrinkled, a pale blue like a bird's egg. Some fancy flip-flops.

"Did you need some help with something?" Al asked.

"How you holding up?"

Al smiled. "Been a bit lonely," he said, opting for honesty.

Howard's smile faded. "I'm sorry, Al. You're welcome…" he said, gesturing broadly at his house, at the carefully packaged garbage.

"Thanks, Howard. Very kind. But poor Marshall here might go into a decline alone."

Howard paused. He was standing in the front walk, a respectful early morning distance from where Al was on the porch.

"I feel a bit awkward." Howard couldn't look at Al.

That's when Al knew. The miscarriage had never been a secret. Not that he and Sarah had shared much with people, but it was hard not to let the news filter out. Sarah had sunk so low with the news of the impending loss, and they had needed some short notice help several times. The evening—that dark evening—when Sarah was hunched on the bathroom floor, weeping, Al had called Norda, who was closest, and she had come and stayed near Amelia's room in case she woke. Amelia loved Norda—her hats and flowing, flowery scarves;

the hodgepodge of perfume bottles in her bedroom; her make-up kit, like a coloring box. Once Norda had let her try a bright red lipstick. Amelia fell in love then. With Norda. With lipstick. With the heady power of being a woman.

"It's wonderful news," Al said. "I'm sincerely happy for you." And he was. He felt something catch, took a moment to get air, but at the same time he felt genuinely pleased for Norda and Howard. "I didn't realize you wanted children. It's the most special thing."

Howard smiled, his face lighter, a wash of joy coming over him. "We didn't plan it," he said. "But we're thrilled."

"Well, let us know if we can help with anything." The more he spoke, the more inadequate Al felt, as though he was speaking lines he had heard somewhere, from a book about how to handle awkward occasions, for instance.

"Actually, that's why I'm here," he said. "Norda isn't feeling well, and I think I should run her in. Our car is dead. That new engine. I am not sure what I did. And the sports car is so low…" Howard's voice trailed off. "I was hoping you could run us down to urgent care."

"Of course," Al said, standing quickly. He cinched his robe around himself. "Give me a few minutes and I'll pull the car around."

Marshall whined, his eyes moving between the men, the air seeming suddenly electric, even to Al.

Later, Al worried as he waited in the car, engine running. Had Norda slept enough? Were people smoking in the house? Was Norda drinking? But it wasn't his business. Norda, though she needed help and looked drawn, managed to get out the door and down the steps. He couldn't see any belly on her, but she was tall and wouldn't show yet, he supposed.

Howard guided her into the backseat and as she settled, Norda flashed Al a wan smile. "Thanks for this, Al."

"Of course, Norda. Absolutely."

Howard had hardly settled into the car himself before Al pulled away from the curb.

The car fell quiet. Norda had closed her eyes and let her head fall against the door, and every question Al thought to ask focused on the baby and asking anything now seemed inappropriate. He remembered too well the inadvertent wrong questions from kind-hearted neighbors and colleagues after the miscarriage, and he remembered the blessed, even tight-lipped silence from family, who seemed to know when to speak and when not.

Glennie, of course, had proven particularly helpful. After Sarah first got the news, and Al had been pulled out of class, he had dialed Glennie as he hurried to his car. He didn't move swiftly or with ease and he had wished for a stout heart to get him the speed he needed and to give him the courage he lacked.

Glennie had taken the call, a stunner. Her middle name was Unavailable.

"Hey, Al," she had said, and he couldn't speak. Then: "Is it Sarah or Amelia?"

"Sarah," he had gasped. "They just told her the baby is dead."

There was a pause. Glennie had not known about the baby. At that point, no one had. "Where is she?"

"Abbot Northwestern."

"I'll meet you there. Al, I am so sorry."

So sorry. Perhaps the kindest words he had ever heard from Glennie, who kept emotions in a special place to which he seemed denied access. She was always cool, in control. He wondered when she broke down and with whom. She had to cry sometime. Didn't she? Not even Sarah really knew.

Of course Glennie had gotten there before Al. Glennie, rail thin and with that gush of hair, that porcelain skin, that perfect complexion and perfectly composed, she stood outside Sarah's door. Dr. Glennie Macmillan, OBGYN.

"She should see you first," Glennie said.

Of course she should. Seeing Glennie might not calm her right now.

But as Al opened the door, Glennie placed her hand on his shoulder and squeezed. He looked at her, and there were tears in her eyes. He stopped. For an instant, he stopped flat. He squeezed her hand back and then plowed through the door to that newly frail girl in the room who held his entire world in her hands.

At Abbott Northwestern now, again, Al parked the car by the doors and stood ready to help Howard get Norda out, but he wasn't needed, and he felt like a large flightless bird, flapping nearby. Then he had the sense to lumber ahead and secure a wheelchair.

Howard nodded, said "Thanks so much, Al."

After he parked, Al looked for them in the waiting room, but they weren't there, despite the crowd, and Al's heart rate picked up. He approached the front desk. "The pregnant couple?" he asked.

The receptionist, a young woman with a stylish bob, eyed him. "Family?"

"Friend. I drove them here."

The woman didn't speak right away, but she pushed back her chair from her desk and said a few words to a colleague around the corner, in the hall.

"They've sent her to emergency," the woman said. "Do you need directions?"

"It didn't seem urgent," Al said.

The woman's expression dimmed. She looked away. He knew she wasn't allowed to share more.

"I know the way," he said. He knew it all too well. How many visits had he made here for Sarah's grandparents? An endless number. And then for Sarah. He turned out of urgent care and began the walk he now hated.

IF WINTER WAS SARAH'S SEASON, fall was Al's. He loved crunching leaves underfoot, football (any football, though he bled gold and maroon for the Gophers), and all the holidays. He decorated the house for each of them in turn, and though he was a natural fit, he never offered to play Santa. He far preferred to be a part of the crowd than its star, to see Amelia's face light up, to be there with her. With them all.

Christmas was the one time each year he felt a glimmer of faith. Neighbors would pass a cup of cheer with a hearty, "This must be your season!" Al would chuckle and raise his glass. But if the season was his, it wasn't for the reasons they expected. He wasn't a religious man, just a Professor of Religion. He wasn't Santa. He was, he realized, a simple man. A happy, simple, quiet man.

Losing a child hadn't fit in to his worldview. It fit no one's, of course, but Al had been singularly unprepared for any loss. He asked for little, and he had been unmoored by the unnatural goodbye, by his insistent grief. And angry. Al had been angry.

Now he sat in a hard plastic chair, flipping through travel magazines and health brochures, waiting. Hoping. Because who would wish ill on a child? He needed, he realized, for this little baby to live. A new loss would unravel him. The thought struck him cold. He understood Sarah's leaving now in a new way. Suddenly he wanted to escape as well.

Across from him, an older man twisted his health brochure endlessly, his mouth a tight line, his knobby knuckles achingly large. An Hispanic family clumped together, heads down, praying. A middle-aged man in a pinstripe suit paced. Al sat. He slumped down into himself. He closed his eyes. He tried hard to think good thoughts.

It was a while before Howard appeared. He looked drawn and tight, and Al's heart skipped a beat.

"You don't need to stay, Al. I just wanted to let you know that they're running some tests."

"I can stay, Howard. Can I get you anything?"

Howard shook his head. Then he said, abruptly. "Isn't your sister-in-law an OB?"

"Yes, she is. I'd be happy to call her, or to give you her number."

"Would you do both?"

Al dialed hurriedly, his thick fingers fumbling over the numbers. He had to redial. He left her a message. "Glennie, a friend of mine and Sarah's is here at the hospital. Howard and Norda. Norda is pregnant and there is a problem. Howard was wondering, I guess, if you could call him."

It was a miracle born from a painful place, a thread of memory, that allowed Al to remember and recite Howard's cell phone number, his voice sounding wooden. Howard, who sometimes worked from home, had been the person Al phoned from work for check-ins after their loss. How is Sarah? Have you seen her? But only once or twice, after those awful few days, and only until Sarah's mother moved from across town and took over.

Howard nodded a thank you, turned quickly and left, tears coming into his eyes. Al couldn't imagine. Yes he could.

It was not long before Al saw Glennie striding across the ER waiting room, that white coat flapping like a flag. She did not look for him, but she caught his eye once, as she turned before going in to the care area. She saw him then and lifted her hand. Once. As though he were a casual acquaintance, maybe another Resident. Then she was gone.

Glennie had been voted by patients as one of the up and coming OB doctors in Minneapolis-St. Paul. She was featured in Minnesota Monthly. Her photo made her look like a goddess. Her honors and credentials were as lengthy as she was tall. And she was single, an absent aunt, a sometimes sister, an elusive personality with a ready, brief smile and a calm voice. She knew her medicine, and she took the extra time to know her patients. Her hands never shook. Not like Al, who was shaking now. Shaking because he knew that it must be serious to ask to see Dr. Glennie Macmillan, who had actually been number one on that list in part because of her even-keeled responses to crises. Thanks to Minnesota Monthly, everyone knew that. Everyone.

IN THE DAYS BEFORE AMELIA, Sarah and Al had said many goodbyes to loved ones. Both of her grandparents, her Auntie Em. His grandfather, a stoic Scandinavian named Anders Anderson. Not even Lars, Al used to say. It was like naming someone Andrew Andrews.

But practice didn't make Al perfect. Every loss was harder to bear, the accumulation of absences loud and unsettling, accentuated by the strain between Sarah and Glennie, which had been going on for so long now it ought to have worn itself out. But wounds like theirs strengthen, Al had learned, in the face of passivity. The most recent goodbye—theirs, the child he always remembered as sound, that thumping, persistent heartbeat—had seemed to allow the sisters briefly to drift closer, which he registered but couldn't absorb.

Sarah remembered other sounds, she had told him—the steady almost determined breathing of the tech, the squish of more jelly across her stomach, the clickclickclick of the tech taking picture after picture. Suddenly she had realized that the tech was searching. Then she caught the tech's glance and knew. She just knew. Sarah remembered the sound of her own loud breathing.

Glennie soon left the ER, her speed walk taking her past Al without a glance. He found himself bowing his head, toward what and for what he couldn't say, all of him suddenly feeling vacuumed out from his core. He bowed, head to hands, hands clasped on knees. He bowed down.

He was interested in faith, always had been, of course. Interested in the hope and calm it provided certain family and friends. Interested in how the ritual and beliefs had shaped his parents cold marriage. Al had always thought his parents lacked passion, but lately, perhaps given his own aging, he realized they had some bond he had not given any credence before. They relied on each other, trusted each other. They had committed to each other and that came in part from faith.

Now he searched his mind for the words that had defined his childhood, the prayer as important to the weave of his days once as lutefisk and football and books. But what he thought was far simpler. *Dear Lord, please protect the babies.*

Plural.

And then Al began to weep.

IT WAS LATE WHEN THEY DROVE HOME. The neighborhood streetlights flickered. Al helped Howard bring Norda inside, settle her on the couch. He put a meal together, a green salad, bread and butter, some pasta, and left it on the table. He made Howard a drink. Then Al left, quietly closing the front door behind him.

Howard had said only that they believed the baby was all right. That, and thank you. The ride home had been tense, Norda curling into Howard, who sat in the back, eyes wide open and unblinking. Al tried not to glance back at them. It seemed impossible.

On the front porch, Marshall stood and greeted Al, his tail wagging slowly, his whine short and high pitched.

"I don't know, Marshall. I don't know if it's okay."

Inside, he put some food in Marshall's bowl and some fresh water in a large clear Tupperware container, and then he lay down in bed, hoping to sleep forever. When Marshall curled in a ball near his feet, Al didn't protest. As Marshall inched his way closer to Al and stretched out, Al said nothing. He didn't care about rules and being sanitary and dog hair. Who gave a shit.

He thought of Sarah and Amelia. They have only been gone one day, Al thought.

One.

He checked the messages. No blinking light, just the steady red glare of a button. They were on the road, they were traveling through the dark, as was he. He felt as cracked open as an egg. Al thought he might stop breathing, and when he cried out, what rose out of him was loud, and raw, almost a scream, and then it became one. Marshall, beside him, whimpered. The women had each other, God, doctors, nurses. Who did the men have? What were their words for this particular grief?

Later that night, Al woke and went out onto the front porch. He was still wearing his clothes. He had not eaten. Across the street, Norda and Howard's house was silent, without lights. The trio of beaters lined the curb, looking, if possible, more forlorn. The streetlights glowed steadily now, dimly but steady.

Marshall followed Al outside, keeping close, pressing his frame against Al and steadying both of them.

Al looked up at the stars. Dear Lord, please protect the babies, he said in a whisper. Then he repeated it, over and over.

AL WAS ASLEEP ON THE PORCH when dawn broke. Sujay touched him lightly on the shoulder as he delivered the paper.

"You okay? Mr. Nelson?"

Al had nodded, tried to make himself presentable and to pretend that no, he was not asleep in his clothes on the front porch, next to a dog, even if it was Marshall.

"Want me to call someone?" Sujay asked. He glanced down the street toward his own home.

It was the last thing Al needed.

"I'm fine, Sujay," Al said. "Fine, thanks. Please don't call anyone."

Sujay hesitated.

"Please, Sujay. It would be embarrassing. I had a rough day. Some friends were in trouble. It bought back some sad memories."

Sujay listened. He was 15. He understood the social implications. Absently, he reached down to pet Marshall, then he handed Al the paper. "I'm sorry," he said. "Um. Is everything okay now?"

"I don't know," Al said.

Sujay bit his lip and nodded. Because for God's sake men only nod. Men and near-men.

"Okay, well, I hope it all works out," Sujay said.

"Thank you," Al said. "I do, too."

Sujay hopped down the porch steps, grabbed his bike, and headed off.

A bike? Al thought for the first time. *How long is his route?*

Anil had come by one night, after the news had made its way. Anil had come by and offered his condolences and a bear hug, then walked quietly away. The hug had shocked Al. It was born of an Anil he hadn't known. He had watched Anil work his way back up the block between the intermittent streetlights. Al had not thought his heart could hurt more right then, but watching Anil make his way home was somehow shattering.

Now as he watched Sujay cycle all the way down the long block and turn the corner onto 15th, Al realized that Sujay was a lot like his father. He understood dignity. Or maybe he understood fragility, Al wasn't sure.

Something in Sujay's kindness and then gentle departure had given Al, for the first time aside from the holidays, a sense of calm, even faith. A small, butterfly-winged hope, fragile, easily torn. But there.

SARAH HAD CALLED SOMETIME IN THE NIGHT, leaving a message. She had called again later, no message. Al didn't want to call her. His head felt full of air. He gave Marshall a head rub and some extra breakfast, showered, drank some strong coffee, and dressed for work. He crammed that new Macmillan textbook into his briefcase. The book weighed a ton. On his way out the door, he made certain to stop at Norda and Howard's and to put the newspaper in the door with his cell phone number scribbled on an attached note. As an afterthought, he added Glennie's number again. He had no idea what the hospital protocols were.

When he arrived at his office, he must have looked off balance because the department secretary brought him the last Danish from the staff room. He thanked her and rather than launch into any unsolicited commentary or confession, simply smiled and reached for his phone, though he had no one to call. Finally, he decided he'd better call Sarah. To his relief, she didn't pick up. He left a message, then he took a deep breath. He wanted to be alone. He needed time to re-establish the whole of himself. "It never leaves," he thought. "The grief never leaves. You just have to learn how to carry it."

Al opened his email to a reminder about a departmental meeting at 10. He spent most of the meeting checking his cell phone, and when it rang, he jumped up and hurried out, muttering apologies about urgent personal business. Al had expected Sarah. It was Glennie.

"There are HIPAA rules," she said, without preamble.

"I didn't ask anything," Al said.

Glennie paused. "Call your friend," she said.

"Can you tell me if it's bad news?"

But Glennie had already hung up.

Al left then. He drove home, to the peace of a quiet morning in a neighborhood in which the houses carried a hint of personality even without the noise that people bring. Homes painted different colors, lawns mannered but not immaculate. The occasional bike visible, the odd, vibrant, defiant weed. It was quiet enough now that one could hear the bees in the flowers. For a moment, Al paused in front of Norda and Howard's door. "What will you say when they tell you whatever it is they tell you?" Al thought, and then, "Who am I now?" He knew and knocked on the door.

WHEN SARAH FINALLY CALLED later that night, Al grabbed the phone.

"Where are you?" he asked. "Are you okay?"

It was a gleeful Amelia who took the call, giggling, unable to adequately convey information. They were in Colorado, about to cross the state line into New Mexico. They were almost there.

Amelia wouldn't relinquish the phone, and Al said, "I love you, and tell Mommy I love her."

His voice sounded worn. He wondered if Amelia could tell.

Al wanted to speak with Sarah about his own journey, across the street. About how he had come to understand that his grief would be there, always. That afternoon, though, he had found a small place inside himself to tuck away his pain so that he could hear Norda and Howard's news, that this little baby was fine, that Norda needed to slow down. She couldn't be a hostess. He wanted to tell Sarah about holding Norda's bony, veined hand. He wanted to tell Sarah that he now understood some of his last thoughts in life would be of the child they had lost, and that at the very end he would be reaching out with some extension of his heart. And that maybe, maybe, there might be someone out there, up there, reaching back.

Amelia was chattering now. About restaurants and ice cream, about steering the car on a rutted back road, about how Mommy looked in her bandanna. Alive, like electricity, his beautiful, beautiful girls.

Going Home
Sarah
2002

SARAH CLIMBED INTO THE CAR. Amelia was already strapped into her car seat, happily jiggling her legs and humming something tuneless, gaze drifting languidly over the view, the scraggly weeds in the parking lot, the fire red in the sky, the slow entrance of a semi into the lot, with the wheeze and thrum of its brakes and gears like a low, drawn-out groan. Low drawn-out groans were about what Sarah had left to offer, especially as she settled, yet again, behind the wheel. This was New Mexico. Dry, flat, open-ended New Mexico. And they had so much farther to go, whole worlds to go, from desert to plains to prairie. They would take them one by one, and when they hit that prairie, something in her blood would pick up, something like a beat from a song or a drum. People might call it Godforsaken and cold. But there was, would always be, a heartbeat for her when she cast her eyes along the endless plains, felt that slow heat from a summer breeze over the grasses. Here, people loved the sage. Loved the red stone and the red sunsets and the brown squat homes. The mysticism. But she loved the bracing clarity of snow and ice and temperatures moving below zero. The way the humidity made her feel tough. The silence in a deep snow.

It's about where you came from, she thought. It's about what you know. And you either love that landscape you were born into or hate it and move elsewhere. But it never leaves you, that first geography. That early terrain becomes the rough view of your heart. That place, the weather, the amount of space. It enters your blood.

Sarah started the engine. Time to go home. Nothing is easy in families. She knew all too well. But nothing mattered more to her than their love. Sarah knew that, too. She would never make it without Al. Maybe someday sweet Amelia would meet as sweet a man, someone as lit from the inside with good nature as Al was. Maybe someday Amelia would have a sibling.

Briefly, Sarah's thoughts traveled to Glennie. She rested her head on the steering wheel. What would it take to reconnect? What list of things did she need to apologize for or forgive? Both lists were worn and thin and long. Too long. As long as their stand-off. She needed to shed her bitterness, but she didn't know how to do it, and hadn't she tried once? A miserable failure, that weekend outside Belton.

"Are we going?" Amelia asked.

Sarah nodded. There were few words now, both of them fatigued and curved into their seats, into the familiar grooves. Readying for the long drive back home, where in the late evening or early morning Al would find them. He would be there, waiting. She knew this. Regardless of the hour. He was hers. His landscape, his terrain, were the world she breathed.

With only the occasional other car on the road and stray streetlight to guide her, she drove in a kind of fog of sleepiness mixed with the slim hum coffee gave her. Soon, Amelia slept in the backseat, covered with a blanket. On the long roads through nowhere New Mexico, with starlight their most consistent friend and scratchy radio stations piping in mariachi, there seemed no promise of bumps.

And they knew bumps.

Sarah thought about what Al was probably doing now, how he had come home and likely flung his jacket across the back of a chair by the kitchen table, sighed as he kicked off his shoes and socks, peeked out the door to see if Marshall was around. Maybe Marshall was, and maybe they shared a companionable moment on the back porch, looking at their own bright stars while Al sipped a beer. But deep in her heart, she knew that Al was busy counting the hours, would soon pat Marshall on the head and head toward the front door and the porch and root himself there, waiting. Waiting for those two dim headlights to rise at the top of the road and make their slow way down, two lights that would through tears become one, like a moon, maybe a sun, rising. A single light of hope and promise, of returning, their light, coming faster now, above the whoosh of tires, on the breath of what might seem a prayer but really, deep down, was the best way she knew how to say, I love you.

They had never had what Sarah thought of as the giggle years, those blissful early years in marriage. Their first years were marked by losses of various stripes. But if her world was repeatedly knocked askew, it only served, when she finally could pause on this trip to think, to remind her where her center was, and her center was always

Al. They may not have had much time for laughter or rosy days. They may have learned early and hard the rough patches of married life, the strains. But it had taught them this: they had the kind of love that endured. Love that held up, and love that lasted. Love that understands compassion. And forgiveness. Love that sent people away, and love that let them come home. Love that knew where home was. Love that traveled the distance.

Who Is Family?
Al
Spring 2003

WE WANTED ONE MORE BABY, but luck had not gone our way, and so we counted our blessing and held want at bay, whispering to one another, We have one. But still we desperately wanted one more and as much as we both fought against the impulse, thought wanting too much—especially in the face of having—was gross, we recognized that want would gnaw and divide and grow like a cancer. We just couldn't find a way to shake the wanting off.

The child was on TV, a little girl, aged six. A string bean of a girl with long dirty blonde hair and a quick, nervous smile. Her name was Beth, and she loved painting, books, and dogs. She liked to run, but she didn't have a yard. She looked too thin to carry the burden she obviously felt, for all of her smiles and giggles in front of the cameras. It was the darting looks left, to whoever was there, that got to me. Her sweetness and hope and fear, her courage and want, we knew all of it, and while the footage cut to my core, it somehow destroyed Sarah, who sat beside me on our tattered cloth couch, crying quietly.

Then she said. "Six!" She turned to me, indignant. "How must she feel, six and no one wants her?"

I shrugged and then it hit me. "No, Sarah. We have no idea about her, or her history. There are horror stories about adopted kids. Aren't there?"

But the idea was planted, and planted in the deepest part of Sarah's heart, and even as I sat shaking my head, I knew that likely we would be opening our doors to this child, creating a larger family. As the adoption agency number flashed on bottom of the screen, Sarah dialed on her cell phone, wiping away her tears with the back of her hand.

Down the rabbit hole, I thought.

Want had won.

SISTERS DON'T HAVE A GREAT HISTORY IN THIS FAMILY, so I argued for a boy. That lasted about two minutes. Sarah had seen Beth, and her heart was set.

Over the next several weeks, we collected information. We considered letting the idea go, and then Sarah looked at our wide back yard and said, "She could run here," and suddenly we found ourselves circling back toward adopting. But I still fretted, and not about Beth.

Finally, one evening I said, "We can't talk any more about welcoming Beth into this family with you and Glennie still at loggerheads, not when that separation still eats you up. If you'd decided to just let Glennie go, say "the end," then fine. But you haven't, and it's not fair to ask Beth to come into a new family that doesn't get along."

Sarah was sitting with me at the kitchen table at dusk, a rosy glow marking the hum of mosquitoes waking. I had called a summit of two, at our own kitchen table, a worn soft maple with navy blue placemats.

"This family isn't whole," I said. "You need to make a decision about Glennie. In or out?"

And then I left, not quite fleeing but like a balloon deflating, trotting out into the bug infested night on whatever air I had left. Marshall met me in the backyard, which was not fenced. I scratched his ears and then took him on a leashless slow amble around the neighborhood. I slow down when I'm with Marshall. I don't rush. I don't think of teaching or grades or how badly the Gophers are playing. I don't think of anything. I hear the birdsong and the old timey love songs my neighbor, Norda, sings while she washes dishes; car doors slamming. I hear Anil calling his kids inside, and the squeak of brakes from anyone's car or the bus. It doesn't matter. This is a neighborhood for brakes. I hear it all, and sometimes I bend down and pat Marshall on the head. I hope he lives for decades.

I already had my theory about the split between Glennie and Sarah, two sisters who look different but have a similar core. Here is my theory: One was never seen because she was not beautiful. The other was never seen because she was.

I'm older now, and I hate to bring it down to looks, but I believe that how they looked shaped how they were treated, and not always in obvious ways. Sarah would clock me if she knew I thought this. She might even call me a pig. But it's a truth I have lived. How I look affected how I was treated, am treated. I have been defined, in part, by my size and, sadly, not the size of my heart. Sarah is a beautiful woman in an unconventional way. Maybe her jaw is too strong. But Glennie is a jaw-dropper. She is a lightning bolt of golden hair and eyebrows, her body that languorous kind of thin, and she has deep blue eyes. You think you have entered a new world the first time you see her. A fairytale.

Until the adoption came up, I'd never considered how it must have felt for Glennie, being her, especially in the world of medicine. How hard she had to fight to get where she wanted. I have heard stories about what surgeons can be like, about how women residents can be treated. How would it feel to be among the smartest in the room, if not THE smartest, and only to be seen, never heard? It must have been a gargantuan task to be recognized for her work, ethics, and skill. How tough she had to be. Perhaps, how ruthless. Maybe that long fight for respect sharpened her sense of dedication and her duty to her dreams into a fine, piercing point.

And Sarah. My sweet Sarah. Overlooked, but matter of fact. Not bitter about the invisibility but instead protective of Glennie and then so bitter when Glennie became remote. Of all people, her own sister turning away. Some part of Sarah paled and froze, soured.

It doesn't take much to see it all play out, in hindsight. But it was near a lifetime for all of us getting here.

Beth will have a different history from Amelia. She will be coming from a place of loss and neglect and maybe even fear. The girls will speak different languages of love and hope. This family has been here already, in a cloud of babble and misunderstanding, hurt and recrimination, and I have to know, I absolutely have to know, that we have the heart and the will and the skills to build bridges to each other before we ask this small, hopeful child to join us. Our track record stinks, and the fact is, among the robins and leafed out trees and the symphony of sound that is my neighborhood, I feel cold.

Marshall grunts, and I look up to catch Sujay racing past on his bike, his blurred wave, and then we are back to our amble. Past Sujay's house, on down the road as far as we can go, for as long as possible.

When I finally walk inside, I'm covered with mosquito bites. I want to shower in Caladryl. I hear nothing, see no one and sneak in through the kitchen, down the hall, toward the stairs. Then I realize: the house is dead silent. I peek out the front door. The Volkswagen isn't in the driveway. My girls have gone.

LATER, DEEP ASLEEP, THEY WAKE ME where they find me on the front porch. I am one giant mosquito bite, and they are chatting about stories and fairies and bedtimes. Sarah's face is blotchy and she gives me a weak smile and I head for the fridge and a chilled dry white wine. I hand her the bottle and take Amelia's hand.

"Let's get this fairy to her castle bedroom," I say.

"Yes," says Amelia, and that is all. We climb the stairs slowly, and I don't even make her brush her teeth. I let her sleep in her clothes, some puffy dress that I imagine she wore wherever it was that they went.

Sarah's still on the porch, sitting on the stairs, and I think I am going to die from some mosquito-borne disease or rip my face off if I go back outside, but I go.

"Where were you?"

"We went to see Glennie."

"At her place? She was home?"

"No, at the hospital. She fit us in."

My mind goes blank, so I wait for whatever terrible news is coming. I probably look calm, but a slow ache has moved past my shoulders and into my chest.

Sarah smiles up at me from the stairs. "We talked some, but there are so many potholes in the road…"

"She fit you in?"

"She told her nurse she had a personal situation."

"So where does this leave us?"

"With trying for the rest of our lives and protecting the girls."

The girls.

She wants to go forward.

God help us.

"What does this all mean, with Glennie? What does trying mean?" Sarah sighs. "Well, we came up with a plan. Like visitations."

The word surprises me, but it makes a strange kind of sense and is realistic, which I respect. The word acknowledges their division and their hope of managing that division. But the word worries me, too.

"No." My voice has an edge. Have I ever said something this blunt? Asserted my own family rights? "No. I want you two to work it out, but adopting Beth is our decision, Sarah. How we handle it is our decision."

"Of course, Al."

I take hold of her hand. "We're not asking her to be available to the girls, Sarah. What we're asking is if she wants to see us all. If she wants to be a part of our family. Because if she can't commit to us all…" I shake my head. "Then I don't want her around. At all."

And I mean it literally. Anger and stress have caused enough heartbreak. No more tears in hospitals while Sarah grapples to escort one relative into the world, or one out, her sister completely absent from filial responsibility. No more missed coffee dates, holidays, birthdays. No more.

Sarah's eyes scan mine and then this woman, who is so deeply committed to her relatives, finally hears me, and abruptly looks away, out into the night. But she does not let go of my hand.

"I want to talk to her, too. I'll try to catch her at lunch tomorrow. The Dean canceled the staff meeting. Can I get an hallelujah?" It's a weak attempt at humor that doesn't hide my tension, but Sarah smiles, and there it is, in that brief look, fear. She's afraid, too.

"Lunch is part of the deal. She has to eat more, not just enough. She has to take better care." Sarah pauses, looking down at my stomach. "You, too," she says, eyeing my paunch. Her attempt at humor falls as flat as mine.

"I can't believe we're really considering this."

"Beth? Or Glennie?" Sarah asks.

"Both."

But we are.

THE NEXT AFTERNOON, I catch Glennie in the hospital cafeteria on her lunch break. It's a surprise assault, but she takes it in stride. Of course she does. She has surprise medical assaults every day of her life. She's not one to flinch.

Glennie sits alone at a small white tabletop for four, facing the windows, and staring at her plate. She has ordered a sandwich. Actual food. It seems that I am suddenly capable of all kinds of blunt because I immediately say, "Good to see more than a salad in front of you!"

I might have been embarrassed by my rudeness years ago, but not now. I think of Beth and put her first.

"What are you getting?" she asks politely.

"A salad."

I expect her to laugh, but she doesn't. She doesn't react. She waits, which unnerves me. Glennie doesn't even blink.

I'm back soon from the counter with my wilted lettuce, three sad cherry tomatoes, and one slice of cucumber, which cost me $6.99, and I'm not at all happy about either the food or the price. I look up at Glennie and perhaps my face shows my displeasure because she starts talking.

"I'll be coming over for dinner every Friday."

I spear a leaf.

"And you are coming to my house every Sunday for an early dinner. Everyone. Mom and Dad. You guys."

"This is what you two talked about."

It isn't a question, but Glennie nods. She takes a bite of her sandwich. She looks miserable. Maybe she is. Is it the food, or the new schedule?

"Holidays? Christmas?" I'm trying to wrangle the conversation toward what I need to say, with as little success as I'm having with my salad.

"I will be there for each child's birthday and on Christmas Eve."

I nod, try to spear a tomato. It slides away, and I stab until I get it.

"And what about us? What efforts are we making?" I ask, uncertain what we can do to equal her effort but wanting to be fair.

"Sarah is going to let me have some of the family memorabilia and stop pressuring me."

I nod like a bobblehead.

"And you are going to arrange for me to see the girls sometimes without Sarah. Or you. To have fun times. To create my own relationships with them."

"Me?"

"You."

"Why me? How?"

"You have to make plans for me and the girls, Al. If Sarah does it, she will already be interfering."

"How often?"

Glennie shrugs. "When you can. Maybe every other month? Three months?"

I fumble with the last tomato. "I think she will have problems. Beth."

Glennie leans forward. "She'll need therapy and patience and love. All of which you guys can provide, if you choose."

I look away. I can, but what if I mess up? What if we mess up? I need to tell Glennie the truth, and the truth has nothing to do with meals or family traditions.

"Glennie, we're applying." I look her dead in the eye, as she would me. That's the only way. To tell her straight. I keep my voice low and as even as possible. "We are doing this, but if you can't be a part of the family, the whole family, we're done. If you can't show. If you add more stress and drama…We'll cut you out." Not my most tactful. Actually, among my worst efforts, but word choice a doctor will understand.

Glennie studies me. She doesn't speak.

"We're serious. I don't think Sarah was clear when she spoke to you last night. But we agree," I tell her. "We can't fuck this up. Not for Amelia, and certainly not for Beth. Not for any of us."

Glennie gives me a steely glance. "We won't."

"I'm going to tell the adoption agency about our bad sister history."

Glennie takes another bite of her sandwich, a determined bite. "You should," she says. "Tell them the truth."

"You know a meal plan isn't going to change the last however many years." My voice has an edge.

Now Glennie laughs. "I don't think I've ever had rose-colored glasses, Al."

I finish my salad and sit with her, not to watch her eat, which is painful, seeing the sheer determination it requires, but to give myself a moment. I moved a mountain today. On a salad. We all moved a mountain. And we still have a hell of a long way to go down the path ahead so I need to sit and contemplate. I stay to gather my strength.

Glennie is still eating slowly. She swallows and says, "You don't trust me, do you?"

I take a deep breath. "I trust that you ladies will try to find a way back to each other before we bring this little girl into our family. Because we'd all like to have you there, Glennie." I'm tearing up. "And we need this little girl to come to a family that can work through things. We need to show her that even when things are rough, we love each other enough to make amends."

At least I got that part out the way I'd planned.

There is no sudden call for her to anyplace, no place to rush or

212

escape, and the words fill the space between us. I'm not sure what to expect, but then I realize this is Glennie Macmillan, who has battled to be the doctor she is. She has heard worse, faced more. She has overcome an eating disorder, though she still confronts that history three times a day, game on. Her expression doesn't even shift.

She carefully places another bite of sandwich in her mouth, and when she is done, she sits for a moment, looking out over the assortment of nurses and doctors and cafeteria workers and motley families that comprise most of her world. Then she looks me in the eye. "Okay."

That one word leaves me cold again. I feel sick to my stomach.

"I mean it, " I say. I shake my finger at her, like my father used to do to me. "I mean it. If this little girl is joining our family, then we all better be one."

I rub my face with my hands and let my shoulders sag. I'm still teary, but she isn't. She looks away again, out into the open. My stomach growls.

"I'm worn out and still hungry."

"I miss my salads."

"We can trade in the future."

"I trust," Glennie says, emphasizing her last word, setting her gaze back upon me, "that you know better." She isn't taking the bait. No jokes.

And then she is gone. No grand exit. She simply leaves. She could be a general or a President or a movie star or a model. She could be anything. She can handle this. But there is something new in her today as she strides away. She wants to handle this.

I DID NOT HAVE A SWEATING PROBLEM until I met with Gretchen, who became our family liaison. Then, I became disgusting. I was drenched.

"She's going to think you are a serial killer, Al," Sarah said.

But Gretchen didn't, through all the forms, through the background checks and home study. Through the pre-placement visits and meeting the foster family and a letter from Glennie. A letter Gretchen did not really share except to say it was a moving tribute to family and what Glennie hoped to be for Beth, an engaged and loving aunt. Through meetings with Beth. Through a process that felt both interminable and exhausting and wouldn't even be over until after we had had Beth for several months, when we would go to court to file the papers and call her ours.

I sweated for months and months. I did not lose weight, just water. I was swimming toward a family of four, and only Marshall stuck with me the whole way. There was not enough deodorant in the world for anyone else but the dog.

But I stopped sweating when Gretchen confirmed that Beth was coming to us. Sarah danced. Amelia jumped up and down. I froze.

WE ARE WAITING ON THE PORCH FOR BETH. It's sunny out but cool, the kind of weather that always makes me happy. Amelia is playing in the yard with a helium welcome balloon that I don't think will last until the big event. She's making the balloon dance, and laughing.

At some point, before I see the car, I take Sarah's hand, and we hold on tight to each other. That's what we do best. Then I see it, up ahead, coming our way, a white Honda. The white Honda which carries our new daughter. I grip Sarah's hand. My breath catches, and I see only the flash of that wicked balloon, its gaudy welcome and the way it splinters the light. I squint against the glare.

The neighborhood seems suddenly, loudly, silent. No one is outside. Even Anil's yard is empty. Because they all know that at any minute, a young child will step out of that car and who needs a ruckus and a party and a sea of faces?

I shiver. How must Beth feel, being whisked away and down the highway and over to us, even though she knows us a little bit now? Is she scared about how it will be, joining us? To start a new school? To find her way places? To be chosen?

That's when Amelia tears out of the front yard toward the sidewalk, running full tilt toward the road, beaming, her giant welcome balloon billowing behind her. She has no fear, of the road or of Beth, no jealousy, just flat out open-hearted joy.

Sarah stands and yells and it's primal, nothing I've heard before. "Amelia!"

"It's okay," I say, rising as well, patting her arm. "She's okay. Let her go."

Amelia hasn't heard anyway. She's already reached the car door and she is breathless, face flushed. She is rocking her balloon back and forth right in front of the window, and then she steps back a bit and squats down, all her little girl pudge not yet gone even at seven and having to sort itself. She is a beaming ball of little girl. She waves at the window and we are walking over to her, almost there, almost there and Amelia says as the door opens, "Hi Sissy."

Long Distance
Sarah
Fall 2005

THE FORECAST WAS FOR RAIN ALL WEEK, big puddles of it. Jumping puddles. Except for a few brides needing last minute alterations, Sarah's bookings were few, and the phone wasn't ringing to announce new clients. Who wanted to hopscotch through the rain into her house, only then to wrestle in and out of outfits for sizing and hems? Seamstresses could wait. Besides, it was almost Halloween, in Sarah's experience, the beginning of the end for autumn diets.

Amelia had torn away this morning in a giant rush, wanting to grab a good seat on the bus, which creaked around the corner at 6:50. Beth had had a friend from her cross-country team, Addie, pick her up. The team was meeting for breakfast at Perkin's, pre-race. Sarah was excited Beth wanted to go. She was even more excited that Beth wanted to go with a friend.

With no appointments, Sarah had a wide-open day. When had that last happened? For a few moments, just heartbeats really, she paused after the bus groaned away and looked around her neighborhood. Marshall was staring forlornly at her from his living room window. Many mornings, Marshall came over to spend the day since Mark worked long days as a legal aid lawyer. Sarah fished in her pocket for her keys, found Mark's, and opened his front door.

"Marsh?"

Marshall, though old now, still had his moments and was a whirlwind of golden retriever gratitude and joy, soft hair and whip of a tail. He was already out the door and trotting gingerly through the rain toward her porch before she had gathered her wits. Marshall was always a tonic.

At her house, she slid the open dog biscuit box under his snout and let him choose a few.

"What shall we do today?"

Marshall led her slowly upstairs because that is where they usually go when Sarah has custody of him. She followed, uncertain.

"Marshall, I haven't even had coffee. And no one is coming today."

Marshall was her ambassador. When a bride was feeling teary or stressed, when an outfit was too small, when anything went wrong and Marshall was on duty, disappointments smoothed more quickly.

Marshall settled on her couch for waiting customers, a navy-blue cloth couch Larch had helped her find when all she had was scraps of fabric and dreams and a budget as thin as a needle. The couch rested along one wall, next to two changing rooms, and faced the sewing machine and large mirrors and bolts of colorful cloth that made up the opposite wall. Marshall stared at himself in the mirror, seemed to approve, and with a sigh, closed his eyes.

Sarah started to scold Marshall (dog hair on the couch for guests!) but didn't have the energy. It was as though he knew no one was coming today and that the couch was his. Instead of getting frosty, Sarah sat with him, then rose, feeling the pressure of silence and her customary schedule. It's hard to just sit. She spent a few minutes cleaning her office, filing invoices and patterns, picking up stray extras. She saved all her extras. Threads, snippets of cloth. She found a good square of white linen. Oh, how she loved linen. For a moment, she ran her hand over it, feeling the slight roughness, the tiny bumps, and then the thought came to her, weakly, like winter light. A perfect white linen square. Maybe off white. She needed her glasses to check.

It's time.

"I agree," she told herself. Out loud. It was time to make her square for the family women's quilt.

What to stitch? What to say? She knew now why her grandmother left only her name. There are no quotes big enough for a lifetime, save one, maybe, the one she has let guide her since she first heard it as a child in the nasally voice of Father Bright. She laughed now, remembering. What a name. Father Bright. She stitched in one letter in a beautiful light blue thread, on the edge, as a test, to see how it felt, to see if she could live with it, but she knew it was right. She wondered what Glennie's square would say, if Glennie would even make one.

"What do you think, Marshall? Do you think she'll make a square?"

His eyebrows rose.

"Glennie," Sarah said, looking at him. "Will Glennie make a square?"

Marshall groaned and stood, tip toeing delicately on the couch cushions until he could flop down on his other side.

Sarah laughed. Someday, Glennie's square would be there or not. Just like her sister was there, or not. Sarah just needed to let it all go, this endless building up of expectation and then disappointment. It was a recipe for bitterness, and Sarah knew that particular flavor, that sourness and rot.

Glennie is Glennie.

"Right, Marshall?"

Marshall lifted his eyebrows and sighed, as sick of hearing about tensions with Glennie as Al, who once got all the hissing updates from Sarah anytime anything happened. Or didn't happen. Sometimes, she still found reason to hiss but less often and only for minor things, like when Glennie was late or gave the wrong kind of gift (make-up? To girls?). Now Sarah chose to stay silent and mutter to herself. She took a deep breath. They'd all been working so hard since Beth had arrived, Glennie especially, having the girls over every month or so to bake or cook. She was religious about making Sunday dinners and attending birthday parties. If all Glennie delivered were babies, meals, and memories with the girls instead of a quilt square, so be it.

"Well," she told Marshall, "I'm making mine."

THAT WEEK, IN THE DIM OF RAINY GRAY MORNINGS, after the clatter of school preparations and the race for the bus, Sarah slowly made her way in thread: Be strong and of good courage, go into the world in peace. The Book of Common Prayer. Sarahstina Ann Macmillan Nelson. As much as she loved that verse, she knew it wasn't a fit. She had never been peaceful, more like a thundering warrior. But one can always aspire, and she has aspired all her life. She has let the verse guide her on many a day, and it seems fitting to let it speak for her, to let it speak after her.

One ancient auntie filled her square with embroidered pictures of birds and flowers, another with Bible verses, another with a recipe. Sarah loved looking at the quilt. She loved seeing who they all were, these otherwise forgotten women who survived the trips from Sweden and Scotland and carved out the plains; who made jam and rode horses and sang hymns in two languages; who toughed out frigid, bitter Minnesota winters. It was not home for some of them. Charlotta missed Sweden keenly, but she never returned.

The thought stopped Sarah mid-stitch. She could not imagine.

Marshall joined her most days that week, unless he had a better offer. Some mornings, Mark left the TV on, and Marshall liked watching the animal shows from the comfort of Mark's cushy French couches.

Occasionally Sarah's phone rang. A bride with eight bridesmaids, wanting to schedule appointments. A businessman who had lost weight who needed his suits taken in. And, at least once a day, her mother, if only to say hi. It was blissfully quiet. Sarah was picky about her stitching, and worked slowly, mapping out her square, testing thread colors.

The next week, as the rains passed and the sun finally came out, Sarah embroidered stars along the square edges, along each one, in different colors. Red, teal, deep yellow, green. The rainbow of her life, every color a memory.

At the end of the week, Sarah called her mother. Her mother spent most of her days on the telephone now calling aunties and library friends and church wardens. She loved to chatter, this woman who had never been much of a talker. But with her bad knees and unsteady gait, she had had to find a new pastime instead of gardening, and she'd discovered the joys of conversation.

"She's killing me," her dad whispered before he handed the phone over.

"Guess what?" Sarah said when her mother got on.

"Oh, what fun. Let me think," said her mother. "Are you pregnant?" Her voice warbled with excitement, and Sarah felt instantly that she had overplayed her hand.

"No, nothing that exciting."

"Oh."

"I finished my square. For the quilt."

"Oh, how nice," her mother said.

It did not compare to a grandchild. It was a custom, a tradition, and a beautiful thing. It was also, in the list of exciting things, a big fat failure. But they made a date for Sarah to come over to share it with her. They would sew it on together, have a cup of tea. That was tradition, too, that the women gathered to add the new square, as many women as could attend. Sarah started to ask if she should invite Glennie but stopped herself.

Her mother seemed to read her mind. "Glennie asked me about the quilt the other day. Asked to see it."

"Really?"

"Really. She even came over and stayed a while. She asked me to tell her the stories of each square so I did. We had a good chat."

Sarah didn't know quite what to say. Her sister was trying to reconnect, and that was good, so Sarah said the only thing that she felt was honest and true. "I hope she makes a square."

"Me, too," and her mother's voice was a whisper. Sometimes, when one wants something awfully badly, it's hard to say the words out loud. Sarah knew from experience. Sometimes she whispered her wishes and prayers because they were fragile, tentative things, like hummingbird wings, like peace.

"I left her with it for a while because Aunt Sue called. You know Aunt Sue. We had a lot to catch up on, and I didn't think Glennie would care. Plus, I was kind of hoping seeing all those squares would make her think about doing one."

"Did she say anything about making one?"

Her mother paused. "Well, she asked where hers would go."

"Well, that's hopeful."

"How's Marshall?" her mother asked.

"Fine. Bored."

"Well, when you bring your square, bring him as well, and he can run in the yard."

"Why don't you get a dog?" They had been without a pet for years.

"We like borrowing Mark's. It's so much easier."

AMELIA ARRIVES HOME FROM SCHOOL and bounds up the stairs, calling, "Mom! Mom!" She's gripping a self-portrait, only a smile taking up the entire space. Exactly who she is, on most days. One giant smile. She gives Sarah the picture.

"Drawn in plein air! That means outside."

She throws herself into Sarah for a hug and then does the same for Marshall, who takes it with good grace.

Beth follows quietly, her hair tucked behind both ears. She wears her jean shorts and a blue t-shirt with a butterfly on it. This is her favorite outfit, or at least, the one she picks most often. She is not used to having a different outfit for each school day.

The only paper Beth has to show Sarah is a behavior summary, all fine. Amelia doesn't care too much about any negative marks, but Beth cares about hers. Amelia gets in trouble for talking; Beth, for not. Beth's participation grades are always mercy grades, except in gym.

"Good day?" she asks Beth softly, scooping her in for a hug, and Beth nods, quiet as ever. But she leans into Sarah, and she hugs back.

Amelia is already thumping back downstairs with Marshall. He knows if he goes with Amelia, she will give him part of her snack.

"No chocolate for Marshall!" Sarah hollers, as she does any day he visits. She turns back to Beth. "How was Perkins?" The team now eats breakfast together every race day.

"It was fun."

"Who did you sit with this time?"

"Addie again."

Slowly, Beth is making friends, mostly other girls on the team. She doesn't talk a lot, except with her feet. Beth roars down any course, this tiny determined little girl. Sarah watches Beth's face when she trains, the hard look in her eyes, the set jaw. Running is serious business for Beth. It's where she rises from being shy to announce herself. It's where she becomes a lioness, a power. It's where she shines.

"I have a neat idea," Sarah says, suddenly inspired. "What about if I make us all brightly colored hair bands? You can wear one to run, so we can find you in the crowd. And we can wear them, too, so maybe you can see us when you whiz by. What do you think?"

Beth bites her lip but nods.

"Should I make some for the whole team?"

But before she finishes, Beth is already shaking her head no.

Sarah stops herself from asking if Beth is sure. She has a bad habit of second-guessing her kids. Beth will let Sarah know if she changes her mind. Sarah bites her own lip, to remind herself not to ask, not to push.

"Would you like to choose the fabric? Or the color?"

Beth shakes her head again. She rarely chooses anything—ice cream flavors, TV shows, school supplies.

"That's fine," Sarah says. She gives her another squeeze, and Beth leans back in. Sarah holds her until she pulls away.

Marshall has come back up the stairs, looking for Beth.

"He's hoping you'll share your snack, too."

"I always give him a bite. Sometimes I give him half."

"So you're his favorite now?"

Beth smiles. "Maybe."

Beth's history was a litany of neglect and transience, with many blank spots because no one knew what had happened exactly, with her original mother drug-addled and now gone and her original father a question mark. They had the reports from her foster parents and therapists and teachers: quiet, sometimes withdrawn, loved to run, anxious, few friends.

Marshall is watching them, his tail wagging lazily, as if he hasn't decided if this is a happy moment or an explosive one. He decides this must be a happy moment and aims for the stairs, but then he pauses, waiting for Beth to reach him.

"I don't think there is any "maybe" about it," Sarah says.

"Why running?" her mother asks Sarah, again, during their next call.

"Because she seems to love it, and because I want her to be strong and go the distance."

"Lots of things can make people strong. Let her be a girl. Let her try dancing."

"Girls can't run?"

"Girls spend their whole lives running," her mother says.

Sarah doesn't know what to say. Is there something her mother hasn't shared?

"Does she like it?" her mother asks.

And there it is—the sudden switch of subjects, the sharpness, the drilled-down-to-the-core vision: this was her grandmother as she aged, as her mother is aging now, that old familiar roughness mixed with love and spiced with fear. Sarah closes her eyes and thinks, no. But it is too late. They are already here. It has already begun.

"Beth adores running, Mom. You know all this. She's good at it. And she hasn't asked to try dancing. A few of her friends dance. She seems happy where she is."

"You didn't run."

"No, but I didn't dance either. Why don't you come to a race to see her?"

Sarah regrets it immediately. How, on a cross country course, will they get her mother to the finish line? She won't use a wheelchair. She'll want to walk out to the shoot.

"When is she running?"

Sarah places her forehead slowly against the wall. Oh no. "Next Monday night, at Cross Park."

"Cross Park?" And then her mother is hollering to her father across the room about going to Cross Park, and her father is on the phone.

"Cross Park?" he asks, as if it is a foreign country, and it is. Suddenly, it is.

THE RAINS COME IN AGAIN for a solid, pouring, soggy two days, and after spending a few hours rescheduling the new bride and all eight bridesmaids, and after assuring the businessman that he would have his suits in time for his performance review, Sarah is exhausted.

Marshall won't come out in the dripping wet, and she can't blame him, but the house feels swollen with silence without him, and Sarah searches for a task. Then she remembers: hair ribbons for the race. Neon green, so they can always find each other.

The fact that she has neon green anything means someone, at some point, needed the color for something. A costume? She can't remember, but she wraps the cloth around her hand, enjoying its silky quality, then slowly slices the ribbon into the tails they will become, tied to a hair band, following Beth as she speeds toward the finish. She makes a hairband for herself, another for Amelia, even one for her mother. She makes a wristband for her father, who will wave. Neon green, so they can always find each other, she thinks, is not a bad idea. And so she grabs her last materials and makes one more, then tucks it into a padded envelope, scribbles a quick note, and addresses it to Glennie.

THE RACE FOR THE GIRLS is at six, so her parents arrive at four, in order to park as close as possible. Tents dot the hillside, and the announcer is testing his radio. Pfft. Pfft, he says, and then a scratchy, booming welcome that is enough in itself to knock her mother galley west. With her father holding one arm and Sarah the other, they inch her mother across the uneven green expanse toward the little yellow cords that define the shoot. Amelia twirls the whole way behind them, green ribbon flashing, until she unsteadies herself and collapses, laughing, midway across. Finally, her father sets up the camp chairs, and her mother sits heavily onto it, eyes on Amelia, who is twirling again.

"How long until the race?" her mother asks.

"An hour and a half. Well, more like an hour now."

Her mother nods. She settles in, watching the volunteer chalk the start line, a young boy with floppy brown long hair. He wears an orange vest and is apparently new at the job because as he comes back their way, finished with his task, there is chalk on his legs. The boy looks gloriously happy.

And this is how they bide their time, watching the event gather itself together, watch the runners arrive and scissor their legs in warmups and practice sprinting from the start line, and the team volunteers hanging their banners in front of their tents. Beth's school pulls up in a yellow bus, number 253, and they see her emerge, hair tied back in a long neon green hair tie. Sarah jogs over to help with her bib and her spikes, to whisper good wishes and remind her of a few strategy points. She wishes Al could be here, too, but he has a class. Sarah forgot to remind Glennie, but Glennie has the schedule.

The air is warm, and there is electricity in the air, tension, as the announcer begins his reminders, asks coaches to pick up their packets. Across the field, her mother and father sit and wait, and Sarah thinks how small they look and yet how solid. They are, she now sees, wearing their neon so Beth can see them, and so she asks Beth to wave in a big way so they'll see her, and Beth does, crossing her arms and slashing the air like she is lost at sea and waving for rescue.

Amelia has made a friend, some random child a few feet away from her parents. The two little girls sit on the lumpy grass, chattering, and making something out of the grass. This might be a new record. Amelia makes friends like some people eat potato chips.

"Good luck," Sarah says, turning back to Beth, putting an arm around her. "If you have anything left after that last hill, try to sprint in the final stretch."

Beth nods. "Place, not time," she replies.

"Place, not time," Sarah repeats. And then, something new: "We're Nelson women. Remember that. We may not always win, but we never give up."

Sarah has no idea where the canned wisdom came from, but the combination of race tension and navigating the landscape with her parents has made her emotional.

Beth looks at her mother. She doesn't play with her lip or look away or cock her head. She doesn't wisecrack. Who taught Beth to listen carefully? Not anyone in her family. Al's mother. Al's father. They hardly speak, they spend so much time listening. But that's unfair. They are good people. Remote, but good people. Stiff, but good people. She has no idea how together they birthed Al, who is a lightning bolt of energy and goodwill in their staid home.

She is a wisp, Beth. She is thin and proportionate with strong, lean legs. She is made to run, and she knows it. A body has wisdom, Al says, and Beth has found some of hers.

"Your legs are wings," Sarah says. She kisses Beth on the head and turns quickly, swallowing tears as she makes her way back to the finish line.

As the teams find their boxes on the starting line, Sarah feels restless. She's always restless at the races because Beth is good, and she wants her to do well. It's a fine line, this wanting. She readies her camera to get whatever she can for Al, so he can at least see part of the race, if only the beginning and the end. And then the girls are off, and her mother stands. Sarah reaches for her and holds her arm. They are all looking, but it is easy to find Beth. She is out front, not in the lead but keeping the leader in sight ("Keep on her shoulder," Sarah had said), and there are neon hair ties flying behind her in the wind.

"I see her," her mother says, her voice determined. By God, she will see this little girl run in this sea of girls. Hundreds of girls.

After six and a half minutes, when the cyclist emerges from the trees, her father helps her mother stand again, even peek over the rope to see. The first girl coming in is not Beth, but hopefully Beth will not be far behind.

"Where is she?" her mother asks, sounding alarmed.

"She's coming."

Sarah holds her breath as another girl bursts from the cover of the woods, and then another, and another. "C'mon, Bethy," she shouts, as if to summon her, and then as if she has, the fifth person speeding out of the woods is her girl, her thin little wisp, like contrail, streaming toward them, an edge of green behind her.

Sarah and her parents are all roaring now, even Amelia, and that will likely be all Al can hear when he watches the video, this cacophony of voices as he sees his daughter fly by. Eyes straight ahead, arms pumping, mouth a determined line. Sarah has an eye on the clock. Fifth place, 6:56. A personal record, and nationally competitive for a third grader. Beth's coach has told them about her times, and Sarah told him not to push.

Beth finds them afterward for kudos and hugs. She's tired, and her legs are streaked with dirt, and she is beaming. No need for neon to find her now, with that multi-watt grin, a rarity, except on the courses. Beth gives them hugs and then heads back to her tent, as required by her coach. Sarah watches Beth go, sees standing by the tent the thin figure she knows so well, the blonde hair, with neon green ribbons worn like a string bandanna. Was she in a hurry? But it doesn't matter. It's like a halo, Sarah thinks, and the thought makes her smile.

"Look! Aunt Glennie came!" Beth turns to yell back at Sarah, jogging backward, her voice lifting, and then she is off, racing again.

For a moment Sarah watches as Beth runs, waving, as Glennie sees her and rushes forward, as they hug. They're holding hands and jumping up and down. She wonders what they are saying, and then she doesn't want to know. It's theirs, their moment. Sarah turns back to her parents. With her father's help, her mother sits back down and keeps cheering for the remaining girls. Her mother stays until the end, perched in her chair, urging them on, the girl who is crying, the girl who is walking. The girl in braces, for whom her mother rises, with help, again, and for whom she cheers mightily. She cheers for Edina, for Hopkins, for everyone. Her father is cheering as well. They are having a wonderful time.

They have found a new activity.

They will go the distance with these girls.

The afternoon that SARAH AND HER MOTHER HAVE ARRANGED for quilting, Sarah arrives without patience or grace and sighing, opens the front door. Marshall enters first, sniffs, and then beelines for the back door, where her father stands, holding a tennis ball aloft.

Sarah expects Mom to be sitting at the yellow kitchen table with a pot of tea, all the lights on as brightly as possible, with the quilt in her lap, and she is, but she's crying.

"Mom? Mom?"

But her mother shakes her head, raises a hand as if to stop Sarah's advance. Then her mother holds one edge of the quilt high so that Sarah can see. There is a new, bright white square attached. It has red stitching that is small, precise, and oddly beautiful in its tight control, just like the stitching on the pocket of a doctor's lab coat. It reads:

Carys Glenn Macmillan

She healed

Wonder

Al

2004, then 2016

IF AL COULD HAVE OFFERED AN EXPLANATION, it might have been easier for Guy to accept. But there was none. Simply put, Al had happened to grab his fishing pole, because the last time there had been a tornado, he'd saved the pole, and in his panic, it became a talisman. This time, though, he forgot the pole in the doorjamb while he raced downstairs, the breath of the storm on his heels. The wild air seemed to reach inside, and later he would learn that the storm had swept up the fishing pole, which caught the power line as it swung low toward the house, deflecting it slightly off course and leaving the wire hissing and spitting on their lawn. A fishing pole had saved their lives. There was only chance to account for the miracle, but chance wasn't enough for Guy, who stared at the rubble of his own home convinced that had he done something else, tried something else, they, too, might have more than memories to sustain them.

Al was astounded that they'd been hit twice. Should they move?

He was astounded they'd walked away twice, but it was just plain old luck. Still, nothing Al said could change Guy's mind. Guy worried it over. And over. The thought festered, until one day, out with Guy for a beer, Al saw the tension ease in Guy's face, and he knew that history had finally been put in its place, and the guilt, and the whole backwash of trauma. A history and guilt and trauma that had slowly shaped this new face and heart and reality—Guy had more wrinkles, carried himself with a heaviness in his limbs, had a heart less sure and more guarded because he had learned what an instant can do. A body holds so much. It is a temple, Al's mother had said once. But it is also the place where we store all of our broken hearts and broken promises, and now Guy had finally cleaned house.

But it took years. The effect on Al was that two memories were imprinted: Guy's letting it all go but even more, even more that moment when Guy had turned to him on the day of the storm, face hard and strained, tears in his eyes, and asked "What didn't I do?" It wasn't the time then to count one's blessings; to note that everybody had lived. Because the fact of the matter, the truth, was that they had nothing else but their lives and while grateful, were shell shocked. No home, no car, no money, no documents. Few friends, since they were new to the area. And so many other issues—like Julie's pregnancy.

Al had understood how Guy felt—how one needed to know that he had lived well and wisely; that chance wouldn't sweep away the savings and the IRAs; that if one made sound decisions everything would be okay. Al had always thought the same things. But staring at the heap of garbage that was once 1518 Magnolia that day after the storm, Al knew that some things were unexplainable, and some luck, unaccountable, like love. He'd had his losses (who hadn't?), but he'd been relatively lucky in his life. When Guy asked what more he could have done, Al stared speechlessly at the pile of boards and the smashed mugs and soggy sleeping bags and a stray sneaker—the scraps of a life—wordless. He began then to appreciate the small, the ordinary, the boring, and the uneventful days, the wonder that any of them survived anything at all.

AL HAD THE HEART OF A PUPPY in the body a bear. That's what Sarah said. The day Guy and Julie had moved in, Sarah had walked down the street with a casserole, and Al had followed with a six-pack of beer. Guy had been unpacking, and when he stood, he seemed to go up for miles, but there was a hard ripple of muscle in every limb, a sense of power and grace in his every gesture. He had a smile as wide as he was tall—as open-hearted—and for the first time Al felt immediately at ease, that he would be friends with this man. Who knew Al could have two great friends, Guy and Anil? Never in his life had he had more than one. He'd often felt lucky to have even one.

1518 had stood vacant for a long time, down on the west end. It was a larger house than he and Sarah had. Theirs was a modest, four bedroom with attractive features—a bay window, hardwood floors, a sloping yard that seemed to cascade flowers down into the street, thanks to Sarah's mother, who had a gift for growing things and a passion for any stretch of solid green.

The Roses had two kids and a loping, silly large dog named Butch who seemed part yellow lab and part everything else. And they had a ranch house that fit the flowing nature of their lives. Another baby on the way, another dog perhaps, since Butch was getting on, so they said, and they thought another dog might ease the strain of the inevitable loss. And that's who clustered on the front yard after the storm, and then filed into the Red Cross van: a tall man made of muscles and his pregnant wife; two small children; and an aged dog who looked as though this day, this aftermath, might kill him right then and there. They had no car. They had no home. They had nothing but each other, and Guy kept herding them, even Butch, pulling them together if one ventured an inch away, a look on his face of horror—complete incomprehension. He was living on instinct as was Al, who walked to neighbor after neighbor, checking on them after the tornado roared through, making his way from his back yard with mild damage to, yet again, devastation further down. Walking toward his neighbors, all that Al could think of was his own family. Safe.

When he heard about Al's house, Guy had laughed. One house with minor repair necessary but a jumping wire tossing about, the other house obliterated. He laughed and shook his head and Al thought he was fine.

"He was in shock," Sarah said later. "That laugh came from the wrong place."

AL WATCHED THE RUBBLE for the hours it took the Red Cross to clear the area. They wanted him out, but he said to take care of others first. He asked if there was a working phone. He asked if someone would deal with that electrical wire so that nobody got hurt. He told everybody about the wire. He inched his family out of the house through the back door and didn't try to go back in, as though something else could be wrong and all his good fortune would disappear. He would trust that everything would be okay, but he would not tempt fate.

And so out of loyalty Al then sat on the curb and watched Guy's rubble, tried to pry a few items here and there and toss them in his car so that they wouldn't get damaged further. A photo album, a shirt, a toy—some stuffed bear that could be washed and made to look all right again. Sarah made the girls stay by the car with her, and she held Alber, who seemed, for once, to be perfectly content to be in someone's arms. But of course, now Alber was as aged as Butch. He cast Al a look that seemed to say, did you do this? But Al ignored the look and worked on what he could for Guy until the Red Cross shooed him away, said he shouldn't be there, that he needed to go. Ordered him to leave.

It took hours, or so it seemed, but eventually they followed a caravan of cars and unnecessary ambulances out the road and onto the highway. How unlucky can one neighborhood be? Al asked himself. He saw himself later on the news—a round man with rumpled clothing and tossed about hair sitting on a curb, a man whose face seemed frozen in an expression he didn't even recognize, as though he'd been slapped across the face, as though, for all his good fortune, he was about to cry.

AL STARTED CALLING THE SHELTERS that night trying to find the Roses, but there was too much chaos. Each time he phoned he was told to call back; people hung up on him—they had no time for questions, they had people to help. Al wondered where they were. There was plenty of room at his in-laws, but Sarah said that maybe it would be better to give them space, to let them talk to other people in similar circumstances. Al couldn't stomach that, but then again, he couldn't find them so he let it go. And when he saw Guy days later, he came with a box in hand: freshly washed bear, photo album, shirt. He believed there was likely something in Guy now that he couldn't share or know or ease. But it had been that way all his life—a failure to find a way through the awkwardness, and a casual acceptance of it for the sake of going on, for the sake of salvaging the connections.

But Guy was different. He wept over the bear. He told Al everything. He took Al through what he had been through. And from then on, they were even better friends—Al felt for the first time that they were friends, as though their earlier relationship bore no resemblance to friendship.

"I tried to find you," Al said,

Guy nodded. He nodded at the box. He said simply, "Thank you."

Al said, "I saw that blue green blouse of Julie's, but I didn't save that because I know you hate it."

Guy chuckled and said, "Lord, that was an ugly blouse."

"It really was," Al said.

And they laughed again.

And then of course the world tripped back in and Guy had to talk with the insurance investigator and begin to sort through his finances. And of course, he needed to find a new home. And of course, it was far away.

AL CONSIDERED THE SITUATION—by chance he'd made another true friend and by chance again the friend, who wanted a fresh start, was swept north almost to Canada. And by luck and hook and crook it hadn't really mattered in the end because they stayed in touch. Guy called when he was in the cities; Al took his fishing pole (not the same one, a new one, bought exclusively to spare Guy) and went up on the water up there and stopped in for dinner afterward. But now Guy didn't fish; now he refused.

It was these small reunions—and the goodly amount of distance— that allowed the balance in the friendship to sustain itself. He hated to admit it, but Al believed that some people, having sustained a blow, can never quite regain their equilibrium. Same with friendships. We all feel we're owed something, he thought, that in the end bad things should not happen to us.

He wanted to tell Amelia these things, but he knew that these were the very things parents tried to explain but which remained best open to experience. And Beth? Beth had already had her world torn apart. Once, she had been the little girl who hardly smiled during her formal adoption and later, in the hallway, took a great heaving breath. Had she thought they'd back out? Beth had emerged slowly from a cocoon of fear to be herself: prepared, focused, hardworking, maybe a little intense. She had the heart of a warrior, and an unexpected humor. She didn't roar across a finish line during races, but from the expressions on her face, Al kept expecting she might. Instead, sometimes she'd stick her tongue out at Al as she ran by. Once, in high school, she even gave him the finger, smiling, while running uphill during a 5K on a steaming hot day. He'd chuckled and waved from his spot in the shade. The older she grew, the more humor and light they saw in her, like they were opening louvered blinds and suddenly, finally, there she was.

As a child, Beth had said that her mother was like a broken doll, but she loved her, and Al and Sarah had respected that love. They saved the information they'd received about Beth's mother from the adoption agency, and they'd shared it with Beth when she was twelve—her meager family history—which triggered a memory, of her mother whispering one night before Beth was taken away, *I can't keep you. But I want to. I want you to know I love you. I would keep you if they'd let me. I love you*—the whispered confession more terrible and terrifying because of its gentleness.

Beth had had nightmares all her life, but then for awhile she wouldn't let herself sleep. On those nights, Al sat in the hallway where she could see him. With him nearby, she'd fall asleep about midnight, but once he sat all night. They'd let Beth stay home and sleep the next day, all of them hostage to her past, none of them bitter.

In his best moments, later in life, as Amelia was sprinting down the stairs to a date or a football game or to school, it was the speed of her flight, the sureness of her footsteps, that moved him. Al called out warnings, things that he imagined she found annoying, warnings like *watch your step* or *check in later* or *stay with your sister*. Always, full of hope that she'd be okay and avoid all the storms that could come, that she would lead the charmed life every parent wants their children to have.

Beth never took the stairs fast, and when he spouted his cautions, she'd come over and hug him and say, "I know, Dad."

Sadly, she did, but Al hoped for her, too. Hoped the scars of her early childhood would continue to fade, the nightmares, abate.

Sometimes, when worry overcame reason and Al began his fretful commentary, Sarah would eye him over her bifocals, never in a way that made him feel embarrassed, only with that same look that Beth gave him as well——the look that showed she was listening, that she'd registered his words, that she understood. And those were the moments and days during which Al most often thought of Guy, a sad man up north who had once laughed loud and then slowly, slowly, had learned to do so again.

We are not beaten, Al often thought. We are lucky. So very lucky. We have had the best luck in the face of the worst luck.

He held each day like a gift, not carefully, not like a trophy, just a gift. A reminder. He just liked to remind other people, too.

"Look out for her," he'd tell Beth, when she took Amelia along with her someplace because although younger, Beth was more responsible.

"Make sure she has fun, too," he'd tell Amelia, when there was a party invitation they shared and he imagined Beth standing along a wall, hanging back.

When they were young, if they all went somewhere together, he'd let the girls run ahead. At the State Fair, the girls would beeline for the Big Yellow Slide, and they'd always go down the slide hand in hand, arms high, both girls laughing and hooting, hair behind them in waves.

But wherever they went, if suddenly the girls got too far ahead, he'd call to them, even side by side racing toward that big yellow slide. Al couldn't help himself. He'd yell with a slight urgency in his voice— and they let him, years past the age of reminders. They let him because of the family stories and the family history, the quilt and the occasional glossed-over pause in the middle of a reminiscence, and because of Beth's nightmares. They knew that life could get complicated and that love was not a given. Always in his loudest voice, which was never very loud and could get a little reedy if he strained, Al yelled to them, and they heard his warning, like a gust of wind, more a prayer: "Stick together, girls! Stick together!"

The Other Side
Glennie
2010

SARAH DOESN'T KNOW that I saw Grandpa's chart or how much I understood of what I read there. She doesn't know that I went to see him a few days before he died, before that massive snowstorm came and blotted out our world.

She doesn't know that there was no reason for me to return, and that he and I knew it.

She doesn't know I said my own goodbye.

I had popped in unannounced, carving time out of studying. I knew I had to. I tried to look presentable, to wear clothes, not sweats, and to comb my hair. The routine felt familiar but odd, like a song I had once loved but for which I had forgotten the words. In the mirror, I saw a brighter me, someone with polish and snap, but I disregarded it. What mattered least about me then was the way I dressed. I could say the same now.

Grandpa was eating his dinner when I arrived, or eating what he could. I helped him get down some of the vanilla pudding. I remember thinking vanilla was unkind. Couldn't a dying man receive the chocolate instead? Food wasn't sitting well but eating gave him something to do. Eating was hopeful. His eyes were watering, his chin was stubbly, and he seemed as though he was biding his time, as though he were waiting for a train to come in or a bus, or the plane he was to board. And he didn't seem bothered or scared by either the delay or the ticket he carried. His calm relieved me. I hope it held.

We laughed about old family memories, and we talked about my hopes, and he knew why I was there. He knew exactly why. For a while, I held his hand, and we said nothing, just sat.

Before I left, he looked me in the eye and said, "Goodbye, Glennie. I love you."

And I said, teary, "I love you, too. I'll see you on the other side."

He nodded.

I walked the long hallway back to the elevator, eyes wide trying to stop the tears, and I couldn't breathe. Every breath hurt. I hoped that the big snow the weather forecasters were promising would actually come, and I hoped it would swallow me whole.

WE STARTED OUT DIFFERENTLY, Sarah and me. We started out carrying light inside us, not needing to gather it. We were two halves of a heart, our Grandma would say, and I'd like to know if she saw what we would become, one with blonde hair, the other an auburn that skewed dark, both passionate but quiet people, both set on a low simmer. I wonder if she knew we would split apart.

When we were little, we were friends. Not inseparable, but friends.

We rode our bikes down Glen Road until it got too hilly and then we'd turn around and ride home, and we weren't racing. We were chatting and laughing and trying to do wheelies. We talked about how it was possible that Evil Knievel could make his jumps. We talked about where the Smiths had lost their puppy. We left our bikes at the top of Logan's Hill and tumbled our way down to the creek to make leaves float to Alexandria, never concerned that our bikes could be stolen. They never were. We sent fleet after fleet to Alexandria on humid days when the forest cool wicked away our sweat. We began there, in that shaded wood.

I've asked myself when it changed, and I'm not sure. I have a feeling my answer would be different from Sarah's. But there came a time when I didn't recognize her. Literally. One day during my sophomore year, after she had graduated, she came over to my dorm room in search of me because I hadn't answered my phone again. She had styled her hair differently, in a bob, and she had new, severe-looking, square black glasses frames. I closed the door on her. I closed the door in her face.

That was when I was starving myself, which she called and called about, and I wouldn't discuss. Sometimes, in revenge for her pestering, I would eat less. I subsisted on carrots and water and yogurt and fruit. Peanut butter if I got weak. I'd eat more before exams and then slide back.

It was a professor who got to me. Professor Harold Ebermeier.

"Macmillan," he said one day. He was young, thin, always dressed in a pressed shirt and slacks. He was a tough professor, demanding. He called us by our last names and nothing else. He did not offer extra credit. He did not give partial credit. He did not chat. He did not hold office hours in his office, but he would meet with at least two people at a time in the cafeteria because he liked his coffee piping hot, and he always had coffee. Among some of us, his name became a swear word. Ebermeier. If I got caught in traffic or overslept, I'd say it: Ebermeier.

But one day, in early April, he caught up with me after class as I was trying to stuff my textbook into my bag. I always sat in the back of the classroom, high in the back seats. The effort to reach those seats taxed me, but I loved getting to see the whole room. The day he called me out, walking up to that last row had taken every bit of grit I had, but stuffing the textbook in my bag at the end of class threatened to end me. The book was huge, a doorstop. Suddenly, I felt like I was winding down, and I let my hands fall to my sides. He strode up into the farthest seats quickly, it seemed to me. I heard him coming in swift, efficient footsteps. Suddenly, I was winding down, and he was there to see it.

"Ebermeier," I said.

"Macmillan," he replied, and I glanced at him, then away. I didn't want to look him in the eye. "I'm worried about you, Macmillan. You're smart as a whip, but, uh, but you're not well. I've called the counseling department. I called last night. Someone will be calling you."

I remember smiling. Half a smile, lifting half my face. And it was not a happy smile. I was caught, and I knew it. He could make a stink if I didn't speak to this counselor, whoever she was. Or if I got thinner. He would make a stink. Ebermeier.

It wasn't a counselor who called. It was a psychologist, and I had to go see her for a whole year once a week, through summer and junior year. I also had to check in with my physician, work with a nutritionist, and join a support group with other people who hated themselves at some level and so were doing damaging things. Cutting. Suicide attempts. Then I guess they worried they were giving me ideas because they moved me to a different group, all girls who had eating disorders. The group was huge, and the minute I saw all those girls, all those strong Minnesota farm girls and wispy fashionable Edina girls, I relaxed. We were tall girls and plump girls, brown girls and white. We dressed well or dressed, like me, in sweats. We were a bouquet of colors and sizes and great yawning need.

I was over 18. They did not have the right to tell my parents I was in counseling. I did not tell them either because I was okay. I would be okay. There was nothing to worry about.

"You can handle this," I told myself as I took a seat my first day. "Lots of girls have this. No problem."

The young can really be so stupid. No problem took a year, and sometimes I even checked in with my psychologist during medical school.

IT'S LATE WHEN I LEAVE THE HOSPITAL after one last round, to check on a middle-aged woman who is alone in the world with only her husband, no children, no cousins, no anyone. Just them, teetering, after her hysterectomy because of uterine tumors. For the woman in the hospital bed, there is always that wispy-haired, bone thin man in the waiting room. He's clutching her gargantuan red leather handbag, and he sits ramrod straight in his chair. We understand each other, he and I. I am to be honest with him, and he will be clear with me. He might be all she has, but she has him, out there, waiting with bated breath. And in here I am going to continue to fight like hell to make sure he can breathe again. But just in case, they can face that dark edge together; they can order their worlds.

The night is pitch, and my headlights remind me of candlelight, flickers in the deep night. It will be Christmas soon, and I need to find gifts for everyone, but in the last few years any joy I used to feel during this season has faded. I am too tired, as though my years of grueling hours are calling in their chits. A tinny Christmas carol plays on the car radio as I drive through ice silent streets. I crank up the heat, take off my wool hat, let my hair fall down. It's a while before I realize I've bypassed my exit entirely and am exiting into Sarah's neighborhood, its quiet, tree-lined streets, the dim streetlights, the God-Please-Help-Them-Last cars.

I don't quite know how the people over there keep this many clunkers, but they accumulate, like litter. Al told me once, in an offhand way, that the clunkers aren't a choice. This is a city neighborhood with the best and worst that brings, he had said. The occasional crime, the occasional sagging house, the glory of bus routes and art museums close at hand, and good food, really good food, just around the corner. And sometimes, humble budgets sprinkled amidst a trophy case of bad home-grown mechanics.

I pull into their drive. Sometimes I think about stopping by Sarah's, seeing how she is, but we have been battling for so long, I'm not sure I'm welcome. I don't have any patience for smart remarks, and I can imagine what Sarah might say. So you miss Thanksgiving and show up now? You think you can just pop in, like we have all the time in the world? But I've been thinking about Sarah often enough lately, and about our childhoods, that arriving at her door is no surprise, though it is. I wouldn't consciously choose to steer myself here. I let my head fall against the steering wheel. My greatest company now is my fatigue. How sad and yet how earned. A body has its own wisdom, Al says. I repeat this to myself often, but never before in this context. The wisdom to guide me here in the dark, when I can run away if I need to. Everything is so much harder with Sarah in the bright of day.

There are no lights on, but I climb out anyway. Al, or I suppose it was Al, has placed a giant inflatable snowman in the yard, and along the edge of their roof, lights blink a rainbow onto the lawn. Most of the yard is covered in snow except where tiny angels have fluffed the snow away to grass. The cold seeps under my coat. A dog barks, and I try to remember whose dog it is that Al takes care of, but I can't. I remember only that it isn't his dog, and Al was adopted by the hound instead of the reverse. Or maybe that dog would be gone now. I knock lightly on the door, and I keep knocking until someone hears me. When the door opens, it's Sarah, dressed in sweats and large, saggy wool socks, her hair matted on one side.

"Who died?" she asks, straightening out of her slouch.

"No one."

"No one?" Sarah feels the cold then and shivers. She ushers me in the door as she speaks, leading me down the hall toward the kitchen. "Then why are you here?"

"Do you remember the Eliassons?" I ask her.

Sarah nods. Al has come downstairs, and he frowns when he sees me. He looks like a rumpled bear. "Who died?" he asks, and I laugh until I realize he's serious.

"Nobody today, Al," I say.

"What's happening?" he asks, looking at Sarah.

"Glennie dropped by," Sarah says matter-of-factly, as though I do this every week when in fact I have not dropped by in years. When was the last time?

"Everything okay?" Al looks at me.

I nod, and so he nods, and then he lumbers up the stairs back to bed, where I imagine he will be unable to sleep, worrying about what fresh hell I've brought in the door. I am well aware of my stature in their family.

"The Eliassons?" Sarah says quickly. "Yes, I remember the Eliassons. Why?"

"Do you remember how they'd send us a candle to light on Christmas Eve?" I ask.

"Of course."

"That was my favorite part of Christmas growing up. Still is."

She smiles, "Mine, too."

In the buttery yellow kitchen, Sarah opens a cupboard, then another, and another, calmly persistent, until she finds a stubby white candle, the kind one keeps in case the power goes out. She lights it and pours me a glass of wine, and neither of us speaks. She hands me my candle, and she sits beside me at the kitchen table, and she waits. For once in her life, she is completely silent, but she's watching me, as if she knows what I have come to say, or maybe, maybe only this: that late tonight, for a reason neither of us fully understands, I have finally come to share something.

"I went a few days before." I hear myself saying, in a voice that sounds aged and weary. My coat is still on. Maybe I should leave.

Sarah is studying my face, smiling, until suddenly, she inhales sharply. Her face is soft, beginning to sag, as would mine, if I had anything to sag. I see the lines in her forehead, around her mouth, the years she carries now, like banners. She is strangely beautiful, this sister of mine who has never credited herself with the fineness of her own features. She has a fierce heart, but she never forgives herself, or anyone else, I once thought. But I see it now in her eyes, the battle is all gone, has been gone perhaps for a long time.

Slowly, she pushes herself up from the table and pours herself a glass of wine, comes back to the table in leaden movements, like she's dragging chains.

I speak toward the light of my candle, away from the flatness in her eyes, toward heaven.

"That storm saved my life because I'd already said goodbye. I'd gone over a few days before, and I had his chart. You know, it was inappropriate for me to have it, and I just didn't care. The doctor had set it down to go get something. I read as much of it as I could, and I knew he had only days. Days. He knew, too, Sarah. He didn't seem afraid, he just seemed so tired. So tired. We had such a good talk, and he knew I was saying goodbye. And he knew I wasn't coming back."

Sarah has tears on her cheeks. "Why couldn't you have told me this years ago?"

I shrug, the shrug that says everything and nothing. "I don't know. Why couldn't you give me credit?"

Sarah lifts herself up, and I think, Oh, God. She shakes her head but when she speaks, her voice is clear. "I get it. I understand. It can be too much, can't it? I can be too much, can't I?"

I nod, but she deserves a real answer to her question and so I tell her the only truth I know. "I couldn't face it again after Grandma."

"But you left me alone, handling him. And Grandma. Hospital stay after hospital stay. Over and over. And you were the one who would have understood the medical terms, what was happening. Mom and Dad were a mess. It was me, dealing with it. Me. With a baby." She's winding up now, the opposite of the way I used to wind down as my energy fled, and I let her go on, but she's done now, save for one last defiant, hard stare.

"I did. And I apologize."

There. There it is. Years too late. I worry that my apology will become her hammer, but Sarah sags into her chair again.

"But I ran you off a bit, didn't I? I wanted things done my way."

I nod and take a slug of wine. I don't drink often, and the wine zips through me and I feel its warmth spreading, like when ice breaks and the cracks free themselves from the center and race out beyond impact.

"Why tonight? Why now?" Sarah asks. She sounds weary, too.

I prefer answering in the dark, but we have a right to see each other eye to eye. "I drove here by accident. I just patched up a woman who could have cancer. She has one person. Her husband. I'm not sure I have anyone, not really."

"Of course you have me."

"Whether you want to be there or not?"

She doesn't answer.

"How are you?"

Her voice is a whisper when she replies. "I'm broken-hearted, and I'm tired."

In the darkness, I hear her breathing, but it isn't a peaceful sound. It's a sound, though, that defines my life—breath or the lack of it. The soft sweetness of it, or the roughness in its struggle. Always present, and then not.

"I don't understand you," Sarah says finally. "I'd like to, though. I've always needed to." She pauses, thinking. "And I understand not wanting to watch someone else pass away. I just wish you could have said all this years ago."

"The truth is that in a way, all you have ever seen, for a long time now, is my face."

Sarah turns to speak, her forehead wrinkled in anger.

"Think about how it would feel," I say softly, "if at a certain point your family was shaped as much by your looks as everyone else. It became a key point of contrast."

Sarah doesn't speak, her gaze searching the dark through the window. She's remembering. She is considering.

"Not all the time," I add, "but it happened."

Sarah's still thinking, her eyes scanning the night, lips a hard line.

I'm whispering now: "I hated myself. Sophomore year."

I take her hand. Her skin is chapped and rough, but I don't recoil. I've held a lot of hands. Hands are something I understand, like the growing prominence of her knuckle bones. I hold her hand and hope she will understand my language, which isn't made up of words. It's made of touch.

She squeezes my hand and tries to move away, but I don't let her. I hold on. Then I try.

"I don't have the words," I whisper. "I love what I do. I live for my work. But I love you, too. I love you all."

Sarah nods. "Okay," she says. "Okay."

I wait, hoping.

"We love you, too. Even if we're mad at you. You're kind of maddening sometimes. But we're proud of you, of what you've achieved."

"I'm glad," I tell her. "Because I don't think I can feel so angry much longer."

"Me, neither." She looks at me, a wobbly smile. "I tried to protect you. In junior high. In high school. Even college. All those boys everywhere, like gnats. I wasn't jealous, not for long, but I see what you mean. I was defining you by your face anyway, wasn't I? For a long time. Until I started defining you by your absence."

I blow out my candle, and the dark softens, like a blanket.

"Remember Logan's Hill?" I ask her. "And riding our bikes? Remember when we had fun together?"

Sarah chuckles.

I WAKE ONLY WHEN AL PUTS A CUP OF COFFEE in front of me.

"Your pager is beeping." He still looks like a rumpled bear. "We couldn't get you to move last night."

I grab my pager and call in, instantly awake and alive, my blood

253

humming. I take a swig of coffee as I listen to the message, but I'm already moving toward the front door. Al follows, trying to help by pouring my coffee into a thermos, but I shake my head no. I'm hanging up and charging through the door when Al says my name. I turn, and I see him: his tatty brown robe and Gopher pajamas, scruffy and large and holding the coffee cup in one hand and a partially filled thermos in the other.

Does he want an explanation? Will Sarah? I could tell him hell froze over, but the tone isn't right. She'll know that I had to go. There is no need to repeat it for the umpteenth time.

I think of the message I have just received.

I think of that goodbye with Grandpa, all those years ago, on a similarly cold day.

I think of how tired Sarah and I are, bone weary.

"Thank you for the coffee, Al, and thanks for letting me crash here. Please tell Sarah that I hope she'll drop by sometime," I say, and I slide out the door toward my car, toward the baby hurrying its way into our world, toward a tiny woman who prays for good news, toward her fragile husband and that oversize handbag, toward joy and second chances. I am running.

Exit Plan
Glennie
2019

In the hospital TV shows that Glennie sometimes watches, doctors' homes are portrayed as sleek, even clinical. Expensive lofts with water views. Glass and chrome furniture. Modern art hanging on the walls. Not to her taste. Glennie likes what she knows, what she grew up having: piles of books, furniture sunk from use and replaced sometimes with second-hand steals, braided rugs, cushions in primary colors. Even when she finally got her MD and began making money, she didn't move to a better building or redecorate and purchase fancy furniture, in any style. She plodded downtown to Larch's bar, ordered a house whiskey, and asked him what second-hand stores were fair.

In Larch's Twin Cities home, and in his almost seedy but spartan downtown bars, and even in his comfy doughnut shop out in the airy suburbs, Glennie could feel the push of history. It wasn't only because of his décor. It was also because of Larch's patrons, others like himself whose parents came over on ships and carved farms and cities from forest and prairie. This was the one detail about his past that he had shared with her personally, and only because his Swedish was impeccable. Larch and many of his patrons were a dying breed. First generation. Second generation. People who still spoke Swedish with friends, at home. Glennie loved Larch and his other patrons. Sometimes, whispering, she would practice her Swedish with them, since she and her older sister had grown apart and no longer tried to help each other remember the vocabulary. In college and later—during the lengthy, clogged days of medical school—she'd go down to Larch's bar to escape her life and to chatter in her broken Swedish and sip a house whiskey, or two.

When Glennie spoke well, Larch's patrons patted her on the arm or back, offered to buy her an Aqua Vit. Hazy after an afternoon at Larch's, the old men would lean in and whisper, "Jag alskar dig," and it never bothered her. She'd tell them, with a firm pat on the back, that she loved them, too, and they took it with good grace. To be kind, she made them family in the best way she knew how: she told them about hers, every little knot of a story that made the Macmillans the Macmillans, because once you knew the stories, you were almost blood.

Macmillan? They'd say. Your dad? And Glennie would nod, and they'd laugh about the girl who wanted to speak Swedish being part Scot.

Larch wasn't blood, but he was still family, and that day when she finally had money and couldn't bear sinking into her couch any-more, she knew he'd help her find better furniture than what the show rooms offered. And, of course, he knew where to go. He was bent over even then, tilting, but with lean, scrawny legs honed from years of keeping himself as vertical as possible. He still had his trademark wild, white bushy eyebrows and clear blue eyes. That day, he threw on his jacket, a weathered dark green L.L. Bean one with a furry collar, and took her deeper into downtown than his bar, to a place she had only ever driven by on a highway overpass, a three-story brick building with faded lettering on the sides for Herman's Beef & Pork. This was Larch's Twin Cities, the dusty gem of a store in the roughest part of town, run by a craggy older gentleman named Mort who looked older than Larch.

"I like you," Larch wheezed to her on that day that he took her furniture shopping, "because you remember your history."

Glennie stopped flat when he said it, cast him a sharp glance. Was he teasing her? She was the one family member always in trouble for missing a birthday or a coffee date. Or a funeral. She was the missing face in how many family vacation photos?

"Get over yourself," he said, waving a hand. He marched ahead of her as though he was out for a stroll in a suburban neighborhood with high-end homes instead of a warehouse district peopled by shadows and cars without plates.

"What city did your great-Grandpa come from?" he yelled back at her that afternoon.

"Which Grandpa?" Glennie asked, desperately wanting to get the right answer.

"Both."

"On Mom's side, Grandpa Olaf came from Vimmerby. On Dad's side, Hugh came from Edinburgh. And they were both troublemakers," she added.

Larch stopped to smile back at her, then started walking again.

"Did I pass?" she asked.

"You always pass," Larch said over his shoulder.

"Sarah knows the same history," Glennie said to Larch's back, partly a whine, she knew, but her sister seemed to claim all family as her territory. Anything family. It was infuriating sometimes. "Why the quiz?"

But Larch was already hugging Mort, and she doubted he would have answered anyway. He didn't like stupid. Or dim. Or people who couldn't keep up, in any capacity. She wanted to ask what his rank had been in World War Two because she could just imagine him as the Navy equivalent of a drill sergeant.

For all the history he shared with her family, his own past was murky. He wouldn't talk about the war. References to his family were few. "We're his family," Grandpa told her when she asked, and that was that. Maybe, she thought that day, all Larch wanted her to do was to hold on. Remember. Keep family close. As close as she was able. Maybe he hadn't been able.

Glennie followed Larch slowly down the broken sidewalk, concrete slabs forced up and together like there had been a tiny earthquake. She walked up them and then down, wanting to feel every elevation, every sinking back. The slabs were like Sarah and her, with their mountain range of hurt and history between them, obscuring their views. She stood on the delicate ridge, surveying, but then Larch waved at her, holding open the door and calling out. Mort was getting irritated. He had another buyer for the couch. She needed to hurry, Larch said, to claim it.

Inside, on floor after floor, amidst the junk, they found real mahogany, real maple. She doesn't trust her memory, but she still believes she heard Larch giggle. They'd been looking at an old side table, and Larch had raised a hairy eyebrow, smiling, and then she thought she heard it: laughter. They bought Mort's couch and also that side table. It was real maple, no paint, a discard from a too hurried or harried benefactor who didn't know furniture from clothes, according to Larch.

They spent several of the next Saturdays together, and he taught her furniture from clothes, and she remembers those Saturdays in detail, how the sun was bright behind the clouds, and how the cold seemed friendly until suddenly it wasn't. She remembers not thinking about diseases or patients or ratios or insurance payments—things that now constantly roil in her mind. She remembers the rumble of Larch's voice and buying him a whiskey afterward at his bar and then leaving, edging through the bar door out into the glare.

And now here she is facing another glare, the fluorescents and gleam in another kind of show room, Larch now long gone. He'd be upset to see her here. She knows that in some corner of heaven, he's pounding over the clouds. She hates to disappoint him, but the Herman's Beef & Pork building was converted into lofts, and her time is limited.

Glennie stares at the row of kitchen sinks, wishing instead for an old hardware store, cluttered with bolts and screws and bobs and wire and staffed by grizzly, wrinkled older men who don't have polish but knowledge. Wishing for Larch. The bright fluorescents here bother her, and though the staff seems kind and knowledgeable, there is something too efficient in their presentation, too glossy, even in this cavern of a store.

The young man beside her wears an orange shirt and a name tag. Paul. Paul looks like he is about twenty and earning money for college. His glasses are squareish and clunky. He needs a haircut, and he wears his day-old beard more with resignation than with pride. Football weight gone soft. Scuffed soft leather shoes.

Glennie smiles at him, a smile that she realizes, even as she makes it, is now the only one she uses. Brief, to the point. A smile that says, with pleasantries now out of the way, we will talk about how the surgery went. Or which appliance to buy.

"Do you have any questions about the sinks?" Paul asks. He sounds like he has added sparkles to his words, cut them from a song, as if his energy level on the floor is monitored.

"Yes, "Glennie says, nodding. "Do you get a commission on the sale?"

Paul blinks. Then he says slowly, "Yes, we do get a commission."

"So. What would make your month?" Even when she is trying to be nice, she sounds like she might bite. When did she get like this? By drilling residents? By once too often fighting the knock of death on some patient's door? Was she now only made up of edges and ice?

"Pardon me?" Paul blinks rapidly.

"What would take the pressure off?" She tries speaking more slowly. She is trying to be kind. She should sound kind.

Paul's eyes grow large.

"Is there a sink I could buy that would make a difference for you, Paul?" Glennie is out of patience. Is this part of the hospital life, too? Expecting speed? She looks down the row of sinks, then squints to see the rest of the appliances. "Do you get a commission on anything you sell, or do you have an area?"

Paul clears his throat. "I get a commission on any kitchen appliance or kitchen item. Like a counter." He seems to be gaining courage now, his voice calmer but louder. "Do you need a counter?"

Glennie laughs then, and Paul, uncertain, smiles.

"Good for you," Glennie says. "I am going to get a counter today. And a sink. I am going to get a whole new kitchen."

Paul's mouth falls open.

"That will help, right?" Why does she ask. Why is she so insecure? Because she has always been insecure.

Because she has always asked. Did I do well? Was the answer correct? Did I leap high enough?

Because she doesn't know how to stop.

She sees her reflection in the sink before her, all glowing long blonde hair, and her face wide. Seeing her face looking full startles her, not because it bothers her but because she is, in truth, still too thin and this reflection seems who she could have been. Fuller—of life, of love.

Glennie sees herself as flinty, thin, monochrome. Save for her hair, which is that blonde that will gray into something classy looking. Her boyfriends have called her an Ice Princess, not because she is unkind, but because she seems to them like a flower blooming in snow, like a flash of sunlight. They tell her these things in fits of poetry and passion, and she listens and smiles her quick smile. And that quick smile—the one she recognizes after it has happened—is what clues her in each time. Not this one. Nope. So far there has never been a relationship that survived her love affair with medicine.

"May I ask," Paul begins, "who you are?"

Glennie gives him her quick smile. "I'm a local doctor," she says. "How old are you? I might have delivered you."

He blushes then, this young man. Just as she wanted. She knows how to shut people down, cut them off. Hide. It's not an admirable trait, but she can't help herself sometimes. Sometimes, she just needs the veil that being sharp provides.

It will be nice to have more light in her condo now, with a kitchen in gleaming white, Glennie thinks. Glennie lives on an upper floor in a small older building that shoots for the sky. The same old building she has always lived in. She'd rather have a home, but she loves her view. She loves sitting in the dark and staring out at the city lights. She doesn't think of them as stars or glitter or jewels. She thinks of them only as lights. And she loves that light, spread out before her, around her, above her.

In the car later, Glennie sits and looks at her receipt. She has made Paul's day, month, year, which might make Larch forgive her for stopping by this store in the first place. Her condo will now have a warm, white wood kitchen like she has always wanted. It will look like a country kitchen. She might even bake a pie. She might even call Sarah and ask her to come over—just her—aim for some deeper connection with her only sibling. The world is full of possibilities.

AT THE HOSPITAL LATER, she loses a patient. Mary Gross. There had been any number of bad jokes about her name among staff and residents. Normal people wouldn't understand the gallows humor, but Glennie never shut it down. The dark humor was a release. Still, Glennie feels guilty. She had liked Mrs. Gross, and she doesn't like all her patients, though the gallows humor isn't fair to any of them. Mrs. Gross had been generous and funny, respectful and hopeful. They had chatted about books and music and the way the Twin Cities had grown. She had a passel of kids, all of whom Glennie had delivered, a round face, green eyes. And she was kind, kind enough to smile at Glennie after her referral on to oncology, which they both knew was a Hail Mary, though they never admitted it to each other. Glennie squeezed Mary's hand and smiled back, a smile that spoke to their long journey, this last effort, their shared great bubble of hope. But then she let her smile fade, holding on to Mary's hand while Mary absorbed the news.

Mary had waited too long to see Glennie. Busy mom. Too many kids. Always someone missing a sock or needing help with math. Symptoms that could so easily have been stress, or tummy trouble. Sneaky symptoms. Everyone heard about breast cancer; ovarian, not so much, and so now those ovaries that had given Mary the army of children she had wanted ("I want a football team") had failed her. Badly.

Mary had asked that Glennie be present at the surgery, which was unusual, but Glennie's colleague, Lisa, didn't mind. Professionally, Glennie and Lisa knew each other well, had worked together for several years now. And in the end, after they lost Mary mid-procedure, Glennie asked if she could join Lisa in informing the family, her heart as exhausted as Mary's had been.

Glennie doesn't pause as she joins Lisa and walks down the corridor to inform the family. She doesn't pause when she sees their faces and they note that hers does not carry a smile. Today Mr. Gross's eyes fill. Her oldest daughter hangs her head to weep, but Glennie still doesn't wait. She begins, "I am deeply sorry to share…"

In these painful moments, Glennie never pauses. She listens. She consoles. She answers questions. She handles paperwork. But she does not pause. Not until she has marched out of the hospital at the end of her day, marched into employee parking and made her way home. Nodded at Michael, the doorman, a recent addition to her down rent building, recently converted to condos but otherwise much the same. Michael is young, like Paul at the home appliance store, and he looks uncomfortable in his uniform, like a bear wearing a pea coat. Normally she makes an effort to talk to him, but today she can't pause. Not until she has opened and locked her door, ignored the light switch, and marched over to look out over the breadth of Minneapolis at night, that wide open of twinkling light. Because it is always night when Glennie comes home. She always stays late. Only then, in front of those windows, does she pause, bending to light the single white candle on her old maple side table. It's held in a ceramic candle holder from Mexico, all bright yellows and oranges and blues, a souvenir that caught her eye on a rare vacation trip. It's the only thing she has on the old side table, that candle and its holder. The flame catches and reaches high.

"Goodbye, Mary," she says.

She does this for any patient she loses, though they are few. Very few. In this moment, she doesn't second-guess herself. She doesn't worry over their care. Not then. That's for later. She is simply quiet. Her grief is always silent.

Somewhere out there Mary's family has gathered, and a part of

Glennie wishes she could be with them, but she is only the doctor, though Mary would have said she was also a dear friend. Still, the family wouldn't know that. Glennie has already set aside money for college funds for the children. Mary knew this and had protested, but Glennie was firm. She gives most of her money away. She has blooming trust funds set up for her nieces as well. No one knows. No one would ever know until her will was read. She would never tell Sarah, who might think, despite their improved relationship, that it was emotional bribery or an apology for her many absences. It was neither. It was simply the right thing to do. It was simply that Glennie had what she most loved and adored, her job, a magical, challenging, mystical, terrifying, rewarding job. What else was there to spend on? A big home? Vacations? She loved Italy. She would go again. But she had amassed a small fortune that had become a burden and she was going to do right by the people she cared about, on her own quiet terms. She told Mary before the surgery only because it stopped her fretting, which was ruining her health.

"They're covered, Mary," she had said.

Mary had stared, uncomprehending. And then Mary's eyes had widened. "You shouldn't," she said.

"I have. It's done. I did it a while ago, before you even got ill." Glennie took her hand and held it as Mary cried because Mary was a friend and saving her was a slim hope, a tiny sliver of light in the deepening dark. How rare to cry. So much easier to give. Anonymous, the donation said. When Bill Gross found out, the only thing he would be told was that the gift was given out of love and admiration for Mary, who would be deeply missed.

Friendship was an occasional gift in Glennie's life, that bright, odd, unexpected joy.

She smiles out into the night, toward the light. Fly on, honey, she thinks.

IN THE HOSPITAL THE NEXT WEEK, she meets with a patient in her twenties, who was just diagnosed with ovarian cancer. The patient wants to freeze her eggs before treatment, and Glennie talks with her about seeing a specialist, about her dreams, her fears. The girl's name is Sarah, and although Glennie is not an oncologist, she certainly doesn't want to quash hope. A fighting spirit is essential, and this Sarah has a fierceness that reminds Glennie of her own Sarah.

"Would you do it?" This Sarah asks.

Glennie looks at her, at this frightened, rail of a woman whose eyes seem dark with a determined hope. When she had started out in medicine, it had startled Glennie to see hope beaming through the bleakness, but she feels an affinity with patients whose very essence devolves into that beaming prayer. Glennie rarely gets personal, but she feels herself slipping toward this young woman. Feels herself slipping toward a kitchen that reminds her of an earlier time, pristine and warm and full of promise. Feels herself slipping. And the word "yes" slides out, like afterbirth. Bloody and wet and filled with relief.

But she does not tell the girl that she has. In fact. Frozen eggs. Years earlier.

Glennie knows now that she would be a remote mother, no matter how much she loved the child. And she would love the child. But she has never been a snuggler or a joker. She is serious and literal and focused like a laser. And having been an aunt for a while, she knows that she is not enough. She believes there is no more important job in medicine, no greater responsibility, than delivering the next generations safely into the world. She just can't raise them.

"It's good to have a plan," she tells This Sarah.

Glennie believes in plans. Plan A. Plan B. Plan Hope. Plan Maybe. Exit plan. Her entire life has been focused on medicine and the planning it required, but as the years add up, she finds herself reaching. She is unclear toward what, but she feels herself extending out. She froze eggs. She ordered a kitchen.

Right now, Glennie has no plan for the inevitable end of her career. Inevitable because there will be a time when she can't keep up or see well enough for surgery. When her joints will hurt more. When getting up in the middle of the night to deliver a baby will not be easy. Who she will be, what she would do, if she were not a doctor? It's the only job she has ever wanted. The only thing she has ever wanted, even from early childhood. She can't imagine, even though she tries. She could teach more, but she doesn't enjoy teaching that much. Too few students share her passion, and she can't relate to those who don't. Not really. Not well.

She thinks she needs an exit plan, but for now, she tries small accommodations. At the hospital, she wears soft-soled shoes, meant for walking. She wears them in the halls, during appointments, in surgery. She doesn't know how many pairs she owns, but they are called Trotters. Still, sometimes her feet hurt now. Her left shoulder aches from her habit of using it to push doors open. She has increased her visits to the eye doctor from once a year to twice. Maintenance. Maintaining. That is her plan right now. What other option is there?

Glennie smiles at Sarah as she leaves, flashing that smile that says, we're done for today. She leaves the taupe-colored room with the autumn painting she found in a thrift store, and she leaves as a lady making accommodations, helping another lady to make accommodations.

HER NEW KITCHEN TAKES A MONTH TO INSTALL, and when done, it is shockingly bright in comparison to the homey dark panels of her living room, stuffed with books and rugs and chairs. She buys a hutch for her grandmother's china, which she only ever uses when her nieces visit. It takes her a few weeks, but once she has acclimated, she calls her mother.

"I got a new kitchen put in. Would you like to come see it?"

"Will you cook?"

Glennie laughs. "Yes, we'll get it messy together."

Her mother wants to make a dinner, and her dad has requested meatloaf. Her parents drive over in their old Honda, arriving at four to beat the rush hour.

"Oh," her mother says upon entering. "It's so you!" She claps her hands in delight, as if to say, Well done, being yourself.

Glennie pours them some wine. She had no idea the kitchen was "her." The only thing she knows that is her, has ever known, is medicine. She has tried to share that fact with people. Long ago, when she tried to make friends, she'd talk about her work. Or she would tell boyfriends, other doctors. No one understood or they felt second place, so she stopped sharing. She stopped trying to make friends. She declined dates, had been for a long time. She even felt alien in her family. But she kept trying to connect there. They love her, though they miss her. They understand callings. Even Sarah, made of fire, quick to anger and blame, even she had never stopped trying. So neither did Glennie.

"Have you told Sarah?" her father asks. He's running his hands over the kitchen table, leaning back and sipping his wine in the wide kitchen chair.

"I called her. Left a message."

Her parents seem surprised, which annoys her. She has made a lot of effort in the last many years. She makes every Sunday dinner, and every few months, she makes dinner with her nieces or they go to a movie or for ice cream. Sometimes, they even spent afternoons baking, only a success when the girls took complete control.

"I do call," Glennie says.

"You're right. Much more than before." Her father shrugs. "You make a big effort on Sundays."

No one is angry. There are no gotchas. There are also no excuses. She is good at bringing people into the world. She isn't adept at handling their hearts.

"Meatloaf?" she asks, changing the subject. "Mashed potatoes?"

"Oh, yes, please," says her father, smiling, and they move on, away from the old sore spot—the absent daughter—which they've rubbed raw and let scab, become a callous. They are together now. They are seizing the moment.

THE YOUNG PATIENT, SARAH, freezes her eggs later that month. On the same day, her oncologist sends a more optimistic report than Glennie had expected to receive. Glennie strides out of her office to tell her team.

"Some good news!" She waves the file, and Avery smiles.

"Who?" she asks.

But Glennie is already gone, down the hall to the next appointment. Striding away from the happiness as quickly as she can. It's just today's news, she thinks. There are so many more battles. She is afraid to hope.

AT HOME THAT NIGHT, Glennie sits in her kitchen, reading cookbooks and drinking tea. The cookbooks were her grandmother's, and they are full of her scribbles and advice. The phone rings, and Glennie knows it is Sarah. Still, she doesn't hide. Not tonight, in her kitchen.

"Glennie? You got a new kitchen?"

"I did."

"Can I come see it?" No anger, no recrimination. Only excitement. "I want a new kitchen. You are so lucky!" Less envy than expected. More joy.

Glennie is quiet and Sarah, her Sarah, is still chattering away.

"Can I bring something to cook? Try out the oven?"

"Yes," says Glennie, finding her voice. "What are you going to make?"

"What do you want to make?"

Sarah is rattling ideas off into Glennie's pause, her own fears running over Glennie's and down the line.

"Let's figure it out together," Glennie says.

"Sure!" says Sarah. "Sure!"

Glennie pencils the date into her blank calendar.

THE DAY SARAH COMES TO COOK in the new kitchen, it snows. Of course. But Michael is on duty and lays out mats, and when Sarah appears, she is carrying her old boots and Michael is carrying her groceries.

"I wanted to cook a steak!" Sarah says, beaming. "Doesn't steak sound good?"

"Of course," Glennie hears herself say, though the thought of steak brings a hiccup in her stride. Their last major argument had been over steaks in an old restaurant like Ponderosa, someplace rural, maybe Belton, an argument followed by near silence between them for years.

In the kitchen now, Sarah is squealing. She is opening drawers and then the refrigerator and running her hands the down the bookshelf of cookbooks. Glennie trails in behind her, after taking the bags from Michael, giving him a tip, and then taking a deep, deep breath. Sarah has found grandma's cookbook on the shelf, and she has it open now, and she is teary.

"Look, Glennie," she says, glancing up from the pages. "It's us. It's our story."

"Favorite recipes are like chapters."

"They are, aren't they?"

And now they pause, awkward.

Glennie takes another deep breath. "It's good to see you," she says. "Wine?"

Sarah nods, but suddenly she is crying, her bubbling enthusiasm caving.

Glennie stares.

"I'm a little overwhelmed with life." Everything spills out, tears, words, her purse slips from her shoulder. Sarah slumps.

Glennie pours the wine. "Well," she says, feeling all her inadequacies tumble into each other in the moment and yet she can manage this with patients. "Let's sit down and talk about it." Bravo, her mother might say. Good job!

Sarah wipes her eyes and settles hard into a chair. "I want another child," she says, "but I think I just need something to fill a space in myself. Aren't I awful?"

"Not at all," says Glennie, who had not expected such big news. "I completely understand."

"You do?"

"Yes."

"You want kids?"

"I considered it once."

Sarah looks around the condo, at the sparkling new kitchen. "Did you decide to get a kitchen instead then?"

"I decided I wouldn't be a good mother," Glennie says. "I have trouble being an aunt. I have trouble with everyone."

Glennie didn't intend to say it. She gets up suddenly and reaches for the cookbook. "Steaks?"

Sarah's look is pensive. "With everyone?"

"What kind of steaks?"

Sarah grabs her hand. "You don't have to be lonely. You could—"

Glennie pulls her hand away, and Sarah's voice is swallowed into a silence so complete it is as though sound simply disappeared.

"Steaks," Sarah says softly. "Let's just do plain steaks and add that spice dad makes to go on top."

Glennie nods, flashes her quick smile. But later, as Glennie cleans up and Sarah surveys the city lights, Sarah returns to the subject of children.

"Is it too late?"

Glennie shrugs. Is this what Sarah really wanted? Free medical advice? Glennie turns from the sink to reply, and she sees that Sarah is neither waiting for a reply nor even listening. She's looking out the windows at the city. Perhaps Sarah's question is only for herself. Perhaps it's time to stop questioning every motive.

Glennie offers what she has. "It's been nice for Amelia to have a sister."

Sarah peeks over her shoulder. "We keep trying, but our history isn't great."

"Our history isn't theirs."

"Why risk it?" Sarah asks, and Glennie isn't clear what Sarah would be risking, her health? The delicate family balance? Then as suddenly as her tears, Sarah turns to face Glennie and takes the conversation elsewhere. "Larch would love your kitchen."

Glennie laughs. "Just not where it came from."

"It must have cost a lot."

Glennie shrugs. "But I never spend so I had some money set aside. I am only ever here or at the hospital."

Sarah's eyes take on a spark, but she blinks it away.

"I had a patient much younger than either of us save her eggs today." Glennie walks to the windows and stands beside Sarah. "I think having a plan is good, thinking ahead is good."

"Are you thinking ahead?" Sarah asks.

"I thought I was, but when I'm honest, I know what my future will be. I'll practice 'til they kick me out. And then I'll probably die from heartbreak." Where is this emotion coming from? This yearning? This kitchen?

"We're both at a crossroads, I guess," Sarah says.

"What will you do?" Glennie asks.

"Probably get a dog." She chuckles. "You can't really mean it, that you'll practice until the bitter end."

"I'll practice 'til the bitter end. It's what I love."

She loves her family, but other than that, she loves medicine. She loves the joy of bringing babies into the world. She has won awards. She has dedicated her life to patient care. The city lights reveal her exit plan for what it is. No retreat. No falling back. No switching to a side road. Always here, after another aching day at the hospital. Always, at the end, looking for these lights. But maybe now, when she gets to her bitter end, Sarah will be there. Maybe Sarah will catch Glennie when she sinks, spare her the landing.

"What do you see?" she asks Sarah.

"I see the lake over there. And there's your hospital. And 28th street." Sarah elbows her, thinking it's a game. "What do you see?"

"Lights," Glennie says. "Just lights. But that light everywhere, I love that."

Sarah doesn't reply. She looks harder out the window, and Glennie turns back to find the wine bottle, suddenly needing to get lost and thinking the alcohol will help. She flashes on Larch at the bar, elbows bent as he scrubbed some spot she couldn't see—but he could—some place he needed perfectly clean. He of the family history quiz she still doesn't understand, though maybe now—considering the question after years of fatigue, with the perspective of age, after tonight— Glennie has come to her own answer. If Sarah has been selfish about family history and family bonds, then Glennie allowed it, which gave her the chance to be selfish about medicine, about her aspirations. About herself. Sarah is the sun, all heat and warmth. She knows every name on the family tree, each wiggly little branch. Glennie is the moon, distant, more muted. She remembers how people carried their babies and the shape of them and the ailments that swept them away. Together they remember the whole, and Glennie is sure that only love binds that combination of memory and blood. They just love differently. Sarah demands loyalty to family, and Glennie to medicine, and they are the same deep down, the same exacerbating, exacting people. It's why they battle.

And maybe it's why they each struggle with loss. When you fight so hard for something, when you work so hard to keep something, any loss is devastating.

It's a relief to finally understand, even though it isn't pretty.

Glennie lets loose a grim laugh and Sarah turns, her smile expectant, her eyes alight, just like the glowing lights behind her in the city outside, all around, her fragile halo.

"What's funny?"

And what can Glennie say? "I think," she begins slowly, "that I finally understand something. About myself."

Sarah's smile is still there, wavering, backlit.

"I don't have any plans for once, except to let go of old wounds."

Sarah's smile fades. "Forgiveness is hard but thank you."

"I think I'm forgiving myself," Glennie says and now Sarah is crying again, loudly, great heaving boulders of grief wrestling out of her, and she says, "Please forgive me."

Sarah's hair is glued to her face by her tears, and Glennie feels something recalibrate in her brain, in her heart. What does Sarah need to hear? And what is true? What connects them now? Everything begins and ends with her sister, with their tangle of love, and rejection, and expectation, and division, and hope.

"Jag alskar dig," she says, softly.

Sarah is still crying. Sarah who holds family history like a whip. She is the shorter, stockier sister who carried high. She's the one who laughs at silly jokes and misses the more sophisticated ones. Her accent is flatter, more nasal. This is her Sarah.

Something has faded, something new grown. Glennie thinks of the arrows of geese pointing themselves south toward the warmth. Maybe, like the geese, they can aim for warmth, too. In this moment, she feels anything is possible and something, some real rapport, is necessary. She sets down the wine bottle, looks into the kitchen, into her bright forever. Into the light she has created. Aim for the light, she thinks. Inside and out. That's your exit plan.

And then she turns and wraps her arms around her sister.

Christmas Eve
Sarah
December 2019

SARAH REMEMBERS CHRISTMAS EVES THE MOST: they would stand in the kitchen at midnight, each with a taper, the lights of which wavered against the heavy dark outside, against the rising cold and chill. Huddled together, they'd wait in a hush for the grandfather clock to chime. This was after church, before bed, a last moment of quiet and reverence.

The candle-lighting tradition wasn't theirs, but one that they shared and then adapted. It started sometime in the 80's with the Eliassons in Malmö sending Dad a single, thin white candle wrapped carefully in crinkly white tissue paper, their Christmas greeting tucked inside on a tiny card. The Eliassons asked that the family light this candle in the spirit of peace and friendship at midnight on Christmas Eve, just as the Eliassons would in Sweden, and Adam would (who had last heard from Adam?) on the rough coast of England, and somewhere deep in the suburbs of Paris, Jean-Paul and his family. And the Macmillans would also, in the bitter cold of a Minnesota winter, surrounded by 10,000 lakes made of ice. And who else? Hundreds. Hundreds of people who knew Jan Eliasson from one place or another, this reedy, even ascetic man from a coastal Swedish town reaching out with his humble gesture of peace. For one night, they all briefly joined the stars, midnight by midnight, connected worldwide.

In that quiet assembly, then, it was a night to believe in God.

When they expanded the tradition, they first included Larch, and much later, Al's parents. Reserved as Larch and the Nelsons all were, tough as they all were, each year they joined, standing in their church clothes at that late hour, solemn, expectant, hopeful (everyone was hopeful) and waiting as the match was lit and the flame slowly passed around.

This is the image that has stuck with Sarah in the rough years. When little else soothed, this was the memory she returns to, this one moment, year after year: Dad turning off the lights in the house, his footsteps creaking over the floorboards, each click of a lamp turning off becoming a complement to the ticking of the clock. They linked arms, all of them silent, their slender candles flickering as the grandfather clock chimed Christmas.

This is the story of Sarah's life, and the image is all: the family in a little knot, hands reaching toward each other in the darkness, their effort a promise to those who have passed, a promise to those who remain. In the encroaching darkness, spurred by hope, the family clustered together with whatever light they each could bring.

THIS YEAR, FOR THE FIRST TIME, she and Al and Glennie are in charge. Which really means that Sarah's in charge. Mom is too thin and weak to decorate; Dad is unable to see well enough. Yet somehow, with less than a week to go, Sarah and Al have bungled things. Today is decorating day. She and Al forgot to buy eggnog on the way over, a tradition. Glennie burned the Christmas cookies and set off the smoke alarm. Her sister has many gifts, but none of them involve baking. Now she and Dad and Mom have given up, and poured glasses of wine. It's early in the afternoon, and Sarah envies them. Their early retreat makes her doubt that Mom and Dad will be able to stay up on Christmas Eve, and something in her heart aches to think of the diminished family gathering at midnight. Who will turn off the lights? Who will light the candle? She will. Or Al. Maybe Glennie.

Sarah used to think Glennie's absences were due to work, that suddenly she had been called to the hospital. But when Sarah had thought about it, really sat down and considered things, she realized no. Sometimes, Glennie just didn't show.

All Sarah knows is that she is supremely irritated today, and everything feels tangled. There is no buffer or distraction between them if their fragile new rapport tears open. As for Sarah, her Christmas spirit is about spent, and it isn't even close to Christmas yet. If the family gives her the job of putting up the lights, she has no doubt that she'll blue the air with swear words. She's not far from doing so now. Still, if she could just be alone for a minute. If she could just catch her breath, maybe she could rally, maybe they all could, and the season would once again capture them at their best.

Amelia has disappeared outside to make snowballs for the snowball fight Sarah promised. She'd been rushing everyone out the door to come here when Amelia, even at her age, turned and asked. Sarah had said yes without thinking. Yes, yes, of course, let's just get everybody out the door. We're already late.

For Amelia, the magic of Christmas is like glitter every day. She is still tow-headed, giggly. Once a squiggly ball of little girl, adorned in warm weather in princess dresses and often trailing a balloon, she has grown into a boisterous, fun-loving woman. She still loves balloons. And in winter, every snow is a gift. Amelia charges through it, throwing it into the air, eyes alight, skin aglow.

If only wonder were contagious. If only she could share it with Beth. If only Beth could teach Amelia a little caution.

Sarah isn't sure where Amelia's joy came from, maybe from Al or his side. It seems doubtful from hers. Sarah closes her eyes. The very thought of a snowball fight tires her, but she always keeps her word. Just like today, when she promised to find and split up the family's favorite decorations, a heartbreaking job. I need to learn the word "no" or rather, I need to learn to say it out loud, Sarah thinks. She whispers to herself, practicing. No. Nonono. Nope. Nyet. No.

But she may as well finish the job. She's spread her parents' ornament boxes out over the cool, worn wood of their vestibule, an assortment of plastic bins and old cardboard boxes and the occasional Dayton's shopping bag. Al has draped the front door with lights, which blink red and green in splotches of color across the wood. She reaches for a box and her arm aches, some pulled muscle, mostly likely. This happens now—she'll be participating normally in a normal day, but her body balks or outright rebels. Age hurts. She has always understood, having seen family member after family member walk this path, but she's shocked to find herself so swiftly following their footsteps. She feels too young.

They can't find the Christmas tree, which is typical of her family. Only they could lose an entire, giant plastic tree. At this very moment, when she is eyeballing the boxes (how did mom and dad accumulate fourteen boxes of decorations?), Al is out in her parents' musty, spider-webbed garage, hunting for the tree. It's freezing, and he hauled his coat from the piles on the back door coat rack and stuffed his feet back into his sturdy workman's boots, carting himself out into the cold to help her parents have their happy holiday.

She'd stood with him in the dimly lit, cluttered back hall, debating whether she ought to be the one to search the garage, once immaculate and organized and now a jumble of boxes and old tools, bent paperbacks and stray bikes, bird feeders and car parts, some for a '57 Chevy, others for an '84 Ford. Her dad used to keep this garage clean. Everything slips so fast once the slipping starts, so Sarah offered to brave that mess of family history and detritus, but Al shook his head as he reached for his coat.

"Stay with your folks," he said. He smiled. "If I found the lights, I can find a tree." His voice was light, and Sarah gave him a smile she imagined many wives have given, of love that has survived the miles of a long marriage and is as full of light as it is apology. But maybe he needed to get out. Maybe it was a break for him, with Mom and Dad and Glennie sipping Chardonnay and watching Bing Crosby in a living room that carried the scent of smoke and the stink of Sarah fretting over traditions. Again.

Isn't that the way it always was? Al will work the jobs on the periphery, open the doors for her family at restaurants, stand within hugging reach at hospitals, always there, but leaving the center for them—so they wouldn't have to reach too far for each other in those terrible moments of grief or loss, or in those moments of celebration. He was always on the edge, which worried her. Doesn't he know how central he is to us? she thinks now, slumped against the wall in the hallway.

"I love you!" She had called out on impulse, as he headed out to hunt the tree, but he'd already closed the garage door and her voice fell amidst the coats and mittens, a soft landing of words without echo, suddenly gone.

Sarah lifts the lid off a red plastic bin, and it comes away with a sharp smacking sound. Inside, in little rows of tissue paper, are the bells that Mom bought one year when Sarah was little—tiny perfect china bells that ring a dull, almost flat, note, but which they love, Glennie and Sarah. Oh, the hissing arguments they used to have about who got to put up the bells, who got the extra one. The bells were more important than the star on the top of the tree, a real evergreen back then, not the plastic pretender they have now, a concession to the realities of old age.

Of all the decorations, for any season, they've always loved the bells best. Sarah picks one up and rings it, and then she sets it gently back amidst its crepe, locks the lid back down, and affixes a label made of masking tape. The label says Glennie. Sarah doesn't pause. She moves on to the next box, a cardboard one, dented in one corner. Here are the recipe ornaments, handmade with ribbon and card stock and scribbles in her childhood hand, then Glennie's. Recipes for love and peace and happiness. The paper is in surprisingly good shape, only a few with curled up corners. She counts them. 52. She divides the love evenly and takes her portion, the symbolism loud to her in this quiet house with the occasional outburst of song from Bing. Her whole life has been about portioning out the love, and suddenly she stands and pushes the box away hard, slams her recipe cards down. Her heart is pounding, and her neck aches from staring down at all these boxes. She feels dizzy, a sweet sinking in her whole body, and it hits her: she is fainting.

GLENNIE IS HOVERING WHEN SARAH WAKES. Glennie's lips are a hard, thin line, her forehead wrinkling, and Sarah sees from the beige wall opposite her that she's not at her folks' house. Glennie smells faintly of roses and coffee, and she's wearing her doctor's coat, the red stitching of her name admirable but off a few strokes. I must be okay if I can be bitchy about stitching, Sarah thinks, and swallows a laugh. Clearly Glennie is not happy, but it's not because Sarah is cracking up at her own silent jokes.

Glennie's eyes catch hers, and Sarah sees instant calculations.

"They're running some tests," Glennie says.

"What tests?" Mom's voice, from somewhere in the back of the room.

"Just some tests," Glennie says and she is gone, a blurred angel out the door, always heading out the door, never one to linger. The disappearing sister, more magician than doctor, all hard lines and difficult vocabulary. A flame. She is fire inside, this woman of blonde hair and slender sleek elegance and stunning blue eyes. She is made of fire inside.

"What?" Al asks Sarah, leaning close, a hulking presence. Her comfort. Sarah repeats herself.

Al's bulk wavers, then settles, and Sarah sees his face clearly. Then he whispers: "We need her fire right now. Take a little bit of it and promise you'll fight."

Sarah's startled, but they promised each other from the beginning to always be honest, always and forever, no matter what. Sarah blinks.

"She's scared," Al says.

And that chills Sarah. She has never seen her sister frightened in her entire adult life. Glennie doesn't show much emotion. She said once that she couldn't risk it professionally, and Sarah had understood. In the past, she told Sarah a few stories. About surgeons making comments. About a resident who forced her up against a wall until a nurse walked past. Comments in class about her being as smart as she was good-looking. Then Glennie stopped sharing battle stories and war wounds, stopped sharing entirely, as if she had forgotten how. She stopped showing emotion, as if she had frozen. Until now, when she let something slip through the cracks, and now they all know: Glennie's heart is not lost, and Sarah is not well.

It's late when Glennie comes back. Someone has pulled the blinds, and Sarah hears the whizz and buzz of machines. Al's asleep in the chair, bent at an angle that will feel painful in the morning. Who is helping Amelia and Beth? But then Sarah knows. Harold and Norda, their relentlessly efficient, perfectly-styled neighbors. Sarah would love to dislike them, but they're just too nice. She wishes she knew their secrets. She always looks slightly mussed when she leaves the house, even on her best days. She smudges a manicure before she even exits a salon.

Glennie is a shadow, but she isn't trying to hide. She moves around the bed, briskly stepping around something, an instrument. She stops beside Sarah and sits down with a thump.

"You had a heart attack."

Sarah is confused. There was no pain that she remembers and then a shiver of a memory, the feeling that her heart was breaking over dividing the ornaments, breaking over waves of loss. But not actually breaking.

"Aren't I too young?" Her throat is dry. Her lips feel cracked stiff. Her breath stinks, but the fact is that everything stinks.

"No," Glennie says. "You're not too young. I'm not your doctor, even though I've pushed the line here. I called a cardiologist named Dr. Henson. I trust him. I know him well."

"How bad was it?"

"It was moderate. It was a warning."

"Did I do something wrong?"

Glennie can take a shot at Sarah here, make a smart remark, but she is a consummate professional.

"I think that is a question for Dr. Henson, but I'm sure family history plays a role."

Which family history, Sarah wants to ask her, the genetic one or the ones we all know by heart, the stories we cherish and wrestle over, the family tree we hold onto so tightly? The resentments and disappointments and battles?

Sarah wilts back into her pillows. She hadn't known that she could wilt more. Glennie takes her hand. Hers is cool and feels small. Sarah feels like she's holding a ribbed leaf, something fragile.

Everything feels fragile.

Sarah has always thought of herself as a tree, or at least the trunk, firm and a little rough on the outside but solid and round and reliable. To her, Glennie was a thin branch, bouncy, distant up there at the top. Hard to see. The gap between them has widened for years. Who knows where it all begins, what year, which unhappy memory? Was there one precipitating event or a slow erosion that leaves nothing but hard, unyielding sediment? Emotional sediment, like plaque, and as bad for her heart. She wants to ask, how do you heal that bad family history? What medicine is there for that? Instead, she says:

"What about Christmas?"

"Let's get there first," Glennie says, and Sarah is a slender candle in Glennie's hand, her light wavering in Glennie's breath. But then, Sarah has always been. Glennie just wasn't aware. Glennie just didn't know.

Al has not moved. He snores grandly and shifts, and as if on cue, Glennie lets Sarah's hand go, pats the top of it, adjusts a tube. "I'll be back," she says.

Tomorrow, Sarah thinks. Tomorrow or the next day, she will come see me. Maybe.

HOSPITALS ARE LOUD PLACES, even when people want to be quiet. Sarah knows this from experience, but she is usually on the other side of the equation. She doesn't like being the one in the bed, and even though she thinks she knows it all, she learns something, being stuck there: sound magnifies with the fear. Snippets of conversation as a door opens. Beeps. Pounding feet. Her own heart, chugging away as best it can. She tries to ignore it, but she can't. Keep going, she tells it. And then suddenly she is talking. Out loud. To her own heart. She is giving it a pep talk when Glennie walks back in. There's a hitch in Glennie's step but nothing else. No laughter, no comment, no odd expression. Glennie pulls up a chair and sits. And she listens. For a moment, Sarah's words elongate as she realizes: Glennie has taken off her white coat. There is no coat, no stethoscope, no agenda, no timer. Sarah is midway through telling her heart that it is absolutely fantastic when she stutters. Glennie has come to spend time with her. Is it bad that she-who-never-visits has settled into a chair? But Glennie doesn't stop Sarah from chatting up her heart, and so Sarah goes on, like she wants her heart to keep doing. She goes on and on and tells her heart all the beautiful things about itself, and that it can heal, and that she respects it, and Sarah talks herself someplace. She doesn't know to where or what, but she's calmer when the words run out. And still, there is her sister, her semi-famous doctor sister, sitting in a hard-backed plastic chair, just listening, and then letting the quiet fall like a veil. But Glennie is listening. Sarah is listening, too. It has been years since they have listened to each other. Sarah thinks, stay calm. Stay steady. Please. Please. Maybe Glennie and I can reconcile. I'd like to live for that. I'd like to live for Amelia and Beth and Al. I'd like to live.

Al stirs and settles. He will never leave this room for long, no matter what he's told to do. He is her rock, her tether. He will not go. Nor would Sarah ever leave him.

"Is there something you're not telling me?"

Glennie shakes her head. "I wouldn't do that to you. It will be okay." Her voice has weight, power.

"You're staying?"

"Yes, I'll stay until visitor hours are over," she says. "And until Henson comes."

DR. HENSON IS A LARGE MAN. Tall and wide enough that he fills a doorframe. A Paul Bunyan style of a man. His voice sounds like a rumble. He is even jolly. Jolly. Glennie listens to him, hands on her hips. Al is taking notes, forehead wrinkled, but Sarah is watching Dr. Henson smile at her sister and pat Al on the shoulder. Sarah is watching Glennie nod at Dr. Henson and then smile. Smile! When Dr. Henson listens to Sarah's heart, it's as though a massive wall looms over her, but she isn't claustrophobic. Sarah feels entirely safe with this man. Any doctor who Glennie respects can only be a good one.

There are handshakes as Dr. Henson leaves, but Sarah can't manage. Al comes over, leans down. "He seems really good, Sarah. Do you like him?"

She's all worn out, but there is something on her mind so she rallies. "Are Amelia and Beth okay?"

"They're with your parents. They are making Swedish meatballs and having a movie marathon. Did you see their cards?"

Movies with her parents? But maybe it is best. Staying with family is best.

Al passes the cards over, construction paper hearts in different colors, linked in a chain, a rainbow chain of four hearts, with Amelia's grand scribble and from Beth, a neatly folded paper card with a heart on the front, carefully drawn. Inside, in a tight cursive, Love, Beth. Just like when they were little.

Glennie sits on the bed. "Looking good, Sissy," she says. She has not called Sarah Sissy in decades. "You'll be okay. You have some work to do, but you will be okay."

"Invite him," Sarah tells her, sinking slowly back into the sheets again.

"Invite who? Dr. Henson? To what?

"Christmas Eve."

Glennie breathes in sharply.

Beeping. Something beeps. Sarah closes her eyes. It was just an idea because it's tough to be alone. Glennie has been alone so long. She thinks Glennie might be angry, say something sharp, but instead Sarah feels Glennie's hand on hers, then Glennie's fingers slowly sliding up her wrist and pressing firmly. Checking Sarah's pulse. So here we are, Sarah thinks, each of them worried about the other sister's heart.

DR. HENSON LETS SARAH GO HOME on Christmas Eve. She's weak and worn through, but resting at home or resting in the hospital is a toss-up, if she understood him correctly. Henson thinks being able to join in the celebration will be good for her spirit, so he lets her leave.

It is a cold day, bitter, and there is no snow, though Sarah keeps looking out the hospital window for it, hoping. Al makes her sit in a wheelchair on the way to the car, and she wants to fight him but doesn't. Illness makes one weary. Being weary makes one less patient but also mercenary. One distills things down to their root essences. There is no more time for minor battles. He takes Sarah to her parents' house, and everyone is there, waiting. Well, not everyone. Al's parents have decided to stay home. Sarah can't blame them, though the shrunken group makes her sad.

Amelia is resplendent in a red fitted dress fringed with puffy white sleeves. She radiates, which catches, and the mood shifts to feeling content, if not festive. Even Beth, dressed in something slinky and dark green, giggles.

"No late nights this year," says Al.

Her mother laughs. "Who can manage it?"

And so at 7 pm they pass around the candles, light them, and say a short prayer. And just before Al wheels her out the door, Sarah strings Amelia's rainbow hearts on the nearest branches she can reach, stands Beth's card against a branch.

"No friend this year?" Sarah asks Glennie at the door.

Glennie pauses, scrunches up her mouth. "I had you," she says finally.

Sarah is teary as Glennie kisses the top of her head and disappears from view, but Sarah tilts her head back as Al pushes her outside, listening, in case there is more. When she brings her gaze forward, she smiles at the twinkling lights on the house opposite. One whole section of lights has gone dark, and Sarah chuckles. A family like her own, which can't quite get their decorations right. When she was growing up, the Halstroms lived there. Now it is a new couple with three kids under age five. Perhaps, sooner than she is prepared to admit, her parents will also make the move to a smaller house and let another budding family take residence here and expand.

But for now, in this brief moment, it's still her childhood home, and she is still here. Beth waits in the driveway. Amelia twirls in front of them, kicking up snow all the way to the car, which requires effort, given the short distance. She is a whirling dervish in a knee-high fog of white.

We got her right, Sarah thinks. Then, squinting to see Beth, and we were right to get her. Sarah reaches for Beth's hand as Al wheels her by, and Beth holds on, walking alongside her, then lets go to give a tentative spin herself, head thrown back to the stars.

Al stops her chair by the car to dig out his keys, and Sarah seizes her moment. She reaches down and scoops up a handful of snow, which burns her palm. I will live, she tells her hand. We will live, she tells her heart. This is not over yet, she says to no part of herself in particular. But then she knows that she speaks to every part of herself—her heart that is chugging gallantly along, the vein that feels weak and worn through, her angry hand, her throbbing toe. We are not over yet, she screams to herself. NOTHING is over yet.

Beth catches on and helps Sarah pack down the snow. When Amelia next dervishes by, spitting up sparks of snow, Sarah leans forward against the blankets and warnings and puffy coat and fatigue, leans forward past her fear and throws the best snowball she can out into their sparkling, hopeful night.

Sisters

THE ATTIC WAS HOT AND SMELLED OF SAWDUST, which was not comforting. Still, the sisters climbed the last rungs of the ladder to peek inside, then to slowly sort through the boxes and crates, as they had been asked. They were older now, lined, in search of a treasure out of necessity, without the joy of adventure. Unlike their own attics, this attic was neat. Boxes stacked, crates secured, aisles formed. Each box or crate had a label, its contents described succinctly: books, photos, wedding dress. Only one box held knickknacks. As they slowly made their ways down the aisles, searching, they called out what they were seeing: Tax documents. The traditional Christmas tree topper. The family history, secured with rubber bands.

The attic had a fair amount of light from two bulbs on either end and one small window, high on the left, overlooking the side yard, and they didn't feel pressured or tense, only companionable, as if being up there together, sorting through their mother's things, happened every day. But it didn't happen every day, and each found herself glancing up at the other more often than not. This wasn't the kind of company they wanted to keep with the other. But they would.

Their mother had clearly made time to sort and categorize in recent years, so it didn't take long to find the women's quilt, a family heirloom and the inspiration for their visit. Together, the sisters carefully freed the quilt from its box, then from its secure, thick plastic wrapping. It unfurled, and they fingered it, not as if it were a treasure but for what it was: theirs. Their history in cotton and thread and patchwork and verse, tracing the women in the Macmillan line back generations. The quilt had always been intended for handling and for discussion. To be shared and to spark stories and to make more memories.

The quilt was all about remembering.

The question today was this: of the two sisters, who should keep it now, with mom slipping steadily, as though she were marching toward that final door? Day by day now, her decline was stunning, as if she were aiming. But yesterday, she had seemed vivacious, present, alert—and she had asked which of her girls would take the quilt home.

The sisters had been unsettled, less by the question and looming choice than by their mother's awakening, which struck them both as a last stand against the dark.

And maybe it was. Mom had feared a final goodbye, in different ways, her whole life, but facing it now, she did not cower. She rose—alight, awake, herself—and asked the one question they could not yet answer.

THE ATTIC HAD QUICKLY GROWN HOTTER, causing the sisters to sweat, and a thin sheen softened the lines in their faces, slicked their hair.

"I don't need the quilt to share the stories." She was the more carefree one, less worried about everything. Less worried about anything. "You keep it. Just keep it safe."

Beth fingered the quilt again. It didn't feel like hers; it never had. She was family but not. She was the one who didn't look like anyone else. She was the one who couldn't give the doctors a family history. She was the grown woman who still had nightmares, though far less frequently. Still, when the nightmares came, now catching her off-guard, they were even more terrifying.

Beth bit her lip and started to tell Amelia no, but then she thought of what her mother often said to her, even in the muddle that was now, had in fact just said to her that very morning, "I love you no matter what."

No matter mistakes or temper tantrums or cold shoulders.

No matter history or her birth mother loving her, too, only poorly.

No matter ripped seams or patched holes.

No matter anything.

No matter blood.

Amelia was already through the attic door and down the ladder anyway, off someplace, finished with their conversation and busy with life. Just like Aunt Glennie, yet not, because Amelia was usually as swift to return as she was to leave, barreling back up the stairs, often breathless with some wild idea for fun. Beth looked around the attic, at the detritus of boxes and crates and hopes and dreams. She hated goodbyes, and she did not want this quilt. In the stuffy, steaming attic, she began to shake.

It happened sometimes when she felt overwhelmed. When it flared up at night, she shook until she fell asleep; during the day, until she was distracted. Before races, she could shut down the panic quickly, focus. But there was a reason she had limited her competitive career, a reason she stayed close to the love and anchor of family. Even after all these years, she still felt the creep of history. Even after all these years, just like her nightmares.

Aunt Glennie had had her talk to a new therapist. Beth was struggling greatly, with mom's imminent death, to let her body know that she was okay, that she didn't need to flee. And so here she was, shaking again, trying to talk herself out of her trauma rut and back to level ground.

Beth wrapped the quilt around herself. It smelled musty, but she relished the softness of the aged cotton, which soothed. She cocooned herself in the threads and histories and stories it was now her duty to safeguard and to share. And multiply. She would need to add a square someday, take her place in the line. Claim her place in the line. The thought was new and calmed her. She had a place. But she got to choose, too. She could accept. She had never accepted. Not really. She had never accepted that she actually belonged. Deserved to belong.

From downstairs, laughter. Amelia was calling for her.

"Sissy! C'mon!"

Oh, Lord. Who knew what this was about, of all days. But Beth could imagine. Amelia had found an old photo album in a bedroom closet, or a recipe in some kitchen cabinet, or their old Halloween costumes who knew where and now she was parading around. Maybe Amelia could get Dad laughing. She always got her students laughing. She had once walked into her Kindergarten class on Seuss day dressed as Thing One but went the extra mile and dyed her hair blue. She always went the extra mile. Like Beth, but for different reasons. Beth needed to remind herself she could make it. Amelia wanted her kids to know they were worth it.

Beth wasn't ready to unwrap herself from the quilt. She stood in the calm, and then she closed her eyes and listened. Her heart was beating. Not fluttering, like hummingbird wings, tiny and rapid. Her heartbeat was steady. This is how she felt when her mom hugged her. Her Sarah mom. How she felt every time Dad trailed behind her, mouthing cautions. She never minded his reminders because she was grateful for parents who noticed. Who cared.

Amelia was still hollering at her, but Beth didn't move. She waited for the feeling of strength to weaken, like it often did when she was stressed and alone. Dissipating. All veneer.

But the calm remained.

I choose them, she thought, and she saw herself then, stepping into place along some long line of women, behind a blue haired Amelia. Beth took her place. And someday, all their little goslings would waddle behind and just like now, the boys would probably insist on staying with their sisters, on getting in line, too. Jack and Evie, Sam and Smith. But only Evie and Smith would get to make squares.

She could hear Amelia thundering back up the ladder, then there was her sweaty head and high beam smile, which age had done nothing to diminish.

"You're never going to believe what I found, Sissy."

"I don't even want to know. A snake?"

Amelia threw back her head and laughed and the sound carried, and then Beth was laughing, too. She was still wearing the quilt.

"C'mon!"

"I need to put the quilt back."

"Oh, just bring it. We can all have a look."

And she disappeared, like lightning. A flash and then gone.

Beth started down the ladder and peeked down to see Amelia looking up, waiting for her.

"Toss the quilt down. It'll be okay."

And so Beth did, and she watched her sister catch it in a tangle, then fold it loosely against her chest. No reverence, just respect.

That's it, Beth thought. That's exactly right.

Acknowledgments

Thank you to Marc Estrin and Donna Bister, for so deftly and kindly shepherding my story into print. Thank you to Marc especially for his keen editorial eye and also for his patience.

Thank you to Rick, Colin, and Alexandra, who are the light in my days, for their unwavering support and love.

My parents, Donna and David Hamilton, have encouraged and supported me in my writing since childhood. Thank you for taking my work seriously when I was young, and thank you for always being willing to read drafts and offer feedback.

David and Trish Hamilton read drafts and weighed in on issues large and small. Thank you for always being there, and for cheering me on.

Thank you to Ann Weisgarber, who always offers both sage advice and wonderful encouragement and who offered critical feedback on this manuscript at a critical time.

Erik Simon, thank you for always being one of my best readers for the last several decades as well as a wonderful friend.

Thank you to Dr. Paul Jones for advice on medical matters. Thank you also to Dr. Debra Campbell for advice on medical matters and, as a writer herself, sharing feedback on selected important passages. Any mistakes about Glennie's medical career and practice are my own.

Ralph Eubanks, thank you for your support of my writing and for your friendship.

I will always be grateful to Dave Fox and Alex Meyer for inspiring me to get cracking and to make time for my writing.

Thank you to Cary Johnson, Carla Steffen, Nancy Huestis, Sara Speth, Elisa Morris, and Kathy Malik for their encouragement and support in the writing of this novel.

Thank you to Nancy Bekofske for taking the time to share important information about the history of quilts and quilt making. Any errors in describing the family quilt are my own.

Thank you to Beth Hoffman, Steve Yarbrough, J. Ryan Stradal, and Andrew Krivak for their beautiful blurbs.

And thank you to *JMWW*, *Belmont Story Review*, *South85 Journal*, and *Long Story, Short* for publishing my stories.

Fomite

More novels from Fomite...

Joshua Amses—*During This, Our Nadir*
Joshua Amses—*Ghatsr*
Joshua Amses—*Raven or Crow*
Joshua Amses—*The Moment Before an Injury*
Charles Bell—*The Married Land*
Charles Bell—*The Half Gods*
Jaysinh Birjepatel—*Nothing Beside Remains*
Jaysinh Birjepatel—*The Good Muslim of Jackson Heights*
David Brizer—*Victor Rand*
L. M Brown—*Hinterland*
Paula Closson Buck— *Summer on the Cold War Planet*
Dan Chodorkoff—*Loisaida*
Dan Chodorkoff—*Sugaring Down*
David Adams Cleveland—*Time's Betrayal*
Paul Cody— *Sphyxia*
Jaimee Wriston Colbert—*Vanishing Acts*
Roger Coleman—*Skywreck Afternoons*
Stephen Downes—*The Hands of Pianists*
Marc Estrin—*Hyde*
Marc Estrin—*Kafka's Roach*
Marc Estrin—*Speckled Vanities*
Marc Estrin—*The Annotated Nose*
Zdravka Evtimova—*In the Town of Joy and Peace*
Zdravka Evtimova—*Sinfonia Bulgarica*
Zdravka Evtimova—*You Can Smile on Wednesdays*
Daniel Forbes — *Derail This Train Wreck*
Peter Fortunato—*Carnevale*
Greg Guma—*Dons of Time*
Richard Hawley—*The Three Lives of Jonathan Force*
Lamar Herrin—*Father Figure*
Michael Horner—*Damage Control*
Ron Jacobs—*All the Sinners Saints*
Ron Jacobs—*Short Order Frame Up*
Ron Jacobs—*The Co-conspirator's Tale*
Scott Archer Jones—*And Throw Away the Skins*
Scott Archer Jones—*A Rising Tide of People Swept Away*
Julie Justicz—*Degrees of Difficulty*
Maggie Kast—*A Free Unsullied Land*

Fomite

Darrell Kastin—*Shadowboxing with Bukowski*
Coleen Kearon—*#triggerwarning*
Coleen Kearon—*Feminist on Fire*
Jan English Leary—*Thicker Than Blood*
Diane Lefer—*Confessions of a Carnivore*
Diane Lefer—*Out of Place*
Rob Lenihan—*Born Speaking Lies*
Colin McGinnis—*Roadman*
Douglas W. Milliken—*Our Shadows' Voice*
Ilan Mochari—*Zinsky the Obscure*
Peter Nash—*Parsimony*
Peter Nash—*The Perfection of Things*
George Ovitt—*Stillpoint*
George Ovitt—*Tribunal*
Gregory Papadoyiannis—*The Baby Jazz*
Pelham —*The Walking Poor*
Andy Potok—*My Father's Keeper*
Frederick Ramey—*Comes A Time*
Joseph Rathgeber—*Mixedbloods*
Kathryn Roberts—*Companion Plants*
Robert Rosenberg—*Isles of the Blind*
Fred Russell—*Rafi's World*
Ron Savage—*Voyeur in Tangier*
David Schein—*The Adoption*
Lynn Sloan—*Principles of Navigation*
L.E. Smith—*The Consequence of Gesture*
L.E. Smith—*Travers' Inferno*
L.E. Smith—*Untimely RIPped*
Bob Sommer—*A Great Fullness*
Tom Walker—*A Day in the Life*
Susan V. Weiss —*My God, What Have We Done?*
Peter M. Wheelwright—*As It Is On Earth*
Suzie Wizowaty—*The Return of Jason Green*

Writing a review on social media sites for readers will help the progress of independent publishing. To submit a review, go to the book page on any of the sites and follow the links for reviews. More reviews help books get more attention from readers and other reviewers.

For more information or to order any of our books, visit:
http://www.fomitepress.com/our-books.html

CPSIA information can be obtained
at www.ICGtesting.com
Printed in the USA
LVHW011509100122
708198LV00019B/97